NO LOOSE ENDS

A.S. MOST

Visit our website at www.StillwaterPress.com for more information.

First Stillwater River Publications Edition

ISBN-13: 978-1-946-30092-8
ISBN-10: 1-946-30092-6

1 2 3 4 5 6 7 8 9

Library of Congress Control Number 2018967401
Written by A.S. Most
Cover design by Kody Lavature

Published by Stillwater River Publications, Pawtucket, RI, USA.
Publisher's Cataloging-In-Publication Data
(Prepared by The Donohue Group, Inc.)

Names: Most, A. S., author.
Title: No loose ends / A.S. Most.
Description: First Stillwater River Publications edition. | Pawtucket, RI, USA : Stillwater River Publications, [2019]
Identifiers: ISBN 9781946300928 | ISBN 1946300926
Subjects: LCSH: Physicians--Fiction. | Journalists--Fiction. | Murder--Investigation--Fiction. | Presidents--Health and hygiene--Fiction. | Presidents--Election--Fiction. | LCGFT: Detective and mystery fiction. | Thrillers (Fiction)
Classification: LCC PS3613.O7885 N6 2019 | DDC 813/.6--dc23

The views and opinions expressed in this book are solely those of the author and do not necessarily reflect the views and opinions of the publisher.

BOOK ONE

COVERUP

CHAPTER ONE

C arl Flood stared at the body on the table, a white male, middle-aged and in fairly good condition. There were no obvious signs of trauma or other outward clues to the reason this person's body was now about to be dissected.

Carl had received the call that he was needed to perform an autopsy under conditions of extreme security and confidentiality. Those conditions were unusual since the results of an autopsy were not widely circulated under any circumstances. Nevertheless, the call was from on high and not to be questioned. As Chief of Anatomic Pathology at Walter Reed Medical Center, it was most unusual for him to actually do an autopsy. A less senior member of the department would normally be assigned the task. As an additional proviso, he was to have a single assistant chosen by him as a person he trusted to maintain the same condition of confidentiality.

As usual, the autopsy room was kept cool at 62 degrees. Unusual was the armed military policeman outside the door to limit entry to the room.

Now that he was gowned and prepared to begin, Carl started, as was the routine, by reviewing the medical chart that accompanied the body into the room. It was quite thin considering the aura of importance surrounding the entire procedure. Until this moment he had not asked why he had been tapped for this most secretive procedure. He intended to keep his role as routine as possible.

It was immediately apparent from the chart why the atmosphere was so somber and security so high. The body on the table was that of Jack Henderson, President of the United States, dead less than 12 hours. According to the chart, his death was totally unexpected and so the autopsy findings would be of enormous interest. Until the results were known the public would only be told that he had died suddenly and unexpectedly.

"This man was the president of our country," he said to his assistant, "but we will accord his body the same attention we would to any other man's body. Let's keep this autopsy as routine as possible. Now, Bert, hand me the blade and let's get on with it."

The two men worked with quick efficiency. The abdominal contents were removed, organs inspected, described, weighed, organ samples were removed for microscopic examination, and the organs then set aside. The liver was heavy and appeared congested. The saber saw cut through the length of the sternum and exposed the contents of the chest cavity. The lungs were heavy with fluid.

"Looks like we're getting close to pay dirt, Bert. Pulmonary edema for sure. Now let's see the heart."

When the congested lungs were moved aside, the membranous sac covering the heart was opened, releasing an excess of blood-tinged fluid. The heart was quite enlarged and diffusely pale. There was no localized bloodless or hemorrhagic segment suggesting an acute coronary occlusion. This heart had the appearance of a diffuse fibrotic myocardial disease, not an acute cardiac condition.

The chart made no mention of any cardiac disease, but Carl could say with certainty that this man had suffered from advanced cardiac disease. It was very likely a diffuse process that had destroyed much of his heart muscle and likely replaced it with scar tissue. One thing was certain; this degree of cardiac impairment would not have gone unnoticed. So why the absence of any mention of it in the note which accompanied the body?

FBI director Krause put the autopsy report in a personal file labeled "Top Secret." It would never see the light of day.

CHAPTER TWO

The smell was familiar and high humidity made breathing difficult. A threesome, each member in bathing trunks and rubber clogs with a blue terry cloth robe, moved briskly down the narrow concrete corridor. The pale-yellow cinderblock walls were devoid of decoration. Frosted bulbs covered by wire protection provided the only light. The grade was not steep but indicated that they were descending to a lower level. There were no windows. Two of the men were in their late twenties, clean-shaven and crew-cut. One of them went ahead and pushed open the heavy glass door. The third man was in his mid-fifties but could pass for forty.

The large room they entered was also windowless with a low ceiling. The pool was Olympic-size and clearly marked with depth indicators on the surrounding blue tile ledge.

The crystal-clear water reflected the blue tile interior of the pool. Its surface was absolutely still. The ambience was that of a well-cared-for facility with tasteful, though non-distinctive appointments. The sparse furniture, chairs and several chaise lounges, were scattered about. Two piles of plush, tan towels were placed on low tables in convenient locations for an emerging swimmer. A large screen, plasma television sat on a stand in one corner with several chairs assembled in a loosely defined viewing area. The threesome walked around the pool and placed their robes on chairs in the television area.

Without any conversation, the older man walked to one end of the pool, hesitated a moment and dove in. He began a smooth crawl while the other two young secret servicemen watched at the pool's edge.

"Usual 30 laps, I suppose."

"I guess. Be sure to signal him when he finishes number 15 and try to keep an accurate count this time."

"Sure. I'll turn on the set and see what's on ESPN."

The swimmer had an easy rhythm and was not the subject of serious attention.

"Spell me in five minutes, Dan." said the man watching the swimmer. He settled into one of the chairs by the side of the pool.

The swimmer's progress was steady and his stroke smooth and easy. He was however, beginning to fall off his usual pace but this wasn't noticed by the poolside observer. For the swimmer, breathing was becoming noticeably difficult.

Breakfast had been several hours ago, and he'd felt fine on the walk down. Yesterday's swim had been uneventful but on reflection he'd been drained when he finished.

Another turn and shortness of breath was making him very uneasy.

Aborting the swim now would alarm his companions and create a stir, but breathing had become difficult and a sense of suffocation was undeniable. He stopped swimming and stood in the shallow end, trying to catch his breath.

The poolside observer was not looking his way but the change in sound coming from the pool drew his attention. He was startled to see the swimmer standing in the water. He quickly rose from his chair and moved toward the shallow end.

"Mr. President, is anything wrong? Do you need help?"

The swimmer began walking with some difficulty through the shallow water toward the stairs at the pool's end.

"No, no, no.....I just felt a bit uncomfortable. So I thought I'd stop. There's nothing wrong."

The swimmer's rapid and deep ventilation was obvious even to the younger man's inexperienced eye. As the other young man joined his companion at poolside, the swimmer sat on the pool's ledge dangling his feet in the water. He managed a forced smile, knowing that the other two were fully aware of his breathing difficulty.

"Sir, I think we should call for some help, maybe Doctor Benson."

"No, no, I'm feeling better already. I don't want to alarm people unnecessarily. I'm fine, just fine."

The three grew silent. The sound of the TV in the distant corner was the only sound in the large room. The swimmer got to his feet and put on his robe and clogs.

"Look, I'm feeling better already. Let's head back." His breathing, though less labored, was still of concern to the two other men.

Slowly retracing their steps, the three left the pool area and began their way back up the long corridor.

"Fellas, let's keep this to ourselves for the time being. I'll see Dr. Benson later this morning, so don't let your consciences get the best of you. I'll take care of this."

"Yes, sir."

"Yes, sir."

They reached the second glass door at the end of the long corridor and pressed the security buzzer to signal their arrival to the guard inside.

The door swung open and the three advanced through the brightly lit, carpeted hallway. The guard saluted as the President and his two Secret

Service bodyguards passed by. The guard noticed their slow pace but paid it little attention as the door to the White House swimming pool swung shut.

CHAPTER THREE

The high ceiling and dark wood paneling made the dimly lit room seem even darker. Heavy burgundy curtains on the two large windows were an effective opaque block to keep sunlight from streaming in. It could be night; it could be day. The green glass shade on the desk lamp allowed sufficient light for that work surface and that was all.

The only occupant had his back to the closed door with the phone held between his bent head and shoulder. His feet were up on the credenza in front of the two windows. The heavy, well-worn leather armchair tilted back. In his lap he held a legal pad on which he drew finely detailed abstract doodles.

Sidney Curtis, balding with well-developed jowls, showed signs of age and neglect both in physical appearance and dress. His expensive tie was loosened and the collar button open on his custom-made shirt. With an approaching election it was a very stressful time for a Chief of Staff and Sidney gave his job all he had. There had been no extended period of relaxation this summer. His pallor indicated just how little sun he'd been exposed to. The lines in his face gave him a weathered look but belied his preoccupation with matters revolving around this dimly lit office. More than once he'd been told he resembled the actor Broderick Crawford. But today, who knew what Broderick Crawford looked like or even who he was? This room had become his home for all intents and purposes. He spent more time in it than anywhere else. Sometimes he wondered if there was "anywhere else." A workaholic but not quite an alcoholic. Work, he reasoned, is what kept him from wallowing in the liquid contents of the lower righthand drawer in the big mahogany desk. That was a convenient liquor cabinet, well-stocked with Chivas Regal. A glass of the amber liquid was sitting next to the phone base while he spoke into the handset. Sidney allowed no ice in the glass to dilute its content.

"The contract for the copters is secure but I can't predict how the vote will go on the spare parts deal with the Saudis. I think the court appointment will ice the parts deal with Burdick and Cassanowitz but it's too early to be certain. The committee vote will be close, but I think if we sew up those two, the vote will go our way. I think we're in good shape. Tell Marv that I said it's a go but not to put the word out to his group of investors quite yet."

He listened idly, kept the doodle going and rocked the chair up and down.

"Yes, buy if you're hungry but I'm sitting tight until it's more certain."

"Okay, I'll know more in a few days and will bring you up to date as soon as it seems solid. Talk to you soon, George. Love to Veronica. Good-bye."

Turning back to his desk, he resumed an interrupted dictation. "Your speech in Denver will be watched closely by the pro-lifers in that state legislature. We have many friends there, so I suggest we have the speech crafted by Nelson to assure the right touch on this one. No sense getting friends upset at this late date. Miriam, have this ready for me in time for my eleven o'clock with the President."

The phone rang, and the screen indicated it was from the upstairs living quarters. A bit unusual this time of day.

"Hello, Mr. President. What can I do for you?"

He listened intently, and a frown slowly creased his forehead. "Sure, I'll be right up. Are you alone?"

The frown only intensified.

"Let's bring in Benson after we've had a chance to chat." The emphasis was on "after." "Two months before the election is no time to make any rash moves."

His head shook from side to side as he listened. "Sure, I understand that Jennifer will insist but we still need to think it through carefully. Remember what's looming ahead. The polls are encouraging, but I don't want to test the strength of our support. Let's talk first and then decide on the next step. Okay?"

He hung up and leaned back with a deep sigh.

Shitty timing. A health issue could be very damaging at this late date. Damage control wasn't good enough. There couldn't be any damage. The President trusted him and, as his Chief of Staff, he wasn't going to let anything derail this reelection campaign.

CHAPTER FOUR

The walk upstairs gave Sidney an opportunity to ponder what he was about to confront when faced with the President and his wife. He'd have to deal with the President downplaying the problem and the wife overreacting. He'd handled these small crises over and over again. By now he was a master at getting all parties to feel they'd gotten their way. As long as he was allowed to manage the problem, assuming there was a problem, he could minimize any undesirable fallout. Whether out of loyalty to the President or the need for personal satisfaction or both, he would do whatever was necessary to see the President through to re-election. November was only two months away and re- election was not in doubt. Nothing would be allowed to stand in the way.

When he entered the President's bedroom suite an anxious wife and a somber husband were seated close to each other on the edge of their king-size bed.

"Hello, Jennifer. Hello, Mr. President," was Sidney's casual greeting.

The President seemed to brighten up with the appearance of his closest confidant and advisor.

"Sidney, I'm sure this is something we can manage. Jennifer needs assurance that I'm going to get the best medical attention and not let any political consideration get in the way."

"Okay, Jack, let me hear it from the beginning."

Jack Henderson was a handsome, well-tanned six-footer. He was a golfer and sailor who looked every bit the country club gentleman he was. His graying hair was cut close and gave him a look a good deal younger than his 56 years.

He spoke with a deadpan expression, but Sidney could tell it was strictly for his wife's benefit. He wanted to appear unconcerned and keep her from becoming distraught.

The story was related in great detail but didn't take very long to tell. Sidney could sense that this was no minor event. There was no question that a doctor would be needed. Sidney's mind was racing ahead. Just two months to the election. He needed to assure Jennifer that her husband was going to get first-class care and that there would be no compromise with his health. Jack would be in his hands, as usual, so the problem was the wife.

"Sounds like a heart or lung problem to me, Jack. It needs to be investigated and treated appropriately." Sidney tried to maintain some degree of control in an area where he had no expertise. He needed to go slow and take time to think through the options. At such moments Sidney had the discipline which allayed anxiety and quelled panic. He focused his attention where he knew anxiety was greatest.

"Jennifer, I can imagine your concern, believe me. I share it. I just ask that you let me handle this so that Jack gets the care he needs, and we keep a very tight lid on whatever is going on until the situation is clarified."

His words had been intended to head off, or at least soften the reaction which was now unleashed by Jennifer Henderson.

The President's wife was a stunning brunette. Her beauty, coupled with a good grasp of politics and the media, had been an invaluable asset for Jack Henderson. Now she was in no mood to be managed by a skillful Chief of Staff and she let him know that in no uncertain terms. Sidney knew she conceded little to him and was a very worthy adversary when he was managing her husband through a crisis.

"I don't give a damn about secrecy, Sidney. I know what's on your mind. You want to keep a lid on this until after the election. Well, it won't keep. Even you won't be able to control this one."

"Come on, Jennifer, I'm not fooling with Jack's health. I only ask that you cut me some slack and let me show you how this can be handled to everyone's satisfaction. Are you with me, Jack?" Sidney was seeking some support for his cautious approach.

"Sure Sidney, but Jennifer is acting in my best interest too."

The President was reduced to a fumbling husband caught between an anxious, determined wife and a clever associate. Sidney stayed focused on the wife. She was the problem and he needed to get her to back off the ferocious protective spouse stance.

"Look. I'd like to get to work on this immediately and share my plan with you both in the morning. If you say it won't work or satisfy your concerns, we'll take it public and let the chips fall where they may. All I'm asking is that you give me a little time to work out an approach that I can present to you. And please, let's not overreact".

CHAPTER FIVE

As Sidney left the bedroom scene, he thought back to the night when he and Jack Henderson became as close as brothers. A young lawyer working for his father's small general practice law firm in Minneapolis, Jack Henderson was a very eligible bachelor with a good future in the law. He was restless, however, and wanted to experience what it was like in the big leagues. Minneapolis was okay, but it wasn't Washington D.C. or New York. He'd attended Law School at the University of Minnesota and this only fueled his desire to finally leave his hometown and see what beckoned on the East Coast. Enter Sidney Curtis.

Sidney and Jack had attended a fundraiser for the twice-elected mayor of Minneapolis. Standing at the bar, far away from the speeches and hors d' oeuvres, the two men struck up a serious conversation. Sidney was Chief of Staff for the aspiring mayor of a small town in the suburbs of Minneapolis. He too was restless and wanted to see what was out there in the centers of political power. It wasn't long before Sidney saw Jack as his ticket out of Minneapolis and Jack saw Sidney as the guy who could get him started in politics. When the junior senator from Minnesota was killed in a small plane crash that winter, it was as if a huge door had swung open. The two of them rushed through before it could close. The neophyte lawyer and the small-town political operative managed to put together an effective campaign and won the fall election against a weak Republican candidate who'd been appointed by the governor to fill the vacant seat.

Sidney saw Jack as possessing the critical qualities he himself lacked: the rugged good looks and charm that gave him broad appeal. If Sidney had Jack's good looks and charm, he, not Jack Henderson, might be President. At least that's the way he daydreamed the scenario after too many scotches. Nevertheless, Sidney could be a damn good second fiddle if that was the closest he could get to the big prize.

Jack, on the other hand, could see Sidney's skill grow as the campaign roared to a conclusion. His judgment was sound, his killer instinct wisely exercised and there never was any question about his loyalty. The bond was forged.

Sidney could see the potential for Jack Henderson on the bigger national stage, so he was determined to ride what he saw as a winner as far as he, Sidney Curtis, could take him. Ending up in the White House did not come as a total surprise.

Back in his office, Sidney placed an off-log call on his cellphone after his meeting with the President. He didn't want to leave any trail and didn't want his secretary to be able to testify that he had made a call, even if she didn't know to whom it was directed. He was suddenly very security conscious. This episode was clearly marked top- secret in his mind and that added to its complexity.

The phone was answered on the fifth ring and a curt, "Hello," came back. Sidney knew that there would be no chit-chat. He carefully explained the situation and then sat back and listened as an analysis of the problem along with a proposed solution was slowly but thoughtfully crafted and articulated back to him. He listened and responded when the speaker was through. It was a clever plan but not an easy one to put into effect. From long experience, he knew that the speaker was a master of strategy when it came to complex situations that demanded tough solutions. He always marveled at the man's instant grasp of the central issue and the ice-cold detachment with which he went about planning a response. The plan was very creative and very illegal. He also knew that it would be his responsibility to pull it off successfully and accept any blame if there was any blame to be dished out.

"I understand what you've outlined. Let me think it through operationally and see if there are any serious pitfalls we should address. Right now, I don't see any but we want to be sure we cover all aspects. I'll keep you posted as I proceed. Oh yes, we'll have to use our local operative on this one, so I just want you to be aware that the circle will widen a bit. Of course, Number One will be kept a sufficient distance from the more delicate actions required so as to be an innocent participant."

Without even a brief pause, the not unexpected response came back to Sidney, "Call me only when necessary. Good night."

Sidney immediately sent a text message to another number. The message was cryptic in the extreme.

"Number Six, this is Number Eight. Meet me at Place B in two hours."

He knew the message would be picked up within 15 minutes and deleted as soon as it was read.

CHAPTER SIX

The cellphone indicated a text message had come in. It had signaled at an awkward moment, so he let the message wait. His partner was oblivious as she rose up and down in front of him in the heat of pleasure. A brief glance at the phone's screen indicated he had to wrap up the current exercise and respond to the message from Sidney. His mind was no longer on his excited partner. She would sleep off the evening's drinks and sex in his apartment. The only question was whether he had time to let her satisfy him before he left. It was too good to pass up but he would have to accelerate the action.

She began to groan and move in more demanding style as her climax neared.

Two months of regular sex and they knew each other's moves very well. She would finish in a minute or two at the most and then after a brief respite would finish him in the manner of her choosing. For her, the latter was a satisfying way to wrap up because it restored to her some sense of control.

Her orgasm over, Leslie lay back, panting from the exertion. Her vigorous workout routines in the gym were no match for the vigor of her sexual activity.

"Steve, you fuck like you were raping the Sabine women."

"Les, your Wellesley education certainly enriches your metaphors. Now show me what else you learned at that nunnery. And let's make believe your curfew is breathing down on our necks."

She reached down and felt his sagging erection. "I think I can get this limp marine to stand at attention." Even in the dark he could see her smile as she took control.

Twenty minutes later, Steve Berk emerged from the shower, quickly toweled himself off and ran a brush through his unfashionable military-style crew cut. Ten minutes later, as he eased the apartment door shut, he could hear Leslie getting comfortable in his bed. The apartment served as both his office and an away-from-home site for liaisons. Steve often thought to himself that whoever said you shouldn't mix business with pleasure didn't understand the advantage of doing just that in his setup.

He eased the two-seater convertible out of the underground garage and drove slowly out of Georgetown to a familiar restaurant in nearby suburban Virginia.

The former Green Beret and CIA operative, now a private investigator, had many government clients. His reputation for success and absolute privacy had made him popular in a very sensitive and covert field. A call from Sidney Curtis was unusual but they had done work before. He knew the assignment would be top secret and probably illegal as hell.

CHAPTER SEVEN

J ennifer Henderson lay alongside her husband in the big four-poster bed. They were both in their bedclothes but were not making any effort to let their bodies touch. Jennifer was visibly agitated.

"Jack, I'm not going to let Sidney handle your health like a political campaign. You're going to get the best care there is, and I won't let you accept anything less."

"Jen, don't think I'm not concerned. I want to get to the bottom of this problem and I won't let Sidney or anyone else interfere. I just don't want to unduly alarm people about what may be a very manageable problem. I've only been faintly aware of it for a few weeks and I'm only bothered by it when I exercise. I'm sure there's an answer and I have no doubt that it can be handled with discretion. If the press can be kept out of this until after the election, we'll be able to proceed with whatever medical action is needed at a time and place of our choosing. Sidney knows how to handle these matters."

"Jack, Sidney has a controlling manner that worries me when he senses any threat to your office. I often wonder just how far he'd go to protect your position. I wonder if that includes your best interest when it comes to your health."

"Jen, Sidney and I have been together nearly twenty years and have shared a lot. He always puts my interests ahead of everything else and that's why we've both been successful. I trust him. There's no benefit to him for my health to be neglected or allowed to deteriorate."

"I wish I shared your faith, Jack. I sense he's always been a bit jealous of me and that frightens me at times."

"Look, Jen, let's let it rest tonight and see what he comes up with. I think you'll see a master strategist in action. That's what this situation calls for. Now, I'm exhausted and need some sleep."

Jennifer gave her husband a weak smile. "I know you've had a rough day, Jack. We'll catch up with each other soon enough. Good night, darling."

His light went out and Jennifer quietly went into the adjoining sitting room for some solitude and reflection on the day's happenings. Her very comfortable and secure world had abruptly become unstable and stressful. She was, however, ready to confront whatever came next. Jennifer Henderson was not one to wilt in the heat.

CHAPTER EIGHT

The dimly lit restaurant was nearly empty at the late hour, so Sidney Curtis and Steve Berk had a good deal of privacy at a corner table in the rear. Their drinks were half-finished, and the scattered remains of a grilled pizza lay on a cold aluminum tray. Berk listened carefully but did not have the look of a man being briefed by the White House Chief of Staff on a matter with implications which could stun the nation. Berk never gave an indication that the conversation was anything more than casual.

"I called you as soon as I thought I might need some quick, covert action on the medical front, Steve. Since that call I've thought this through carefully. I'll manage the entire affair myself with you acting only at my request, sometimes knowing very little and knowing only what I want you to know. There'll be no written records. None. You'll act as my agent and will only release information to people as I agree it's absolutely necessary.

The less you know, the less you can reveal. That's the safest way. You'll have to know some top-level stuff, but I know you'll keep that to yourself at all costs. Believe me, secrecy here is essential. The presidency is at stake, and there's a value I'd put on that which is hard to measure in just dollars and cents."

"You know my policy on secrets, Sidney. Me, you don't have to worry about. You know that. Our secrets die with me. My concern about maintaining secrecy is the President and his wife. He may be controllable but she's a wild card."

Sidney leaned forward for emphasis, "You're right, but she won't buck me if she thinks I'm acting in her husband's best interest. I must say that they're a very devoted pair. There's been no mess in their marriage for the eleven years they've been together. Her private life before the marriage was less inhibited than Jack believed. She knows I have some stuff on those earlier years. Trust me. She can be contained. But that's my problem, not yours."

"I hope so, Sidney, because she's gonna have a lot more information about what transpires than either of us would like her to. I don't like loose ends and she's a very loose end. Sidney, you better not underestimate her." Steve Berk shook his head from side to side as if to emphasize his concern.

"I don't, and I won't. Trust me."

"All right, Sidney. It's your ass even more than mine.

It seems the next step is getting this medical problem diagnosed and treated without letting anyone outside you, me and the White House couple, in on the matter. Shouldn't be any problem since every major newspaper and TV reporter in the country watches every step the President takes. That eliminates every major medical institution in the country and every leading heart specialist. I'll be watching you on this one, Sidney, with more than casual interest. If you can pull this off, I'll never doubt you on any scheme you propose."

Sidney knew Berk was serious. Berk viewed every assignment as a challenge to be accomplished with total secrecy. The fact that the plan had been conceived and "ordered" by a third party was none of Berk's business and so he was not made aware of their distant partner.

"I didn't say it would be easy, Steve, but I don't call you in on the easy ones. It may call for some work on the dark side, so be ready. I have to go all the way on this one. I have to."

Sidney smiled broadly to indicate the serious talk was over. "Now let's finish these drinks, Steve, and figure out if the Nationals will ever put together a winning team in our lifetime."

Berk also smiled at the segue from a top secret White House issue to the matter of a lame ballclub. "I guess you'll be giving away your tickets to me for some time, Sidney. You're too embarrassed to take your big shot friends out to see the Nats."

CHAPTER NINE

Leslie Nugent's apartment building was full of singles who liked the cache of a D.C. address but lived the limited lifestyle of coeds in a college dormitory. The building itself wasn't unlike a dormitory. Most of the apartments were one-bedroom affairs and had little style. Leslie's own one bedroom was like all the others in the building, a galley kitchen, a small living room-dining room area and a single bedroom with a double bed that occupied almost the entire floor area of the room. That bedroom was in the same confused state she had left it in the night before. The bachelor girl's wardrobe was half in the closet and half sprawled across the bed. The daily battle of picking out an outfit always left her room in a shambles. Although she prided herself on being a neat person, that could only be proven at her workplace.

Returning from Steve's place to shower and change into a fresh outfit for the day, Leslie listened to her voice mails while she tidied up a bit.

"This is Ron, Leslie. Your story on the governor's second home in the lake district will run on Sunday in the Metro section. He won't like it, but that's the price he pays for extraordinary greed. Simple, old-fashioned greed wasn't enough for him. Good job. See you at the Press Club at five-thirty for a drink."

Her editor was a good Joe. Still trying to make it with her, but too nice a guy to press what was obviously a losing cause.

The voice mails droned on with familiar voices.

"Hi, Leslie, this is Joan. Guess you had an all-nighter. I tried you until midnight. Lunch is still on if you're sufficiently recovered to eat. See you at the Potomac Diner tomorrow at noon." Joan was her best friend and former college roommate. She was still single and ever available for friendly anything. They were inseparable.

More messages followed but the clean-up was monopolizing her attention.

Reporting news for a small daily paper across the Potomac in Virginia wasn't a bad start for a girl with limited prior reporting experience. An occasional White House story added "spice" to the job, but she had to discover those stories on her own. The paper she worked for concentrated on the nearby Virginia suburbs.

Recent months had been oddly pleasant. Dating Steve Berk was undoubtedly the reason. Odd and pleasant. Steve brought little emotion to their relationship. She wasn't sure she even wanted to see his emotional side. He never talked about his work and never, no, never, about "Them." His marriage was not a success, but it wasn't on the rocks, either. For some reason, Steve stayed married but lived single. Maybe that was part of his attraction. He was immune to entangling relationships but perpetually hunting for women like a bachelor. She didn't love him, so his seeming commitment to his marriage allowed her to see him without forcing them to face the painful issue that beset many affairs. So, what did they talk about? She smirked.

Not much. Why was this closed, unemotional, married guy still a part of her life? Until Steve, romance and sex were standard stuff for her, and guys moved in and out of her life as if there was a fast-revolving door. With Steve, something else kept her coming back. She enjoyed sex with him more than she wanted to admit, but there was something else.

Their last date was a case in point. A long dinner in a dimly lit and unfashionable restaurant was followed by mischievous foreplay in the cab while discussing Washington politics with the driver. After that, a long evening of endless entwining, positioning and lubricating. She knew it wasn't love, but for the moment, the physical aspects were sufficient to keep her from looking elsewhere.

But there was one other thing. He did keep her well supplied with Washington insider gossip and enough leads to make her the paper's number one political insider. That would be hard to give up. Where and how he got all that dirt and all those insider rumors was a complete mystery to her. He never revealed anything of a very serious or consequential nature. Just some juicy leads for her to follow-up and make her insider column very popular. So, a date with Steve filled her needs on more than just the primal animal level.

Leslie had grown up in New York, on Long Island, the youngest of three sisters in a very comfortable house in a very competitive suburban town. She had enjoyed the freedom that came from being the "baby" in a household where the parents were tired of holding tight reins on successively more emancipated daughters.

Her sisters were married, and each had launched a successful career in business after obtaining an MBA. They each had bestowed two grandchildren on their parents, so the heat was not on Leslie to deliver anything. She was free of that obligation and liked it that way.

Like her sisters, she was an attractive, highly intelligent and fearless woman. Her light brown hair was kept straight, shoulder-length with bangs and parted to the side. Her green eyes worked well with her sensual full lips and perfect complexion. Her figure was every man's ideal and she knew how to clothe it to maximum advantage. She was never lacking for male companions and many had tried to get her to take them seriously, to no avail. Unlike her sisters, she had slept with a dozen men or more and her 35th birthday was only two months away. For her, sex was never an indication of strong affection, only a form of sport that she enjoyed.

In high school and for a time in college, she had been a star soccer player. She was aggressive and very cagey on the soccer field. The woman's professional soccer league had made overtures to her and she was strongly considering giving that a try until her left knee was badly injured in a collision on the field. From then on, she had to consider other options and newspaper reporting seemed to match up well with her independent spirit and skill at sniffing out stories. The present job was her first and she was now being watched by the *Washington Post* as she occasionally scooped their own veteran reporters. Steve was definitely helping to jump-start her career.

She'd never been close to a truly serious romance and Steve was not likely to ever get close to her in that sense. At times she wondered why real romance had evaded her, but she never let those thoughts linger very long. That was a subject her oldest sister had tried to discuss with her, but Leslie found it too threatening to explore deeply. Friend Joan had been equally unable to engage her on the subject. It was the one nagging uncertainty that clouded her otherwise happy-go-lucky existence. She knew it was the one bolt that needed tightening, but the process was too painful to consider. It was a lot easier to brush it aside and continue her life almost oblivious of that flaw.

CHAPTER TEN

O nce again, he spent the night in his office. Sidney's wife, Elaine, had been a rock of stability in his life. His tendency to over-work and have shady dealings, albeit profitable, had been held in check by Elaine. Her death from uterine cancer two years ago had been a massive blow.

He'd never fully recovered. His job had become the surrogate for Elaine, but without her steady hand, his propensity for wanting to win at all costs was unchecked. It was as if his conscience had died with her.

Sidney Curtis had not excelled in his days of formal education. A middle-of-the-class student, his lack of honors belied his A-grade instincts for making deals and keeping his more financially privileged associates ea-ger for his advice. A lucrative career on Wall Street or K Street was certain to follow his White House days. He and Jack Henderson had immediately sensed a comfort level that culminated in Jack's election to the Senate under Sidney's careful guidance. They were now as close as brothers with regard to their careers.

The late summer morning sun was unsuccessfully trying to invade his dark office hideaway. Sidney likened it to a cave, albeit a plush one. Two books were open on his desk. *Aviator Doctors* and the *Directory of Medical Specialists*.

Sidney had formulated his strategy in keeping with the plan broadly outlined to him over the phone less than 24 hours earlier. Planning in minute detail for complex operations was the reason he rarely failed. It was probably the single most determining factor that had brought Jack Henderson to the White House. Now he needed a heart specialist who flew a private plane. How he would pull off the entire operation was a challenge he would deal with once he had his man.

Cross referencing narrowed his list down to three men and he chose the one who practiced just over 300 miles away.

"Jeffrey Oldham," he whispered to himself. "Forty-two years old, board-certified in Cardiology, graduate of Duke University School of Medicine and trained in Medicine and Cardiology at the Mayo Clinic. Specialty: Interventional Cardiology." A made-to-order profile for his needs.

"Jack and Jennifer will surely be satisfied with this choice," he opined to himself.

Now to bait the trap and catch the prize.

He placed the call himself on his private phone line. Once again there would be no logbook entry.

A friendly secretary responded when he introduced himself as Doctor Nolan, calling long-distance.

"I'll put you on hold while I try to find Doctor Oldham."

A brief wait.

"Hello, this is Doctor Oldham. What can I do for you Doctor Nolan?"

"Thanks for taking my call. I have a most unusual request. Do you have a few minutes to talk with me?"

"No, I don't, but why don't we give it a try anyway." He sounded friendly and curious. A good combination.

"I represent a V.I.P. in Washington who, I believe, has a serious heart problem. By the way, I'm not a doctor. I only used that ruse to get through to you. Anyway, we want to get a top-quality consultant to see him and possibly even do a cardiac procedure, if necessary. The only catch is we want to do it very privately. Any news of his illness could be disruptive for many people at this time. I thought a cardiologist from out-of-town, flying in and out on a private plane would be as private as we could hope for. Of course, we would arrange for any procedure in a quality facility with a good deal of similar privacy. How does it sound so far?"

"More than a bit unusual, I must say. How did you pick me?"

"Well, there aren't many cardiologists with their own planes who live within easy flying range of D.C."

"I see. I have a lot of questions." Oldham was nibbling the bait.

"Fire. I'll do the best I can within the obvious limits of security."

"When do you want this to take place?"

"As soon as possible, no later than the end of this week. Don't worry, I anticipated your schedule concerns so let me assure you that we'll make it worth your while. For the one day's work and your promise of absolute secrecy, we're prepared to pay fifty thousand dollars plus expenses. Does that sound reasonable?"

"It's sounding more interesting all the time," was the positive response Sidney had anticipated.

"Trust me, Doctor Oldham, I'm very serious about the offer. The patient is very VIPish."

The call ended on a very positive note. Sidney leaned back and allowed a faint smile to cross his face. He'd reeled in a key player and could now move on to the implementation stage.

CHAPTER ELEVEN

Jennifer Henderson stared back at herself from the mirror on her vanity. Her husband was sound asleep next door in their large king-size bed. It was three in the morning, but she was wide awake, pondering the past twenty- four hours and the implications for the future. Her husband was suddenly a lot older than she was. She should have paid more attention to the warning signs that Jack was not well. They were pretty clear in retrospect.

Just a few days ago she was straddling him and enjoying the moment. Any question of Jack's health seemed remote indeed. As she approached her climax, he began to cough.

The mood broke. His coughing continued, and he struggled to sit upright. Jack was clearly in distress, gasping for air. She helped him sit up and gradually he began to breathe easier. The episode was frightening for both of them, but Jack had insisted that they not call the White House

31

physician. He obviously wanted no one to know about the episode, even his personal physician. Jennifer had argued the point with him, but he was adamant.

He agreed to discuss the best course of action with Sidney in the morning. The next day was the episode in the swimming pool.

Now, as she saw herself in the mirror, their age difference was painfully apparent. She was a youthful appearing, sensual woman in her early forties and he suddenly seemed very old in comparison at 56.

When they met eleven years ago, Senator Jack Henderson was one of Washington's most eligible bachelors. She was an aspiring news reporter on the most popular TV station in the region. Her healthy good looks and subtle sexuality had helped earn her a coveted spot on the evening news. Then, at a ski lodge in Vail, a large crowd of Washington celebrities had gathered for the evening in a rathskeller rented for the evening by a wealthy supporter of the senator. A trio played soft music in one corner and a bar did brisk business at the opposite end. The place was crowded with many guests who knew each other either by sight or reputation.

She was in Vail on assignment and trailed some better- connected network friends to the party. In her tight jeans and navy cardigan, she caught a number of eyes, even in a crowd. Jack Henderson made his way over to the table where she sat with several station colleagues. They immediately recognized him and made room for him to sit in with them.

It wasn't long before the object of his attention became apparent. Jack and Jennifer seemed to be drawn to each other the way iron filings were drawn to a magnet. The friends gradually moved along, leaving Jack and Jennifer alone in the booth. They talked while the crowd thinned out. The evening grew late and serious skiers left for an early bedtime.

Conversation came easily to the two of them, so it wasn't long before both sensed a rapport bordering on intimacy.

"Where did you ski today, Jennifer? I didn't see you on the big mountain and I'm sure I would have noticed you."

"I spent much of the day on the far side near Little Indian. It's a bit quieter and more compatible with my skill level. I'm just a nervous intermediate who avoids challenges. If I end the weekend in one piece without any plaster on my legs I consider it a triumph." She flashed her killer smile.

"I understand completely and agree that it doesn't pay to ski out of your level. Did your partner stay with you all the way?"

The segue to her personal situation was quite obvious but she was glad he asked.

"No, I lured him over the edge at an icy turn and even the ski patrol had trouble bringing the body back up."

Jack stayed in the rhythm of her humor, "So that means you're unattached tonight." He put both palms forward as if to apologize. "Forgive me, that's the punch line to a joke I've told too many times. I won't inflict it on you."

By now, the two of them were growing weary of the gentle small talk and were looking for a way to break some new ground and test each other's interest in moving this casual banter into more serious territory.

Jennifer could see Jack's gaze occasionally take in her cleavage. Her cardigan was open just one button more than fashion dictated, and she only wore a low-cut silk undershirt underneath. When she reached forward for chips or dip, his eyes would glance downward and catch a glimpse of her breasts. She enjoyed the game and played it expertly. Moreover, he knew she knew he was looking and that made it doubly enticing for each of them. They both were getting excited by the game and wondered how to take it to the next level.

Jennifer was hoping he would ask her to dance. She also wondered whether his eyes were the only part of him reacting to the game. She could find out on the dance floor. For her part, the game was also having a very definite effect on her arousal system. Three highballs and a few beers had really loosened her up. She decided to take the initiative.

"Would you care to dance, Senator?"

On the dark dance floor, he led her nicely in a slow fox-trot. He held her tighter than she'd normally expect but not tighter than she found enjoyable. They were floating on an alcohol cloud and feeling no inhibitions. The trio played gentle standards. The crowd was running a very high blood alcohol level and could only handle slow stuff on the dance floor.

She fit against Jack snugly and determined with no difficulty that he was aroused.

"Mmmm," was all she said as they shuffled a slow, heavy-footed two-step. This wasn't even a first date, but they were already on intimate terms. She moved even closer to him, rolling her hips ever so gently. There was no pretense about what they were doing. They couldn't have cared less about anything or anyone else at the moment. His hand on her back explored her rear cleavage whenever her back was to the unoccupied part of the dance floor. She offered no resistance.

The liquor was loosening her up even more. She made a brazen decision, having decided that there was nothing to lose.

"Senator," she whispered in his ear, "I think you're going to wet your jeans if we keep on dancing like this." She was driving now, and he was a very willing passenger.

Her hand on his shoulder moved to the back of his neck. Her hips continued their gentle massaging action. He said nothing, but his deep breathing said enough. "Stardust" would be a tune they'd remember for all time. After ten bars more, he began to lose his dance rhythm and she maneuvered them to the darkest part of the dance floor. They were barely dancing now. She mused that this dance step didn't have a name. Her hips continued their gentle grinding movement and then he shuddered several times. She whispered into his ear, "Oh my. That's nice. That really is."

They stood apart after a minute or so while the music continued.

"You're quite a dancer, Senator. I like a man who feels the music and lets it show in his dancing." Her tone was both warm and mocking. "Want to sit the next one out?", she asked.

He surprised her with his quick recovery, "Well, I owe you and I'd like to return the favor, but in my room. 317. Be there in five minutes. I'll go on ahead of you." He left.

She found his room and they resumed where they had left off on the dance floor. They were sexually compatible and then some. She never knew a man who enjoyed her enjoyment more. For him the dance floor event was the start of a torrid weekend and a relationship that he could not conceive of ending. Two weeks later they announced their engagement and now, eleven years later, a marriage of complete fidelity was at a crossroad.

Fidelity had come easily since they greatly enjoyed sex with each other. What would happen if either lost interest or ceased to satisfy the other, was a question she had never faced until the episode two days ago. The romance in their lives had mellowed a bit in recent years, but she was not without a strong sense of loyalty to her mate. They'd been through a lot together and were very close.

One thing was certain, though. She knew that masturbation would never fully satisfy her.

CHAPTER TWELVE

After arranging for the consultation with Jeff Oldham, Sidney set about planning for the clandestine visit.

The doctor would fly into Ridgewood airport in northern Virginia, just 30 minutes from D.C. Sydney would pick him up personally and explain the mission to him on the way to the White House. He was sure the doctor would be overwhelmed by the situation and would do as he was asked. He would be introduced at the White House, by Sidney, as an economist, expert on the Middle East, who was here to help the President with his understanding of Palestinian economic problems.

First, he would examine Jack. Then, if needed, Sidney would explain the arrangements for a cardiac catheterization procedure. The Doctor had suggested on the phone that a "cath" would be the fastest and most reliable way to sort out the cardiac condition. He agreed to do such a procedure, if it was indicated, but expressed reservations about doing it in an unfamiliar facility. Sidney said he would deliver a facility with equipment similar to what he worked within North Carolina. Staffing, however, would be kept to a minimum to assure secrecy.

Sidney had gone to work and, with Steve Berk's help, found a facility in the vicinity that met the equipment requirements. Berk had scouted the facility and arranged in private for two cath lab workers to help Jeff Oldham. A nurse and a tech were to be all the staff in the room with the doctor. Jeff would have to keep the President's identity to himself and not allow his assistants to know the patient's identity. This would be tricky but was doable.

Berk would maximize security, including the identity conceal-ment. They would be doing the procedure on a Tuesday evening. Chance encounters would be at a minimum.

Berk had made arrangements with two hospital security people on duty that evening to give them several hours of privacy. It hadn't cost as much as he feared, and he had given them a minimum of information. They were made to understand that this was a very private affair and under no circumstance were they to leak any information. All they knew was that they were to assure a period of absolute privacy for the cath lab suite. Since emergencies were handled in another cath facility in the emergency department there was no reason to believe the lab they were "protecting" would be called into action. Berk was pleased to see that these security people were quite comfortable with being tight-lipped for a price. So far so good.

CHAPTER THIRTEEN

The small plane landed at the tiny airfield right on time. Jeff Oldham's estimate of the fly time had been right on target. The sun was just beginning to set, and the small airport was deserted except for the attendant who manned the desk and checked planes in and out.

The plane taxied into a space in a row of ten or twelve similar one- and two-engine planes. The pilot emerged and entered the small building to make arrangements for the plane's stay and refueling.

Sidney observed this from his car a short distance away in a small parking area. When Jeff emerged, Sidney left his car and greeted him with a friendly handshake. The doctor's bags were put in the trunk and they took off for the White House.

Their conversation during the trip held a big surprise for Jeff. He was now informed that they were heading for the White House and the

VIP was indeed the President of the United States. He was stunned, much as Sidney expected.

The total picture for him was both scary and intriguing. Sidney gauged the doctor's character and concluded that he was a good choice for such a weighty adventure.

Sidney assured him that he and the President expected nothing more and nothing less than a very thoughtful analysis of the President's health situation. Just the kind of work he did routinely in his practice. The secrecy aspect shouldn't interfere with his work. That was Sidney's responsibility and he assured the doctor that all bases would be covered. By the end of the day, Jeff would be on his way home with a big secret and the promise of a very generous payment.

The examination was thorough, lasting less than an hour. The President's bedroom had been the exam room. The President, Sidney and Jeff were the only attendees.

Jennifer Henderson had agreed to honor her husband's wish and kept her distance. Sidney had convinced Jack Henderson that security was essential, and that Jennifer would be better off knowing as little as necessary at this point.

Jack was impressed with Sidney's confidence that he could pull this off with utter secrecy. Sidney betrayed none of his own personal anxiety.

Jeff finished his exam. The findings were not conclusive, but the differential diagnosis was obvious. His portable electrocardiogram had been instructive. Either the patient had advanced coronary heart disease or an inflammatory process of the heart muscle, myocarditis. In either case, he was in a mild degree of heart failure and the outlook was guarded. The long-term prognosis would be easier to predict after the catheterization procedure. The treatment options could be spelled out after the diagnosis was established. This was all explained to the President and his Chief of Staff in the President's bedroom. Jack took the news well and wanted to know what the next step would be. Sidney explained the plan to him and answered a few obvious questions about security and how it would affect their immediate schedule of campaign visits. Jack was satisfied with the answers and gave Sidney the green light to proceed. Sidney had never doubted that Jack would be easy to convince. Jennifer would be informed when the procedure was over.

Getting out of the White House required a ruse. The pretext was a secret meeting with a Palestinian leader at an area hospital where the Palestinian was falsely staying as a patient. Jeff, the would-be expert on the Palestinian economy, was needed as an intermediary. The three of them would travel with limited escort. Berk was going along as a shadowy bodyguard, and even now managed to stay at the very fringe of the group, barely noticeable. Earl Jensen, head of White House security. intensely disliked such adventures, but the President was Commander-in-Chief, so what he said went. Since Sidney was going too, Jensen felt a bit more comfortable. Jensen respected Berk but was still uneasy that standard safety precautions had been thrown to the wind.

Security people would remain at a distance sufficient enough that they would be unaware of the actual event but close enough to keep the general area under close surveillance. They would help rather than hinder the operation by keeping stray visitors and workers away from the meeting area. When Jack Kennedy had left the White House for late evening trysts, the Secret Service had been obliged to look the other way. There were ample precedents for this type of executive freedom. No one liked it, but who could argue with the President?

CHAPTER FOURTEEN

Berk had done his job. There were no hospital security people at the chosen side entrance and the halls of the hospital were clear all the way to the elevator that took them to the fourth floor and the cath lab suite. Berk met Sidney, Jeff and the President at the elevator. The President's disguise was a simple one but would suffice. A thick mustache and tinted glasses would do the job. Berk had applied the make-up with professional skill. His line of work made disguise an integral element of clandestine operations. The staff would not know who the patient was as long as Jeff remembered to refer to him only as "General."

With few words exchanged, the President undressed and donned a hospital gown. He was then directed to lay down on the x-ray table. The patient's groin area was prepped by Jeff and the room set up for the procedure by the nurse and technician. Jeff was satisfied that all was in order to proceed.

He knew the nurse as Karen and the tech as Darryl. They knew him as Doctor Allison. The well-disguised and distant observers were identified as security personnel from the Pentagon.

"Let's put the sheath in, Karen."

Within a minute a sheath was expertly placed in the femoral artery and a catheter was visible on the TV screen. It snaked its way around the aortic arch and easily found the left coronary artery.

Jeff spoke to himself as information began to surface. "No calcium in the coronaries. I'm betting against coronary disease."

He gave the go-ahead to begin acquiring images. "Let's take the first shot, Darryl."

Contrast medium filled the left coronary system. The vessels were normal. Several more shots followed at different angles and all were normal.

"Let's change the catheter, Karen, and get on with the ventriculogram."

Again, a catheter snaked around the aortic arch but this time it made an abrupt move downward.

"Okay, we're in the left ventricle," Jeff informed the staff. The catheter in the ventricle was relatively still and this gave Jeff a premonition that all was not well. A bouncing catheter was a sign of vigorous contraction.

"General, you're going to feel a hot flush. It'll pass off in a few seconds so don't be alarmed." He signaled the tech to inject the dye.

A large, poorly functioning ventricle appeared on the screen.

The dysfunction was generalized and quite significant. Jeff had seen enough. "I think we can stop here."

They had agreed in advance to do as little as necessary to minimize the trauma to Jack Henderson. Sidney's principal concern was getting out of there as quickly as possible and he wanted Jack mobile as soon as possible. So far everything had gone according to plan. The lab procedure had taken under twenty minutes.

The tech applied twenty minutes of compression on the groin puncture site. The patient was ready to move. A wheelchair was used as a precaution. The staff then put the lab back exactly as they had found it. Everything was disposable, so that simplified the task. The disposable supplies would be taken away by Darryl to be disposed of far away from the hospital. No one was to know that the room had been used. The digital x-ray pictures were erased while Berk watched. A handsome bonus was to be paid to Karen and Darryl in two days if Berk could verify that no one not in attendance was aware that the facility had been used. There were to be no tracks left behind.

The workers knew what they'd done but they had no idea who the patient was.

While the technician compressed the groin, Jeff wrote a detailed note describing all of his findings and added a list of medications to be used and the basis for adjusting doses.

He was completing a very hasty consultation but was as thorough as he could be under the circumstances. This patient had a sick heart and treatment was essential to slow progression of its dilatation. Entry into a heart failure program was strongly advised. Sidney took the note and assured Jeff that the President's physician would receive it. Most likely he would want to talk to Jeff over the phone in a day or so. Jeff agreed with the plan and the group left the suite the way they had come in. They met no one on the way out.

Berk would drive the doctor to the airport. Sidney and the President would return to the White House in Sidney's car. Before Berk and Jeff left for the airport, Sidney took Jeff aside and summarized the findings to be sure he had it straight.

"Jeff, you found an impaired heart with normal coronary arteries. You believe that some virus may have damaged the heart muscle. You also think that there's little or nothing to do that will fix the damaged muscle. He should be treated for heart failure and may some day be a candidate for a heart transplant. With proper medications, the problem might stabilize for a period of time and even allow the President to complete another term in office. There is no certainty about the course of the illness, however, so a second term might not be completed."

Sidney was very sober. He appreciated that he was discussing a grim situation. Jack would handle it if he, Sidney, put the right spin on it. That was his job, as usual. The "spin doctor." Jennifer would have to cope, and her reaction was more difficult to anticipate.

"Jeff, let me thank you again. Your detailed outline of drug treatment will be a valuable aid to the White House medical staff. I'm glad you took the time to spell out your recommendations. Jack's personal physician may consult you from time to time, although I suspect he'll need to develop a relationship with a local team of experts. You're a real professional so I know your discretion as a physician will suffice to keep this episode forever secret. You just played a very important role in the function of the government. Jack and I are deeply grateful and won't forget what you did for us tonight."

"I was honored to be asked. Frankly, all the intrigue made my head spin. I never dreamed I'd be involved in anything so secret yet carried out with such finesse. I'm very impressed," Jeff replied.

"Your cash payment will be hand-delivered to you personally in a few days. Thanks again for everything."

They shook hands all around and the two cars left in opposite directions.

CHAPTER FIFTEEN

The single-engine Cessna taxied down the runway and rose easily in the windless night air. Anticipated flying time to Burdick Airfield in North Carolina was less than two hours. Jeff figured he'd be in bed by two in the morning.

Reflecting on the events of the day, Jeff could scarcely believe what had transpired. He'd examined the President of the United States in the White House, performed a diagnostic catheterization procedure on the President and was now airborne back to North Carolina. No one had blinked or thought anything out of the ordinary had taken place, except him. Or so it seemed.

He understood the need for secrecy but wondered how the information was going to be presented to the public. He continued to turn the events over in his mind. What exactly was the need for such secrecy? Actually, he thought, you'd have expected the President to seek high profile care and not the clandestine care he'd received. It didn't add up. As a matter of fact, he thought, there might be more public distress about the way they'd gone about the whole affair. It didn't add up.

At 3,000 feet the semi-liquid "bubble" in the fuel line began to expand. By the time he reached 4,000 feet, the fuel line was occluded.

Berk had carried out his assignment with great care and precision. The small airport was nearly deserted when he'd first arrived, and the doctor's Cessna was easy to find.

The "bubble" was an old CIA device used to eliminate unwanted, inconvenient political leaders in third world countries. There was no way to detect it after a crash.

Jeff Oldham never suspected that he was being eliminated as a potentially dangerous witness. Those handshakes had felt genuine enough. His last thought was incredulity over the engine failure he was experiencing. In the next moment, the Cessna and its occupant were spread over an area larger than a baseball infield.

Berk, sitting in his office, heard news of the crash on his shortwave radio that picked up air traffic control communications. A small plane had gone down in Virginia.

No survivors. He rang up Sidney. The conversation was brief and only comprehensible to the two involved parties.

"Went as expected. Any hitches on your end?" Berk was emotionless as he reported on his assignment.

"No. Goodnight." Sidney hung up. He had one very brief call to make before he went back to sleep. He and Berk were now the only ones fully in the know. It hadn't been easy. Careful planning had paid off, though.

Sidney would have to tell the President's wife an abridged version of the night's events in the morning. News of the doctor's fate would not be shared with her nor would the President be briefed on that aspect of the episode.

Sidney knew how best to protect those involved.

Earl Jensen rolled over in bed and squeezed his wife. Thankfully, the President had returned safely to the White House after an out-of-the-ordinary, barely secure venture into Washington, D.C.

In Tucson, a phone rang in the penthouse atop the building which housed the offices of Covington Industries. The person in bed set down his novel and picked up the receiver. He heard a very brief message. His only words were, "Good show." He hung up and resumed reading.

BOOK TWO

THE INVESTIGATION

CHAPTER ONE

Alan Seibolt was on call, so the bedside telephone awakening him from a deep sleep was not a surprise. The State Police were calling to let him know that his colleague's plane had crashed. There was no reason to believe Jeff had any passengers with him. It was not official, but they were letting him know since Alan was listed on the flight plan as the person to contact in case of an emergency.

"Are you sure about the identification?" Alan asked.

"There was no doubt about the plane. Absolute identification of the body will take a few days, but all indications are that it was Jeff Old-ham," said the caller.

"Where did this happen?" was Alan's next query.

His surprise was evident when the caller indicated that the crash site was in Virginia. He didn't even know Jeff was going out of town. He had agreed to cover for him and hadn't asked any questions.

"What was the cause of the crash? Was the weather a factor?"

The caller's answers were of little help. Weather was fine. The plane just fell out of the sky.

That didn't make any sense. Jeff was an excellent, experienced pilot with a well-cared-for plane. There had to be some explanation.

The caller indicated that there would be more information after the aviation authorities had an opportunity to examine the wreckage and do an analysis of the circumstances surrounding the flight. That would take a few weeks. The flight had originated in northern Virginia, just outside Washington, D.C. and the plane was registered to Jeff Oldham. That was all the police knew at this time.

Alan turned off his light, but sleep did not return. His partner and closest friend was gone. Just like that. Jeff was no more. Their plans were now irrelevant. Jeff didn't exist anymore. Two bachelor doctors whose lives were entwined, as if they were brothers, had been abruptly torn apart. Jeff had a not-too-serious girlfriend whom Alan would call. The call to Jeff's parents in Oregon was the one he dreaded.

What had happened? Something was going on that he didn't know about. Jeff and he were close friends, yet Alan had no idea why he had gone to Virginia or Washington. That didn't make any sense. He had to know more. The group would have to cover for him while he went to Washington to retrieve the body and find out anything he could about Jeff's trip. It might take a day to make plans to leave but he had to go. This was just a friend's blind curiosity, but in this case, it was a powerful driver for Alan Seibolt.

CHAPTER TWO

S idney Curtis met with Jack and Jennifer Henderson in their private suite. The President would have to resume a modified schedule that day and they all needed to be on the same wavelength. Sidney had tried to anticipate Jennifer's reaction but her relaxed affect was a total surprise. He'd expected a fierce struggle over the management of Jack's medical care. Instead, she was complacent.

"Jack had an extensive workup yesterday. We had it conducted by an excellent cardiologist. Jack underwent a cardiac catheterization, Jennifer, under the most secure circumstances imaginable. The result of the exam is that we know Jack has sustained damage to his heart that explains his recent shortness of breath. The cause is not coronary artery disease, but rather a viral infection of the heart muscle."

Jennifer's concern was evident but not overly emotional.

"What does this mean for the long term? Should Jack consider leaving office?"

Her husband failed to take note of her well-maintained composure and instead, tried to ease her anxiety over his condition.

"Jenn, Sidney and I have discussed the options and feel that there is no reason to consider pulling out. Moreover, there is every reason to believe that a second term is in the cards and is very doable."

Sidney cut in and tried to solidify his control of the situation. "Doctor Benson will be handling his medications in conjunction with a cardiologist expert in heart failure management. Treatment should be very helpful in allowing Jack to resume his duties. We'll scale back the physical demands of the campaign and that's where we'll need your help, Jenn. We'll be asking you to do more campaigning on the road while Jack does more from the White House. It's not that he can't campaign on the road. He will. It's just that we don't want to push him any harder than is absolutely necessary."

Sidney had no intention of widening the circle of information beyond Dr. Benson and Jack had agreed. Benson would get a condensed version of the problem. He was going to feel hurt that he'd been bypassed in favor of an outside doctor, but his personal loyalty to the President would be crucial and hopefully that would be sufficient to get him on board to manage the necessary medications. He would be asked to contact a local heart failure expert and use him as a supportive consultant on a colleague-to-colleague basis. The patient would be discussed in the abstract. Just enough information would be shared to allow conversation between Jennifer and the President's physician without giving either of them any reason to doubt their understanding of the matter. Once the election was over, a more open and relaxed approach would be developed, and the public gradually allowed to share the news. Benson's involvement would then expand, and direct expert consultation would be brought in. The circumstances surrounding the catheterization procedure would be explained away as necessary to minimize public alarm and excessive questioning by the press that could have endangered several highly sensitive talks being carried out in secret.

Jennifer was trying to get on board. "You know I'll do what's necessary, Sidney, but you can't keep me in the dark. Just how bad is the heart problem?" Jennifer needed to know enough to keep her from committing any faux pas in public.

Sidney wanted to assure Jennifer that he was not painting a rosy picture.

"Bad enough to prevent Jack from doing any strenuous exercise at this time. We certainly don't want to test his limit in public. If the medications are as good as we've been led to believe, he should be sufficiently active to carry out his regular duties. The campaign will need some redesign but that's my problem."

"And that's it?" she asked. "How do you feel about all this, Jack?"

"Sidney said it the way I feel. I plan to stay in office." His tone was tinged with veiled impatience.

Jennifer sensed the subtle change and backed off.

Sidney got up and walked toward Jennifer slowly. "There is one more thing, Jennifer. Secrecy. This is OUR business and no else's. At this moment, we three are the only ones in the White House who know any of this. We've been very, and I mean very, careful."

"What about the doctor?" Jennifer asked.

"Benson can be trusted to keep the information very private. It's covered by the doctor-patient confidentiality rule. He only knows what we tell him and that's being kept to a minimum. He'll access specialists as he feels the need."

"I don't mean Benson, Sidney, I mean the doctor who was here yesterday. I notice you haven't referred to him by name. Am I being given the same abridged version you're giving Benson?"

"Jennifer, trust me. This will go a lot better if we just let that slide. Let me be the manager. The less everyone knows the better. There'll be fewer slips that way. If you need to know something and feel I'm holding back, say so. Don't be curious, though. That's usually not in the best interest of maintaining secrecy. Can I, I mean we, count on you?"

"Of course, you can, Sidney. Curiosity sometimes gets the best of me. I've been in this game long enough to know how it plays. Especially where the press is concerned."

The President was growing impatient. "O.K. Sidney? Can we get on now with rearranging my schedule, so the day can begin?"

"Certainly, Mr. President."

Sidney was not taken in by Jennifer's compliant attitude. He knew her too well. There'd be more turns in this road and he was sure she'd be the cause of some of them. She was an attractive woman in her mid-forties, enjoying the fruits of her older husband's powerful position. What must she be turning over in her mind at a time like this? That's the stuff novels are made of.

CHAPTER THREE

L eslie's editor called about the plane crash and gave her the assignment. She headed out to the small airport to get as much information as she needed for a very brief story in the next day's edition. Small airplane crashes weren't very stimulating, she thought, but there had to be a story in the paper and it was hers to write. The story usually required some technical details about the airplane, the weather, the pilot, crew, passengers and some information about the flight's purpose and destination. To the extent that there was some human-interest aspect, all the better. It usually was cut and dried without any interesting twists. So be it.

The airfield was hung over in a low morning ground fog. As a consequence, the place was nearly deserted. The only office building on the field was a small one-level cinder block structure built sometime in the late thirties. No charm, no style, just gray unpainted cinder blocks.

Leslie parked in the dusty, unpaved parking area adjacent to the building. There was only one other car. "Must be the last parking lot in America without spaces designated for disabled drivers," she thought upon leaving her car and heading for the lone door in the building's front face.

The door was unlocked and the pleasant smell of freshly made coffee invited her in. Behind a gray metal counter sat a thin man in his seventies in a tan, loose-fitting chino shirt and matching slacks. His nearly white hair was neatly combed, and his face sported a very clean shave. A tabloid newspaper was spread over the desk, so the Goods-For-Trade page could be scanned for hidden treasure.

"Good morning, sir," was Leslie's opener for the morning.

"What can I do for you, young lady?" The man flashed a broad smile and let his dentures sparkle in the fluorescent light.

"I'm Leslie Nugent, a reporter with the *Sentinel*, and I'm looking for some information about the plane that crashed last night." She put on her most friendly face and leaned on the metal countertop.

"Oh yeah, the crash. Gave it all to the troopers, but I guess you want to hear it from me again."

"You're right. Maybe we could start with your name."

"John deAngelis, Miss Nugent. It's spelled with a small 'd' and a big 'a'."

"Well, John, what happened?" Leslie asked as she opened her notepad.

"Not much to say. Plane, a single-engine Cessna, came in yesterday morning around eight from North Carolina. Parked over there near the hanger, alongside the twin. Checked in. Young pilot, about 40, hard to be sure, asked for a gas fill-up, paid with a Visa and went outside to wait for a ride. Car came along a few minutes later and took him away."

"Did you see the person who picked him up, John?"

"Nope. Just a gray car. No one got out. Couldn't tell the make but it wasn't some big fancy car."

"Could I see the log? I'm looking for some information about the pilot."

"Can't see why not. Help yourself." He turned the thick, hard-covered book around so that she could read it. A simple log with very basic information. Leslie copied down the data verbatim.

The pilot was Jeffrey Oldham, and the flight had originated from and was returning to Burdick Airfield in North Carolina. The times were given and a Visa charge receipt for fuel was attached to the page with a paper clip. The reason for the trip was given as "pleasure."

"Mighty short pleasure trip," thought Leslie.

The information was sparse, but so were all the other entries in the book. Leslie turned the book back to the attendant. She visualized the piece she would be putting together in the next hour.

"How did he return?" she asked.

"Same way he left. Car dropped him off."

She was probing idly, looking for any information. Anything at all.

"Was it the same car?"

"Nope. Different one. Sportier."

"Did you see the driver?"

"Yup. A man. Different one. Couldn't see the face very good but it was a different man. He never got out of the car."

"Local car? Did you see the license?"

"Not sure. Could have been a D.C. plate but I'm only guessin'. I've got cataracts so my night vision ain't what it used to be."

Leslie sensed she had drained this well of all its water. The crash report would need some basic information about the pilot, so the police station would be her next stop. She thanked the attendant and went out to her car.

"Not much of a story so far," she mused. "Man flies in from North Carolina, for 'pleasure,' is picked up and returned the same day in two different cars, takes off and dies in a crash less than an hour later. I'd just as soon cover a local crafts fair," she thought.

An hour later, back in the office, she put the story together. The only additional information the crash report added was the age and address of the pilot and the fact that he was a physician. It was his personal airplane and he was fully licensed to pilot it. The cause of the crash was listed as "mechanical malfunction." There was little likelihood that any additional information would be forthcoming. The police didn't show particular interest in the crash and the wreckage was particularly hard to retrieve and put back together. The story ended here. It made page four, ran for four inches on the same page as the story on tarring the county roads.

CHAPTER FOUR

In the days since Jack's acute episode of apparent heart failure, Sidney had managed to radically revise the President's campaign schedule. The strategy called for him to make frequent appearances in the Rose Garden and Oval Office, meet with congressional leaders, foreign dignitaries and members of the media. Jack was not in the least troubled physically by these activities and it allowed the public to see their president looking hale and hearty. What was avoided were any physically taxing trips out of Washington where it would be difficult to maintain complete control of the physical demands and the possibility of exposing Jack's limited capacity to endure physical strain. His medications were having a beneficial effect and had improved his ability to endure low-level stress.

The reason given to the media for the reduced travel was a recurrence of an old back problem that made prolonged sitting in an airplane, bus, or car difficult to manage.

Hope was held out that the back problem was mending, and that travel would be resumed as soon as it was deemed advisable. With two months to go in the campaign and the debates set for one month ahead it was expected that the President would be ready to resume a more active schedule by the time of the debates. Sidney was encouraged by the benefits of the drug regimen and he planned on phasing in some more traditional campaigning within a month or so.

Jennifer began to do some of the traveling for her husband. She was media savvy and enjoyed jousting with the press on the road. She especially looked forward to getting away from the White House where Sidney and her husband were frequently closeted away in the Oval Office having very private discussions. Jack shared less and less with her and more and more with Sidney. "So be it," she mused. These were the longest periods away from Jack in their entire marriage, but it didn't seem to bother her at all.

Houston was a routine stop for her. She'd be there two days, make several appearances, speak to friendly audiences and have some time to herself.

The afternoon bath was very relaxing, and the nice complementary bottle of chilled Sauvignon Blanc was good company. The hotel suite was a generous gift from the Houston branch of the Right to Life organization. Her staff knew that she liked her privacy and had left her alone in the suite after her afternoon speech before the Texas Sheriffs' Association. Mildly high on her third glass of wine, Jennifer lay carelessly on the king-size bed in just a thin white cotton robe.

The telephone ring was a jarring interruption. She rolled over to the bed's edge, picked up the receiver and heard a vaguely familiar voice.

"Jennifer, this is Howard Westlake. How are you?"

She hadn't heard that voice for over ten years, but the years suddenly shrank. She abruptly sat up.

"I'm just fine, Howard. What inspired this call? It's been quite a while, but it's really nice to hear your voice." Her own voice reflected genuine pleasure which she hoped he appreciated.

Howard continued the upbeat mood, "I saw in the paper that you were in town and without husband. Thought you might like to get together, have a drink and talk about old times. I know what you've been up to, but you might be interested to hear what's been going on in my life."

Jennifer's reaction shocked her. She actually was eager to see this guy from her past.

Jennifer and Howard had been a natural fit or so her friend Alice had thought. Getting them together was not very difficult since they both were in the television news business and haunted the same watering holes after work.

They made a handsome couple and quickly became romantically smitten with each other. Jennifer took the lead, and Howard was her puppy dog. The relationship started out very heated. Their friends assumed they had each found their life partner and so did Howard. Jennifer didn't exactly see the future quite as clearly. Although they each had a fire in the belly over their respective careers, for Jennifer the fire burned more brightly. It was difficult for her to meet Howard halfway when he attempted to draw her away from incessantly climbing the career ladder. She was aware of this gap in their relationship. It wasn't that she wanted his fire to burn more brightly; she just didn't want him to cool hers down.

The gap widened and each recognized that it was insurmountable. Jennifer began to meet colleagues who felt similarly about their careers and decided that she and Howard were not the perfect match their friends had idealized. After a painful discussion about their respective career goals, they agreed to part.

Two months later, she met Jack at a ski lodge.

She and Howard hadn't spoken since, but she did have an occasional daydream about Howard. And this past week, she had thought about him more than in previous years. Jack's illness had triggered an interest in her old flame, a kind of rescue operation. Rescue? From what? She knew. Her need for male companionship weighed on her as she realized that her future with Jack had taken a rather abrupt turn toward a less physical relationship. And just like that, Howard Westlake called, almost on cue.

"Of course, I'm interested, Howard. Why don't you meet me in the bar of my hotel. The Westin has a very nice lounge. It's quiet but sufficiently public that my entourage of Secret Service men won't be uncomfortable. They'll give us plenty of private space."

"Sounds great, Jenn. I'll see you at six. I'm going to enjoy telling you all about my transfer to D.C., which is coming up this week."

The lounge was crowded with businessmen and women beginning to unwind after a day of on-the-road business dealings. The setting was businessman-friendly with lots of leather, low lighting, attractive waitresses and bar nuts on every table and along the bar. The bar was three deep with business-suited drinkers and the piano playing in the corner was barely audible above the din of conversation. Some were on the prowl and others just happy to be unburdened of the day's challenge. It was a jumble of marrieds, ex-marrieds and never marrieds. They were all tossed together in this mildly excited state and some would end up paired off for the evening.

Jennifer was a thoughtful observer of the scene. She could barely remember back to the days when she was a card- carrying member of this crowd, which felt barely connected to their real-world obligations, and could cut loose a bit, at least for that evening. She empathized with the palpable level of both relaxation and latent excitement.

For her, however, there were two discrete Secret Service men nearby watching to assure her safety. They were used to a relatively young first lady who insisted on getting out into the quasi-normal world for some social contact outside the White House circle. Tonight, she had told them that she was meeting an old male friend for drinks in the lounge and for dinner afterward in the rooftop restaurant. They would coordinate the security essentials with the hotel staff and see to it that the evening's activity flowed seamlessly. Jennifer respected their responsibilities and kept them in the loop at all times.

They appreciated her show of respect for them and that kept both parties on their best behavior.

Howard Westlake was on time. Jennifer easily picked him out as he threaded his way through the crowd toward the corner table where she sat alone. He was as she had last seen him over a decade ago, tall, lean, slightly gray and very handsome. In his college years his eight-man shell had rowed to an Olympic silver medal and he looked fit enough to do that today. Although he'd once done some on-camera work for her network news station, he had ultimately preferred to move into program planning and direction. He had been an immediate success, or so she'd heard.

He lightly kissed her on the cheek she offered and sat down next to her on the soft leather love seat.

After a few pleasantries he was telling her about his upcoming move. "The network has decided that you and I have been apart long enough, Jenn. So, they're putting me in charge of programming at the D.C. station, news and everything else. It starts this week. I was going to call you tomorrow when I'm due in Washington, but this was too fortuitous to overlook. That's the story."

"Howard, I'm very happy for you. I knew you were destined for the big time and so I'm not in the least surprised. I am pleased that you'll be in D.C. We should be able to share a few drinks from time to time. I had heard about your divorce several years ago and wondered if you'd ever remarried. I don't see a ring so I'm guessing that you haven't gone down the aisle again. Of course, in this room the absence of a man's gold band doesn't have the same meaning as it might in a different environment. I'm just kidding, Howard." She smiled with a slight tilt of her head.

"Well, now you're really up to date on Howard Westlake. When I come to Washington tomorrow, I'm coming free as a bird. No entanglements to undo. A clean slate. With the possible exception of an old friend who also lives in Washington and looks even more beautiful than she did over ten years ago."

"Howard, is that my cue to blush and flutter my eyelids? You're too kind. but I don't want you to stop."

Jennifer listened to herself being so demure. She had tried to put some distance between Howard and herself, but she didn't feel the distance.

"Okay, Jenn, let's end these sound bites, finish our drinks and move on to dinner. Maybe we can find a way to keep this rekindled friendship alive even as you play the role of First Lady. I need to hear about your life and how much of it really is yours."

Howard was being very upbeat and friendly. She could sense his more serious inclination behind the façade, but she was restraining her own more serious interest at the same time.

CHAPTER FIVE

A l hadn't carefully thought through his fact-finding trip. He knew he had to go to Washington to claim Jeff's remains and in the process, he hoped he would find out why his best friend had undertaken the ill-fated trip without letting him in on the reason for it.

Standing outside Reagan Airport, he realized he had no plan for how to begin looking for answers. A rental car and motel reservation were the easy part. He'd arranged with a nearby funeral home to send the body, or what parts of it had been recovered, to Jeff's parents for burial.

The police had collected whatever they could identify as articles belonging to the pilot and saved them for Al to review before including them with the remains for Jeff's final trip.

Al's first stop was the police station where he looked over the articles that consisted of Jeff's medical bag, his wallet, and little else. No clues stood out, although the fact that he had his medical bag with him raised the possibility that the trip had a medical purpose.

Al next decided to visit the airport Jeff had flown into and out of. Al had followed a very conventional path during his entire adult life with one exception. As a senior in college he'd been recruited by the CIA through one of his professors. After graduating from an intensive training course, he was assigned to a covert operations section. The romantic notion about what he was doing wore thin after a few months of actual on-site work. For four years he was deeply enmeshed in highly classified operations in sub-Saharan Africa. It had been exciting work and extremely dangerous. It was not at all like what he'd expected. The experience had made him tougher and more hardened than his collegiate good looks suggested.

After five years he'd seen and done enough violent acts to fill a lifetime. He decided to call it quits. It wasn't easy to reenter "normal" life but he was determined to put all that behind him. He decided that medicine offered a far more appealing life. Growing up in a middle-class home with two academic parents, he had always excelled in school and found medical school much to his liking. It seemed like an ideal career and cardiology had confirmed the wisdom of his decision. One brother, a few years older, had preceded him into medicine and practiced general surgery in California.

Al was a bit older than the usual trainee colleague, a consequence of his time in Africa. His maturity distinguished him from his younger and less-seasoned colleagues.

There hadn't been time for many women in his life, but he had experienced several long and draining relationships, none of which had come close to marriage. The women had been interested in permanence, but he hadn't been, so the relationships had dissolved.

He was recognized as an outstanding marriage prospect in the North Carolina town where he and Jeff Oldham had chosen to set up practice right out of fellowship. They had developed a thriving cardiology group practice that now numbered seven doctors, with Jeff gone. After twelve years in the practice, Al was sure that some in the community were questioning his sexual preference. That was inevitable. His most recent steady could give testimony to his robust heterosexuality but that was hardly necessary since he had never been lacking for female companionship. At present, there was no significant other. The loss of Jeff was a major blow both personally and professionally. He would recover from the latter, but the loss of his closest friend was something else. The trip to Washington was as much to say good-bye as it was an investigation. He dreaded the return home and the empty space in his life left behind by Jeff's death.

An hour or so later, Al's Taurus turned into a small airfield, the point of origin of Jeff's return flight. The small airport terminal office was the only building that seemed occupied. He learned nothing from the attendant behind the desk that he hadn't already been told by the police who filed the report and called him. Well, maybe just one thing. Jeff had been picked up by a man in a gray sedan and returned in a sports car with a convertible top.

"Thanks for the info," was all Al could offer at this point.

The man behind the desk was friendly and acknowledged having been through this line of questions twice before. "Sure. You could've saved your time by just reading about it in the local paper. Gave the reporter all the same stuff"

"Really? What paper is that?"

"*Daily Sentinel*. Copy probably lying there on the table."

Al went through the mound of papers and magazines sprawled on the low table in the small area in front of the coffee machine. He found the paper dated the day after the crash. On page four, there was a brief story about the crash with little additional information. The brief biographical stuff on Jeff was painful to read. He scanned the byline under the headline.

"Leslie Nugent, staff reporter." She'd be the next stop on his so-far uninformative investigation.

CHAPTER SIX

Errol Jensen, head of White House security sat in Sidney Curtis's office talking to the Chief of Staff.

"I mean it. There hasn't been anything like it since the Kennedy days. She left the White House late at night and met a guy who has no security clearances. She told me about it at the last minute, so I was able to follow her at a distance with her knowledge. The President may know, but I don't think so. I don't know what to do, but I know it's dynamite. And it only just happened yesterday."

"I'm glad you came to me, Errol," Sidney said. "You're right. It would be the mother of all scandals. A First Lady stepping out on her husband. The country has come a long way, but I don't think it's ready for this. There's not been a hint of a First Lady's infidelity. In the Clinton case, it was the guy straying."

The two men went silent in the dimly lit office. They each sipped their scotch and sank deep into thought.

Jensen broke the uncomfortable silence, "There's no evidence that anything took place other than a few drinks and some conversation. But, if she's carrying around any important government information I don't think we can allow this to go on for very long. Mr. Curtis, that's going to have to be your call, but I do have some responsibility here."

"I understand, and I accept full responsibility, Errol. By the way, how many other people know about this?"

"Well, only me, I guess. At least as far as what went on after she left the White House. As luck would have it, I was on duty that night and kept the entire episode under my personal review."

Jensen had no problem keeping matters such as this to himself. He was the ultimate loyal soldier.

Sidney, however, was uneasy. Managing the President's atypical campaign was stressful enough. Adding this to the script was more than he needed.

"Give me some details, Errol."

"There's not a lot to tell. About 12:30 in the morning, I got a call from the upstairs security guard that Mrs. Henderson was seen leaving her room and was heading downstairs into the West Wing dressed for an evening out. I told security that I would handle it and walked over to the door that leads out of the West Wing. Neither I nor the upstairs guard had any idea what was going on. We had no advance warning. This was not her routine behavior.

"She greeted me pleasantly enough as she exited the West Wing and told me she had a car waiting. She saw the stunned expression on my face and tried to calm me down.

She said something like, 'It'll be okay, Mr. Jensen. I know what I'm doing so please don't make it difficult for me to leave. You may follow me if you like, but I want my space.' I followed her outside where she casually walked past gate security, out onto Pennsylvania Avenue. I couldn't believe what was happening. The gate staff was stunned. I quickly got them under control and let them know I was in full control of the situation. It was also to be kept off the record."

He paused for breath and seemed to be excited as he told the story. Undoubtedly, this was something that Jensen needed to share with someone and Sidney was Jensen's choice to hear it out. He continued with his recollection.

"She got into a waiting car and I followed in one of our unmarked cars. The car dropped her off at the Sutton Hotel. I was able to follow her inside and upstairs and saw her enter a room on the sixth floor. The hallway was very quiet at that hour, so I fixed my ear to the door and listened as best I could. I never saw the other person in the room, but there certainly was another person in there. A man, I think. What I heard was unrevealing. There was no indication that other than simple conversation was taking place. I couldn't make out many of the words through the door. After an hour or so she came out alone, looking entirely composed. I followed her back to the White House in an exact reversal of the trip to the hotel. The same car took her back and forth. It's registered to a reputable car service in D.C. That's the story. And, oh yes, I'm sure she knows I followed her out and back. And one more thing. I obtained the identity of the party who had reserved the room with the cooperation of the desk clerk. My badge helped but I didn't identify myself to him."

He handed Sidney an envelope from his briefcase. "This is a written record of what I observed that night. It's the only copy. The clerk had no idea who I was or who the lady preceding me was. I felt it was best to leave it that way.

"Errol, that's quite a tale. Quite a tale. I need you to keep me fully informed. As a matter of fact, I want you to call me as soon as Mrs. Henderson makes another nocturnal trip. You have my private cellphone number. I want you to call me at any hour. I need to be on top of this along with you. Of course, you'll keep this under the tightest security wrap. That means no other officers should be involved in any intimate way. No leaks, Errol. I have one more favor to ask. I'd appreciate it if you would temporarily move into the family wing and be available 24/7 to cover her back if and when she goes on another 'trip.' I know this will take you away from your family, but it will only be for a few weeks, and I'll see to it that you're thanked generously. Any questions?"

Errol could only wonder what "a few weeks" really meant.

Sidney saw the Head of Security to the door. He'd make sure that Jensen received some significant reward, off-line.

For Jensen, security meant security no matter what the content. Sidney knew it had been a stroke of good luck that Errol had been on duty that first night. Steve Berk had described Jennifer as a "wild card" and he couldn't have been more insightful.

Sidney had not figured on a twist like this. Who could? His only worry was that Jennifer might leak her husband's condition to her "friend" as an explanation to him for her liaison. It would be the truth and that scared him even more. She wouldn't be lying and might feel justified. This required Sidney's closest attention, but he didn't know if he could effectively muzzle her. She was difficult before, but now she was verging on out-of-control. He knew that Jack and Jennifer had enjoyed a very close relationship, but he never realized that she might seek companionship elsewhere so fast if Jack became disabled. Her husband had only been out of commission for little over a week, and she was already acting like a lonely young widow.

Maybe he was over dramatizing it. There was no evidence that sex had been involved so perhaps he was blowing things out of proportion. What worried him was the possibility that sex might soon follow and with that, more shared intimacy and pillow talk.

Sidney leaned back in the worn leather chair and sipped his scotch. There was no telling how close they were to a dangerous explosion. He didn't like the sense of helplessness. This had to be brought under control or at least kept under close surveillance to assure that it didn't go any further than it already had. A small smile crept into the corners of his mouth. He was beginning to see a way to turn her behavior to his advantage. He would ask Steve Berk to video tape the next trip of the First Lady to meet her "friend." He wasn't sure how Berk would do it, but he was expert at such covert operations. Such a record would come in handy if he needed to put pressure on Jennifer for any reason. It would be his trump card.

Sidney reasoned it through in his methodical and calculated manner. "Jensen'll call me and I'll promptly get to Berk. No need to have Jensen know why Berk is involved. I'll see to it that Jensen gives Berk enough room to maneuver without making Jensen too nervous about letting the First Lady out of his sight or hearing range. With enough lead-time, Berk should be able to get some conversation recorded and possibly some pictures. If the liaison matured, a record of it could be powerful leverage over Jennifer," he mused.

He now opened the envelope Errol Jensen had given him. He thought to himself, "Dear God, don't let this get any more complicated."

CHAPTER SEVEN

The day was turning out to be very uninspiring for Leslie. She craved some excitement, and the *Sentinel* was not the place to find it. Her answering machine had a few messages but the one from some doctor who had known the dead pilot had the highest potential. She called him at the cellphone number he'd given.

"Al Seibolt here."

"Doctor Seibolt, this is Leslie Nugent of the *Sentinal* returning your call. How can I help you?"

"Miss Nugent, I was a very close friend of Jeff Oldham's and I'm trying to find out more about the circumstances of his death. I thought you might be able to help me. Could we meet somewhere for lunch and talk?"

Thirty minutes later, they were sharing a booth in a diner. Leslie had tried to picture the caller before she met him. Voices on the phone could be misleading. She'd been pleasantly surprised. He was a good-looking six-footer with a full head of sandy-colored hair and what looked like an athletic build. Had to be married or divorced, she mused, and he just didn't wear a wedding ring. If not, he had to be gay. He was too good to be sitting unattached in the booth opposite her. His age was not easy to guess but she gave him about 40 years, give or take five. With some effort she refocused on the discussion of the crash.

No, she had no idea why Jeff Oldham had been in Virginia.

No, she had no idea whom he had seen or who had picked him up.

No, she had no idea how to get the information he was looking for.

No, there was no reason to do any more work on the story.

On the other side of the table, Al saw a slim brunette with a very nice figure and a teasing smile. Her hair was shoulder length, straight with short bangs. Her make-up was simple, and her eyes were deep gray. Nothing unusual but it all came together very nicely. The initial chemistry was right, and they each could feel the power of it. Her lips were one of her best features, full and almost pouting.

Al tried to figure her situation. Not married or at least not wearing her ring. Could have a steady or a live-in.

Must be in her mid or late thirties. She flashed that smile and let him see her perfect, pearly white teeth. No doubt about her smile. That was her weapon of choice.

Leslie didn't want him to leave, so she tried harder to keep up her interest in the story. Al was growing more intense. He was asking her to try and put some hypothetical story together with the few available facts even if the story was far-fetched.

She desperately gave it a try. "Well, let's see. Guy's a doctor so he flies here to play doctor. He's not very well-known so who would want him to doctor them in Virginia? That doesn't make sense.

"Try this. He flies up here to see some girl he met on a trip somewhere. Never mentioned it to you, because it wasn't anything serious. She called on short notice and brought him running or flying. No, doesn't make sense either. Why was he only here for a short day's stay?

"Try this. He is being looked over for a job with a medical group and didn't want to tell you until it became a real job offer. Didn't want to hurt you unnecessarily.

Flew up for an interview, was picked up by one of the members of the group or their business manager, spent the day looking the practice over. I like it. It fits."

Al shook his head.

"What don't you like about it?"

"It doesn't fit with all the planning we were doing. We just took out a loan for some expensive testing equipment to expand our practice. Jeff and I were very close. He wouldn't screw me. No way."

"Well, there has to be an explanation," said Leslie, "and no one should be better able to figure it out than you."

"I'm coming up dry."

He looked a bit closer at her. Cute. Yes, definitely cute. Worth a try for dinner tonight since he had no plans and they could both pretend it was business.

"Could we continue this over dinner tonight?" He gave it a direct shot.

Leslie was relieved to sense his obvious interest. "Don't see why not. My calendar is open, and I'd like to pursue this a bit with you. I'm curious myself and I'd like to see if we can make any progress toward an explanation." She tried not to sound over-eager. "Where are you staying, Al?"

"I haven't made any arrangements but there are plenty of motels nearby. I'll check into one and pick you up around seven. That'll give us each some time to change and give me a chance to get settled. I think I'll be staying here a few days, so I'd like to unpack."

"Okay, seven it is. Here are directions to my place."

CHAPTER EIGHT

S idney Curtis was successfully managing a most complex political campaign. To his frustration, no one knew it or appreciated it. The President seemed committed to conducting what many considered a reasonably active campaign. The answer was television. The need to reach out and physically touch the electorate was a dated concept.

Television reached many more people and the time saved from travel allowed the President to spend many more hours doing personal campaigning from the White House. Instead of local fund-raisers on behalf of local candidates, he brought them to the White House and televised the meetings for the faithful either live or on tape.

It worked. The President was perceived as doing his job and the campaign was viewed as secondary in importance. The result was image enhancement. The few trips out of Washington were carefully structured to minimize physical stress on the President. And local politicos loved to go to the White House and be photographed with the President. It also helped that Jennifer was out on the hustings making up for the relative absence of her husband. She was proving to be a powerful campaigner. Her direct conversational stump speeches were dynamite.

"Damn it. I've run a helluva campaign. Six weeks more and we'll be home free. Then the President can 'acquire' a heart problem and reveal it to the shocked public whenever it seems appropriate or advantageous," he thought.

Sidney wasn't relaxing. Not yet. Not with the first lady suddenly turning randy. Fortunately, the President wasn't even faintly suspicious.

Berk said all was quiet on the cover-up front. Sidney trusted Berk, but he didn't like another person out there with the same information he possessed. Could he leave Berk out there after it was over? More loose ends than he liked.

So far only five people were in on the secret, four plus himself. The President had a lot to lose if it leaked out, so he was okay for now. Jennifer was a loose cannon. She would have to be carefully kept under his thumb.

Recordings of her nocturnal meetings might do the trick, but he couldn't be sure. There had to be more certain silence. Berk was okay, but he represented another potential source of information leak. Last was Sidney's source of support and guidance out in Tucson. No worry there. He was even more secretive than the others and wouldn't hesitate to sanction anyone who posed a threat.

CHAPTER NINE

Dinner was going great for each of them. The popular seafood restaurant sat on a lakefront with a long porch overlooking the water. Tables lined the open side of the porch and offered a breathtaking view of the sunset across the lake. Both Leslie and Al could sense the interest each had in making something happen between them. A lot was going unsaid. Her first impression was being strengthened by the minute. He was a sensitive guy who also drew looks from women in the restaurant.

"Jeff and I were classmates in med school. We hooked up after fellowship training and decided to chance it in North Carolina as partners. Two single cardiologists with one big bank loan. We worked hard and played hard. We built the practice into a very successful small group of eight and planned to go on forever. Funny how things can change so quickly."

"Did Jeff have a love life?"

"I guess you'd call it that. Holly Anderson was his special girl on and off for the past two years. I don't think marriage was under discussion. We had no secrets on that score. He wasn't here on the trail of a woman."

"Seems we've ruled out business and women, Al. What's left?"

"I haven't the foggiest but there was something sufficiently compelling to bring him to this area for a one-day stay. And someone prearranged it, because he was picked up and delivered at the airport."

"Well, let's think a bit more expansively," said Leslie. She was now genuinely interested in the mystery. A beautiful evening, a good meal, a handsome guy and a mystery to boot. She felt heady, but that could have been the second apple martini. Drinks there were huge.

She thought out loud, "Why Jeff? A doctor? Dime a dozen in the D.C. area. A doctor who flies his own plane."

Not a dime a dozen. Who would want a flying cardiologist? A flying cardiologist from North Carolina? Any ideas?"

Al suddenly grew quite serious. "I like that approach, Leslie. A flying cardiologist who kept the reason secret even from his very best friend."

"Now we're back to a secret, Al, with no Jeff to tell us about it." Leslie was getting both stimulated by this mystery and disheartened since it was keeping Al and her from paying more attention to each other.

"There must be some way to pick up his trail, Leslie. We're just not being clever enough."

Al's mind was firmly fixed on the mystery. Leslie decided to move away from it and get them onto more social matters.

"Let's give it some rest. Maybe something will come to you or me if we just keep it on a back burner for a while. Right now, I see a brick wall in front of us and there's no use banging our heads into it."

"Okay, you're probably right, Leslie. How about some dessert?"

"Why don't we have some coffee and frozen yogurt back at my place. We can pick up some yogurt on the way to my apartment."

"Sounds great. I'll get the check and we can get going."

Leslie smiled to herself. He obviously welcomed her suggestion, so this was going to be a pleasant, long evening. As Al reached in his pocket for his wallet and credit card, Leslie excused herself and headed for the ladies' room. She put on a fresh coat of lipstick and brushed her hair. Funny, she mused, how things worked out. Could have been some other reporter who had drawn the plane crash story.

CHAPTER TEN

The cool evening air sped up evaporation of the afternoon shower, leaving a low-lying mist along the road. The drive to Virginia gave Sidney an opportunity to think in absolute privacy. Some nights he just cruised around and enjoyed the solitary, enclosed space of the car. It was his favorite time for silently talking to himself and fantasizing about problems he was going to solve in short order. Tonight was no exception, although drivetime was going to be limited by the proximity of his destination. He only smoked in private, and there was no better time for a cigarette than these drives out of the city. He'd been a Marlborough man for 40 years. Tonight was a two-cigarette drive.

In spite of his unease about having a co-conspirator, Sidney knew it was essential. Berk was as good as he could possibly hope for. They agreed to meet for a late dinner at a remote, underrated Chinese restaurant in Virginia. The restaurant was almost deserted. One Chinese family was still eating at a corner table, but the restaurant was beginning to close down. No additional customers were likely at this hour. The place was familiar to them both.

Sidney had eaten there with Berk on numerous occasions. It offered the low visibility he sought for his evening meetings.

Sidney got right to the point, "So far, no hitches. Or at least none I'm aware of. Do you have any information for me, Steve?"

Berk was his usual disinterested self. Or so he seemed. "Nothing since our last meeting when you told me about the wife's night time outings. I am concerned about her behavior. It can only lead to trouble. Does the President have any idea what's going on with her, Sidney?"

"No, not the slightest. Doesn't mean he won't find out though. Right now, he's obsessed with the campaign and keeping his condition a very closely-guarded secret. That's taking considerable effort on my part but so far, with his help we've succeeded in maintaining the fiction. He travels on a limited basis and exerts himself as little as possible and always within a narrow, safe range of activity. We faked a leg injury and even had his leg put in a light–weight cast. The cast has afforded us an excellent excuse to avoid strenuous exercise.

"His sex life is of little or no consequence to him for the moment, but that may not be Jennifer's view. We need to be planning ahead."

"What does that mean, Sidney?" Berk leaned forward with a quizzical look on his face.

"Steve, I have a plan that may help us keep Jennifer under my control. It involves some technical surveillance on your part when she next takes a trip to visit her secret boyfriend. A visual record of such a meeting in a hotel room would be a club I could hold over her if there was ever a need to assure her cooperation in our secret venture. Let me tell you how I envision this working, and you tell me if you see any holes in my plan."

Sidney spelled out the details of Jennifer's wandering and the role for Berk in obtaining a visual record of her indiscretion. When they were finished going over the plan in broad strokes, Sidney could see that Berk actually was stimulated by the challenge. Sidney was encouraged. There had been only two instances of Jennifer going out at night, both observed by Errol Jensen. The meetings had taken place in the same hotel room which was apparently being rented long-term by her gentleman friend. This suggested that subsequent meetings would take place in the same venue making Berk's job that much easier since a set-up could be planned in advance.

The steamed wontons arrived and allowed them to change the subject to something less serious.

"Pass the soy sauce, Steve, and ask the waiter for some more hot tea, will you?"

CHAPTER ELEVEN

Leslie's apartment was unusually well-ordered. She'd anticipated or at least hoped for their return and had taken great pains to straighten up the place. What she hadn't anticipated was that they would act like two high school teenagers and begin necking furiously on her living room sofa. The frozen yogurt was slowly melting on the kitchen table. Still clothed but very rumpled, Leslie disengaged from Al's arms, got up and turned to go to the bathroom.

This was Al's first good look at the woman he'd been looking over ever since they met. Only her back was visible, but he was not disappointed. As she walked away, he saw a very sensual woman with a well-proportioned figure. He was aroused, and she undoubtedly knew it.

Leslie returned after only a few brief minutes and had obviously removed her brassiere. That was an invitation he couldn't refuse. Their necking resumed, and Leslie wondered how far to let this go. When his hand ran down her back cleavage, inside her panties, she decided to slow down the process and preserve at least a modicum of female modesty.

"Al, maybe we should slow down. Let's not let this physical thing get too far ahead of our personal relationship. We need to get to know each other a bit better."

"You're right, Leslie. We've gotten off to a racing start and that can have a life of its own. I'll try to rein myself in, but I must say I liked where we were heading."

"Me too, fella. But maybe we can get there at a slightly slower pace."

"Fine. I'm anxious to move that personal relationship forward on a fast track so the physical thing you referred to isn't left too far behind. Now how about that frozen yogurt?"

They finally got back to the serious question that was never far from their minds.

"Leslie, let's pick up the story where we left off. I think we were on to something. A flying cardiologist comes to Washington to see a patient who wants utmost privacy.

But why Jeff? Because he flies! That's it! He can get in here unnoticed and leave unnoticed." Al was getting excited as he began to see some scattered pieces of the puzzle come together.

"And it was just a coincidence, Al, that his plane went down?" Leslie was also in the game in earnest. "Could it be that his plane offered a convenient way to keep the episode extremely private?"

"You're suggesting that the crash was no accident, Leslie?"

"Well, Al, it certainly would have been convenient for the patient to have his out-of-town doctor go down. No witness, no bill, no trail." Leslie extended her arms and turned her palms up.

Al picked up on her lead, "That's a pretty high-stakes game. It would have to involve a very important person who needed his condition kept secret in the most certain way." Al was on the edge of his chair and his mind was racing ahead. "And there would have been no need for the crash if the doctor's findings were not significant. We can probably assume that he found the person's condition serious enough to scare the person into wanting the doctor permanently shut-up."

"The story has a scary ring to it, but it makes sense, Al. Maybe we've seen too many movies or read too much Ludlum and Forsythe. But we haven't a shred of evidence to support the conjecture, so where is this getting us?"

Leslie fell back in her chair and gave a sigh of exasperation. She felt Alan's eyes on her as she lay back. Her sweater was taut across her breasts and she could feel his eyes on the outline of her still hard nipples. The thought began to arouse her, and her nipples hardened even more as she allowed the thought to gain a foothold in her mind.

She sat up abruptly and tried to get their minds back on the serious matter at hand. She could read his mind. "There'll be more time for that later, Al. Let's try to stay focused on the story."

"Very professional, Leslie."

"I'm not always so into my story. This one has me very turned on, same as you are. I'm just trying to keep some balance here. When I cover a story, the facts are usually out on the table and there's not much mystery. Here we're all conjecture with no facts other than the crash."

"If we knew the name of the patient, we would be all set, Leslie. So, let's try that as an objective. How to identify a Washington big-wig who is seriously ill and anxious to keep the matter under wraps."

"That's a good idea, Al, but the list could be lengthy and then, how do we check out all the possible candidates?"

"I know it's a bit of a leap, Leslie, but we have to start somewhere. Do you have any other ideas?"

"No, I'm up against the same wall, but I like your approach. We should just start and see if we come up with anything. Maybe just getting organized will lead us somewhere."

"Okay, let's start with a list of Washington VIP's and see how we can get a handle on their health status."

CHAPTER TWELVE

S leep was a welcome respite from the day's intense and very secretive planning. Berk fantasized about the challenge of eliminating Jennifer Henderson. He and Sidney hadn't even discussed that eventuality but still it raised some intriguing challenges. The First Lady was no simple target for elimination.

The plan would have to be foolproof. An assassination that was an open and shut accident. There must be no investigation which could uncover any clues about her recent dalliance. That could unravel the whole ball of string.

Berk had grown up in upstate New York where unemployment was a perpetual hangover. Leaving the area was the career goal of most young people. His athletic ability was impressive for the small-town high school league in the area but would never be a passport out into any quality school with money for athletic scholarships. His family was always broke and his father's job at the glass factory held no future for him. His good looks and cocky demeanor had gotten him involved with a few older married women in town and they had provided much of his advanced education.

The military was an obvious way out, so he took it. Three tours with the Marines included two with the Special Forces as a trouble-shooter in several dangerous parts of the world. After ten years with Special Forces and the CIA as a covert operative, he decided to go out and capitalize on the many connections he'd established in the world of covert activity. He put himself out to bid and found many takers who knew of his skills and willingness to work in absolute secrecy. He worked alone and liked it that way.

No one to answer to, and no one to bail out of difficult jams. His reputation generated a constant stream of business along with generous payments. He worked without a contract and never left a paper trail.

The bedroom of their apartment was dark, and sunrise was barely a few minutes old. Steve's wife Terry was still fast asleep. They had no children, and her job as an attorney with a big D.C. lobbying firm let her make her own hours. Their marriage was very tired and lacked emotion, much less passion. Terry knew her husband was running a play life outside their marriage, but this didn't bother her. Her own private life was not monogamous either. Two ranking members of Congress currently knew her in the biblical sense and juggling them was as much a challenge for her as her job. Her marriage was just a shell, but neither she nor Steve had the desire to shatter it.

He wondered why he hadn't heard from Leslie for several weeks. That was unusual. They had agreed that she would call him only at his office to avoid any embarrassment for him at home. Their relationship was still alive after nearly a year, but she had shown signs of tiring of him.

Now this silence. What they had together was purely physical, but he did enjoy giving her an occasional inside tidbit for her column. They discussed Washington gossip a lot in bed and he derived an occasional insight he otherwise might miss in his travel around town.

Now, lying in bed, with Terry breathing deeply next to him, he began to fantasize about Leslie. He was going to initiate contact with her even though it was out of character for him. For now, though, there was the matter of the growing erection in his sleep shorts. Terry wouldn't mind an unexpected workout and this erection was going to last a while. He reached over to his nightstand, squeezed some lubricant into his hand and greased her between the legs. She began to awaken with the application of the cool jelly. "Just make believe I'm newly elected to Congress, Terry," he whispered in her ear. She gasped as his fullness entered her from behind and he began familiar motions.

CHAPTER THIRTEEN

Sidney was getting used to working very late hours. In fact, he often woke up in his office at the start of the workday. The adjacent shower made the office a home away from home. More and more, the job was becoming all-consuming. Last night had been no exception. The Jennifer Henderson matter weighed heavily on him. He had stayed up very late working through a series of scenarios that would follow from her demise. They all said the same thing: make sure it looks accidental and leave no reason for a deep, probing investigation.

There were plenty of loose ends already, like the White House Chief of Security who knew about Jennifer's evenings out. Somehow the event would have to offer no reason to tie her recent behavior to the accident. Then there was the boyfriend she'd begun seeing. He too had to see the accident as just that and nothing more. A bit of bad luck. More and more it became apparent that the manner of accident would be critical to the strategy of total innocence for all involved. It was time to call on Steve Berk again.

He also needed to share his thoughts with the other party to this complicated cover-up. The funds in the campaign chest were under Sidney's control so money wouldn't be a problem. There was plenty of cash on hand but it would have to be sanitized with expert care. The money was easy; the actual elimination was more challenging.

He called Berk and arranged for a rendezvous.

The days had become exhausting and he felt a need to wash up and eat. Even though it was late in the evening he wanted to take a break from the tension that was beginning to fray his nerves. He thought about the cocktail waitress in the Willard bar to whom he had spoken a few times. That might be the change of pace he needed.

Sidney had experienced a very normal childhood, growing up in a wealthy, small-town, Alabama family. Road paving was the family business, begun by his grandfather and greatly expanded by his father. Lucrative government contracts were exchanged for generous political campaign donations, many of which never found their way into campaign chests. Sidney was too restless to follow in his father's footsteps and decided to try college outside the deep south. Dartmouth College seemed as far away as he could go and still be at a socially acceptable institution. As it turned out, Dartmouth had many features that were fully compatible with his white, quasi-aristocratic southern upbringing. He became editor of the school newspaper and began a career in journalism.

A "gofer" job at the *Boston Globe* got him to the Minneapolis *Current* and a political beat which brought him into contact with the mayor of a small Minneapolis suburb who was launching a re-election campaign. Sidney became that mayor's Chief of Staff. He and attorney Jack Henderson met and became good friends. It thus seemed perfectly appropriate when Jack asked Sidney to run his campaign for the tragically vacated Senate seat. Ever since, they'd been inseparable. Sidney's instincts for politics and Jack's amiable personal appeal made for a very successful team.

Jack was totally dependent on Sidney. When Jack had met Jennifer and rushed into engagement, Sidney did the necessary "due diligence" on her background. The picture he presented to Jack was that of a bright, ambitious young woman who came from a very modest home. Her intelligence and good looks had helped her rapidly climb the ladder of success in TV journalism. Sidney could see that Jack was not going to be interested in any negative news. He deleted that portion of his report suggesting that several relationships with influential males may have accelerated her climb up the career ladder.

She knew where she wanted to go and saw no reason to deny the value of her natural attributes. One senior executive saw no reason to fault her in her pursuit. It was more natural than Machiavellian.

Marriage had followed, and so had election to the highest office in the land. Sidney Curtis was now considered the Chief of Staff par excellence.

CHAPTER FOURTEEN

The *Sentinel* office was almost deserted at night. Only one staff reporter was assigned to desk duty. Al and Leslie were deep into lists and cross-references. They'd agreed to start with the VIP's and only expand the search once the list was exhausted. The crude filter they had agreed upon was two-fold: elected individuals with high status in government for whom recent news reports made it unlikely that serious heart disease was a consideration or there was no information one way or the other. Another list contained 52 bigwigs who either had known heart disease or for whom it was reasonable to consider significant heart disease a possibility. The cross-referencing with various sources of information was critical. Al's cardiac knowledge was helpful, but he was given little information to work on.

There were several individuals who had physically undemanding jobs and no known exercise routine. These would require special scrutiny.

They were beginning to feel the excitement of tracking a suspect but also were beginning to see the enormity of the undertaking. The whole search could be a wild goose chase, costing them countless hours of worthless labor.

Nevertheless, they had no other approach that remotely offered a comparable possibility of breakthrough.

The phone rang on Leslie's desk. "That's weird, who would call me here at this hour?

Hello, Leslie Nugent." She immediately recognized the voice and sought to conceal her relationship to the caller from Al.

"Hi, Steve. Yes, it has been a while. I've been on assignment and haven't had a free moment." This unexpected interruption put her on edge. She wanted to keep it brief and not let Al suspect any intimacy between herself and the caller. "Sure, we can get together. How about lunch tomorrow? The Georgetown DeliWorks sounds great. Noon is fine. See you then."

Leslie felt the damage was negligible and put a finishing touch on the call. "A fellow reporter whom I see every so often and exchange leads and other reporter gossip. Gotta keep the lines open," she told Al.

Al seemed satisfied with the explanation, so she let the matter drop. Actually, she was hoping to try out their theory on Steve and see how a clever security pro would piece it together.

CHAPTER FIFTEEN

The White House family wing allowed the First Lady to occupy her own bedroom if she chose to. In the past weeks, Jennifer had moved into that room. Jack didn't make a fuss. He respected her decision and took it as an understandable consequence of his recent disability. She could sense his depression over their state of affairs and didn't want to clutter his life at this point or add to his sense of failure. Once they could deal with the problem in an open and honest manner as a health problem and nothing more, they both would feel a weight lifted off their backs.

In the meantime, a slight degree of separation made it easier for each of them to avoid the problem as much as possible.

Howard Westlake had been a help to her. He served as one person she could have a friendship with who needn't know any more than she wanted him to. He wasn't nosy. He enjoyed their late-night meetings and hadn't pressed for a physical relationship. Jennifer knew this was her call, but she wasn't ready to bump up their relationship to that level. She could honestly say that so far there had been no physical intimacy. Knowing Howard, however, she knew he would welcome an expanded relationship. It was just a matter of time before that issue would have to be confronted. She thought about it more than she wished she did. It was easy to rationalize some minimal physical contact, but she knew where that would lead. She was no fool and didn't want to start down the slippery slope and get caught in a full-blown case of infidelity at this point.

Their meetings had been all food, drinks, and talk. Yet, her urges were growing stronger with each meeting. Howard was attractive, and her need was undeniable. If he pressed the issue, she felt she might be a compliant partner. That pressure came one week later, and Jennifer proved to be the compliant partner she feared she might be.

Sidney had received a call from Errol Jensen at midnight. Jensen had followed Jennifer to the usual hotel and he was now in the lobby. She was in room 524, the usual room. Sidney told him to stay put and just follow her back to the White House when she came down. He immediately called Steve Berk who headed for the Sutton Hotel. Several similar recent calls had been followed-up and had yielded no juicy material.

One useful bit of information was that the two so-far platonic friends continued to meet in the same hotel and same room. Apparently, this was where her friend was living, possibly while he searched for permanent living quarters. For Berk, this was a godsend. Sidney gave the go-ahead to rent the adjacent room on a monthly basis. It enabled him to have his video equipment set up and ready to go when needed in the adjacent room. He had a good view of Westlake's room by using a fiberoptic cable with a leading lens that he threaded through a small aperture he made in the wall common to the two rooms. That night, he'd missed the opening act, but the best part was likely to come in the last act. And it had.

Sidney took a video disc from his wall safe and put it on the DVD player. He sat back to watch with a glass of scotch in his hand. The quality of the recording was just fair, but considering the circumstances, it was damn good. Berk could be counted on. Was this the original? Were there copies? Was Berk saving some for his own security?

This was bothersome.

The video was focused on a bed in a high-end hotel room. He'd watched this tape several times already.

Jennifer Henderson was seated on a large king-size bed with the quilted cover turned down. The camera was behind her, so her face was visible only when she turned away from the window. Flesh-colored bikini panties were her only cover. She was watching someone off screen. A man appeared and walked over to where she sat. He had only undershorts on.

He put both hands in her loose hair. She drew him close to her. She leaned over to one side and fell off the screen. In a few seconds she reappeared on screen and now had a condom in her hand. Next, she playfully fitted it over her partner's engorged organ. They both fell onto the bed and were off screen. She next reappeared and was clearly straddling him. They settled into a very slow rhythm, but only Jennifer was visible on the recording. Just watching her was erotic so Sidney imagined that the guy underneath must really be aroused. There was no soundtrack. She bent over and again was off screen for a moment. Jennifer shifted her tempo into the urgent range and began her own slide into orgasm. It was explosive, and then they were off screen again, probably lying together on the bed.

He removed the disc and put it in his briefcase. He'd return it to Berk tonight for safekeeping. Berk could store it more securely than he could, though Harlan needed access to it in the event that Berk came to an unexpected end. It was a very limited record, but the activity and the performers were unmistakable. The note attached to the disc indicated that the guy was a 50-year-old TV executive recently transferred to Washington from Houston. He knew Jennifer from her past days as a TV reporter. Berk had done his homework and had hit the jackpot.

No question, Jennifer Henderson was one helluva sex partner. No wonder Jack had been faithful all these years. Sidney only now became aware of his own erection. The tape was very disconcerting in more ways than one.

CHAPTER SIXTEEN

The White House was jumping. With the First Lady about to leave for a campaign swing through the Southwest, staffers strained to manage the details of a presidential campaign without much of the usual presidential availability for personal appearances.

Sidney met with key security people in his office to review Jennifer's itinerary and head off any possible mishaps or political missteps. The heads of White House security and the Secret Service sat opposite Sidney on his aging, very comfortable leather sofa. Two other Secret Service men were seated in the room, one of whom was assigned to the First Lady. The buffet cart was the only evidence that this was a breakfast meeting. Its contents had been picked clean during the first twenty minutes of informal discussion.

Sidney took the lead. "O.K., I've got the itinerary clear in my mind now. Both days. I assume the usual security precautions are in place, same as we did for the trips to Michigan and Wisconsin."

"That's right, Sidney, you can leave the security to us. Just make sure that your staff, and I might add, the First Lady, adhere strictly to our programmed events," said the Secret Service lead man for the trip.

"It's comforting to know that the First Lady is a respected and much sought-after speaker." Sidney was fishing for any suggestion of danger.

One of the younger men spoke up. "If I may, Mr. Curtis, there are concerns. You should be aware that there are elements in New Mexico that view our President as insensitive to their deeply held positions on abortion, gun control, and prayer in school. The FBI has been watching several so called 'patriot groups' for signs of possible violent action. I just want you to be aware that there are dissident elements out there that could be dangerous to the First Lady. Remember, she has been out front all along on the abortion issue. We just need to be vigilant."

Sidney didn't let the warning slide by. "How remote and how real is the danger? Is this just a very hypothetical risk or is there any substance to it? Of course, I'm aware of dissidents. The question is how hard should we work to defend against every remote possibility?"

Sidney was probing for a situation that could be exploited to advantage by Steve Berk.

"Well, I don't have anything of substance, just a hint in the air."

The head of trip security was a bit uneasy at the presentation's overtones, but he was also proud of his staff's thoughtful background work. He sought to assure Sidney. "Mr. Curtis, we'll be taking all necessary precautions. We just want to discuss all aspects of the trip's security. These trips are never a piece of cake. We've assigned a cadre of security men to pay particular attention to these dissidents. We're coordinating our operation with the FBI, so I think the itinerary is security tight."

"Thank you, Bob. I'm impressed as usual with your staff's preparation." Sidney showed his guests to the door.

Alone in the room, Sidney removed the audio tape of the meeting from the hidden recorder and put it in his pocket for delivery to Berk. The potential for an "accident" had received a boost. Well, if not an accident, an incident that could be attributed to people far removed from the White House, even if they weren't the perpetrators. There was a potential opportunity here to discuss with Berk.

CHAPTER SEVENTEEN

Berk was bothered by something in the plans but was having a difficult time putting his finger on it. The old coffee maker on his office windowsill was still full even though he'd already been in the office several hours. Deep in thought, his cup of coffee was too cold to drink, but he was too engaged to throw it out and get a refill.

Steve mused, "Four of us know what's going on. The President, his wife, Sidney and myself. Sidney sees Jennifer as a threat, but eliminating her leaves me as the remaining risk. Sidney might very well be planning my exit, once I conveniently eliminate Jennifer. Even if I don't, I'm still a liability." Steve didn't like the way this played out.

What if the alignment changed? He could eliminate Sidney. Certainly, that was easier to arrange and wouldn't be traceable to the President's health problem. Actually, it would eliminate the one person in Washington who knew the most about Steve Berk's covert operations, including the cardiologist's death. Yes, this was sounding better all the time. With Sidney gone, an inadvertent slip on Jennifer's part would be difficult to corroborate.

A cup of coffee now seemed in order. The plan made some sense even though it was a strictly preemptive action. And it offered him maximum security. No need to plan a complex accident in the Southwest. This plan was far simpler. Sidney was barely protected by security. Jennifer and the President would never know Steve's involvement, so the secret would be in his hands for the most part along with other aspects of the plot. The election was less than two months away and after that, the ruse could be wound up. The drama would fade with time and never come to light.

So now, he was involved in two operations to secure the cover-up. Each one involved shrinking the ring of "conspirators" and he alone was aware of the particular conspirators being considered for elimination. He'd have to become familiar with Sidney's routines in order to determine a possible course of action.

CHAPTER EIGHTEEN

H is stay in Washington had been longer than he'd anticipated. For Al Seibolt, his attraction to Leslie had been an even bigger factor in prolonging his stay than the unsolved mystery of his friend's death. After a week away from home, he returned to North Carolina to stay current with the practice and arrange for coverage when he was away in D.C. on long weekends. He knew this couldn't go on indefinitely but for now it was the best he could do. He and Leslie were not ready to discuss any commitment, so long weekends were the best he could manage. They avoided talk of the future, since their careers presented formidable obstacles. Each had invested heavily in their respective local situations. It would be a wrenching move for either one of them, and neither wanted to enter into that discussion at this early stage.

Al was at once relieved by Leslie's willingness to put off talk of any commitment and yet was uneasy by her lack of such concern. He tried to understand her better. How could this beautiful, intelligent, sexually aggressive woman be unattached into her mid-thirties? Was there a problem that he was unaware of? On the other hand, what about him in his early forties? Maybe they were more alike than he realized.

The large newsroom was only lit by a few desk lamps. It was full of shadows and the air was heavy with humidity. Air conditioning went off around 5 o'clock and little of its cooling effect remained.

Leslie and Al had worked late into the evening, but no leading suspect had emerged. They were growing impatient.

Leslie offered a tentative optimistic comment, "I know we haven't hit the nail on the head, but I just have the feeling we're on the right track. It feels right."

"I agree, Les, but how are we going to reduce this huge list of unknowns down to a workable few to check out? And how do we know what to look for?"

"We have one large plus in our favor. You. You're a cardiologist. You tell me what we're looking for. Your partner was the doctor on this case. Is that a lead? We can narrow it down to heart disease. What else can we dredge from this limited data base?"

"You're right, Leslie. That's an approach we ought to follow."

"What about Jeff was attractive to whomever recruited him? Aside from his pilot skill." Leslie pushed Al. "Was he special in any way?"

"Well, Jeff was a highly skilled cardiologist. He could do all sorts of procedures. He could implant pacemakers and do cardiac invasive procedures. If they brought him here and then had to eliminate him, the findings must have been devastating. Very probably he would have needed to do a cardiac catheterization. How the hell would he have arranged that? No, that's above and beyond even your prying reporter's imagination."

"Well, maybe so, Al. But don't put it past these operators. Nothing's too tough to try when the stakes are high enough. Remember, they operated on President Taft on his private yacht and never let the press in on it. Trust me, anything's possible. As I recall from an article I wrote last year on health care economics, there are ten facilities in metropolitan D.C. which have the capacity to do a cardiac catheterization."

Leslie continued, "And I'd bet they wouldn't want to travel too far out to the suburbs. That would eliminate a good 50% of the facilities." She paused. "Maybe that's the lead we should follow up on."

"How the hell do we do that, Leslie? 'Say Doctor So and so, has Senator So-and-so been in your lab lately on the QT?' This seems a bit of a stretch if you ask me."

In Leslie's mind, that would be a good query to put before Steve Berk. Right up his alley, undercover inquiry…very discrete.

"Well, Les, I could visit a few labs just to find out if it rings remotely possible. Maybe the lab was used on the sly and the personnel haven't a clue. We'll have to run this through a few times to figure out a likely scenario. I mean, let's have an idea what might have happened so that my line of questioning makes sense. I feel foolish already, so let's not make things worse by chasing a preposterous hypothesis."

"Look, Al, you want to have your patient studied in a sophisticated hospital facility. but you want his identity kept secret. That doesn't sound too difficult."

Al was still not convinced. "I guess not, unless he's a very well-known person whose identity is difficult to hide. Then you'd need to do the procedure in relative secrecy. In addition, Jeff would need some trained staff and they had to be kept in the dark about the patient's identity. That would be a trick of considerable difficulty."

Leslie stayed on the track. "Seems the question is whether they did a procedure and whether it was necessary to do it in secrecy to conceal the patient's identity. See, it's not really very hard to piece together."

"Leslie I've got to hand it to you. You certainly have a good mind for fiction. This whole line of conjecture is built on the presumption that a local bigwig needed a cardiologist and was willing to murder him to keep his medical findings secret. Quite a plot. Maybe you think we should call in the police or the FBI? I'm kidding. I do like the tactic of trying to construct a plausible scenario to follow up with at area hospitals. I'm just struggling with all the conjecture and wondering how we can ever begin to flesh any of it out."

Al leaned back in the well-worn swivel chair, put his hands behind his head and smiled in Leslie's direction. "How about pizza at your place and then continue this discussion along with other matters? You do remember other matters, don't you?"

CHAPTER NINETEEN

The street glistened with the last hour's rain and traffic was light. A weekday night in downtown Washington was usually a quiet affair. Steve Berk waited patiently in the doorway of a deserted storefront. He'd followed Sidney to the hotel across the street and had seen a youngish woman follow him. He figured Sidney would spend about an hour with the woman, since he usually liked to be asleep before eleven on an evening preceding the President's cabinet meeting.

He'd decided to follow Sidney and establish his pattern of nocturnal outings before deciding on a foolproof plan of elimination. The act had to arouse no suspicion of anything other than a routine mugging and murder, with robbery as the only motive.

There was still some lingering doubt in Berk's mind about the whole scheme, so he'd decided not to rush this along until he was certain it was the right move. The death of the President's closest friend and advisor would not be without considerable interest to the press, the FBI, and the White House staff. The plan had to withstand very close scrutiny.

Sidney emerged from the hotel and headed up the street toward his parked car. Steve was ready to wrap up the evening and head home. A sixth sense told him something was wrong. Sure enough, a figure emerged from a doorway and was walking behind Sidney. At first it appeared casual but before Berk could cross the street to his car the man had caught up to Sidney and forced him to stop and move back against a store window. Berk moved behind the row of cars on the opposite side of the street from where the two men were standing in a shadowed portion of the block. A holdup? That's what it looked like. What should he do? He didn't want to break in and reveal himself to Sidney.

Sidney handed his wallet and wristwatch to the man who had his back to the street. Suddenly there was gunfire. Two shots and Sidney went down. The gunman fled. Berk wanted to leave in a hurry, but he didn't want to leave Sidney if he was just wounded. He quickly crossed the street and reached the victim in a matter of seconds. Funny, a few minutes ago he was contemplating his murder, and now he was acting out of compassion. It didn't matter. He was very dead. Two shots in the chest and he was gone. Berk decided to take off before the police arrived. He quickly returned to his car and drove off unobtrusively.

What a coincidence, he thought. The thug did the job for him at no cost. He couldn't have asked for anything better. It made the decision for him. Driving slowly down the wide street with the lamplights reflecting off the thin cover of water, Berk began to consider the events of the evening. Was it as simple as it looked? Did the gunman act like a standard holdup man? Where was he hiding? Had he been there all along? Berk had been waiting nearly an hour and had not seen him come down the block and enter the doorway across the street. How did he get there? And why that particular spot?

As he turned it over in his mind, it added up less and less. Why shoot the victim? There had been no resistance. The shooter didn't seem to be a kid, although he hadn't gotten an even halfway good look at him.

He did seem to have been a man and not a boy. Very purposeful and very effective. An adult holdup man wouldn't murder an easy victim on a city street. It wasn't worth the risk. So, maybe it wasn't a simple holdup.

No new thoughts occurred to him during the next few minutes of driving. Not a simple holdup? Then what else could it have been? The question wouldn't go away. But the answer didn't come either. Berk nearly missed his apartment building. Not a simple holdup?

The questions followed him inside and through his getting-ready-for-bed ritual. "A murder? But who would want to murder Sidney? Who? Me. That's who. But who else? No. No. Not the President. His closest friend. No way. It wasn't even like the man. No, there's an angle here and I've just got to figure it out," he thought.

CHAPTER TWENTY

The catheterization laboratory directors were professionally friendly to a fellow cardiologist. The first three visits, however, had been unrewarding. It was not easy to steer the conversation toward the subject and when he did, Al sensed a degree of poorly disguised, mocking humor in the response.

"Clandestine use of our cath lab? Out of the question."

The inquiries were not without value, however, as it was becoming easier to broach the subject and get to the heart of the matter.

Gordon Axelrod was about Al's age and easy to approach. Sitting in his office adjacent to the cath lab in St. Anne's Hospital, the cardiologist was relaxed and talkative. His blue scrub suit indicated that he was a working director.

The office was small with one window facing an adjacent brick wall. Piles of papers and journals were scattered on his desk, the windowsill, and the shelves in the lone bookcase. The atmosphere was casual and reflected the busy work schedule of a high intensity professional. Both men sat with mugs of coffee in hand and spoke lightly about mutual acquaintances.

"I knew Jerry Randolph in med school, Gordon. We lived on the same floor during our first year and even dated some of the same nursing students. I wasn't surprised he went into urology. He never seemed to study and yet managed to survive." Al was trying to stay on a casual tack.

"Well, he made it big here in Washington, Al. He's operated on every big prostate in Congress. Working on his third wife and not likely to stop there, if you ask me. But you're not here to gossip about Jerry. You mentioned something about a cath lab mystery on the phone. What is it you're after?"

"It's a long and uncertain story, Gordon. Basically, I'm looking for a lab where a cath may have been done with the intent of keeping the patient's identity a secret. The procedure itself may have been kept secret. My assumption is that a high-ranking person inside the beltway has good reason to keep his medical history very private. I'm looking for any leads. Anything remotely suggestive that could provide me with a lead."

"I've read a lot of mysteries, Al, but this is the first time I've played a role in one. Let me bring our head tech in here for a moment. Actually, there is one matter I'd like to have you hear firsthand."

Axelrod leaned over his desk and spoke into the intercom phone. "Lou, could you come into my office for a minute?" He turned back to Al and said, "My head tech and I have been trying to solve a mini mystery of our own for several days now. Maybe you can help us as we help you."

Another figure in a blue scrub suit entered the room and stood in the doorway. The head tech's olive complexion and dark black mustache suggested a Mediterranean or Middle- Eastern origin.

"This is Doctor Seibolt, Lou, and he thinks he may have some ideas about the unexplained minutes on our x-ray exposure meter. Why don't you fill him in on the details?"

"Nice to meet you, Doctor," Lou said. "There's not much to tell. A meter in the cath lab tells us how much time has passed during a study with the patient and staff exposed to x-rays. We write down the meter reading when we start a case and the reading when it's over. Last week there were over 10 minutes unaccounted for. We haven't the foggiest idea how the meter moved up over 10 minutes. It's never happened before."

Alan leaned forward intently and tried not to sound too excited. "What alternatives did you consider? What possible explanations are there?"

"Well, we couldn't find any meter malfunction to account for the excess minutes. That left only one other explanation. The x-ray was run for a period of about 10 minutes without anyone in the lab aware of it. I asked every tech and nurse for another explanation. There is none."

Al restated Lou's observation. "So you think the x-ray unit might have been used and you were not aware of it? Is that possible?"

Axelrod answered the question, looking at Lou, who nodded his head in agreement, "Possible, yes, but highly unlikely, Al." Axelrod continued, "Who would have the balls, excuse my French, to do this? Vandalism I could understand, but the use of such a high-tech facility for a very secretive activity is unheard of. Or at least I've never heard of it."

Al remained calm, but he had the feeling he had just unlocked a very important door.

Axelrod went on, "Failure to reset the x-ray indicator was a small detail and easy to overlook in a clandestine operation. It makes me wonder what else might have been overlooked."

"I think this could be very helpful, Gordon. I just need to ask some crucial questions, like when would this have occurred and would someone on the inside have to be in on the plan to make it possible to get away with such a scheme?"

The two men in scrubs stared at each other for a few moments. The implications of this theory were beginning to sink in, including the possibility that powerful people would not like amateur sleuths sniffing around in their affairs. Al could sense his colleague's unease and tried to put him in a more secure position.

"Look, Gordon, I'll do the asking around and keep you two out of it. Just help me get started and help me when I get stuck. Okay?"

"Sure, I'm almost as curious as you are but my game is not playing detective. What do you need to start?"

"First, tell me when this happened?" He knew it had to have been the day Jeff had flown in and out of the area if this was to be the key first fact in solving this mystery.

"Two weeks ago Tuesday. We noted the discrepancy on Wednesday when we started the first case. Since the last case we did was on Tuesday afternoon, that means it had to have happened Tuesday night."

Al found it difficult to conceal his excitement. It fit. Yes, it could be a coincidence but more likely it was the first piece of information that confirmed their theory. He turned to Lou and asked for additional information. "Okay, let's start with the names of staff who work in the lab. One of them may have been here the night the x-ray unit ran itself."

CHAPTER TWENTY-ONE

The murder of Sidney Curtis was big news in Washington and around the country. His death was reported as a mugging gone bad without witnesses. Why the President's Chief of Staff was in that particular neighborhood at night was not revealed, but the police had no difficulty learning from the hotel desk clerk that a man fitting Sidney's description had been with an unidentified woman in the hotel for a little over an hour. The obvious conclusion sufficed, and the matter was discretely dropped by the police and the White House security people.

Leslie Nugent was interested as a reader and not as a reporter. Her interest focused on her lunch meeting with Steve Berk and any information she could glean that would shed light on the matter she and Al were investigating. She was not concerned about Steve's continued interest in her, but she was determined to keep this meeting strictly business. His interest added undesired complexity to the matter at hand.

Driving into Georgetown, she rehearsed some lines of rebuttal for his likely advances. Her choice of dress was calculated to give him no ambiguous message. She was no longer interested in him and wanted that to be very clear. The prospect of meeting her former lover on these new terms made her jittery and even raised a slight sweat. Steve didn't let go of anyone or anything he liked with a gracious good-by.

Parking was always difficult in this area at lunchtime, but she lucked out and found a metered spot two blocks from the restaurant. Before getting out of the car, she gave the situation a last-minute going over. She would run the story by him and ask for any leads he thought worthy of pursuit.

She would not bring Al into the discussion, and she would not give Steve the idea that she wanted to partner with him in solving the mystery. This was just a chance to pick his brain.

The restaurant was packed with the usual Georgetown lunch crowd: students, tourists, locals, and D.C-ers looking for a reasonably priced meal. Leslie scanned the crowd in search of Steve and finally spotted him at a far corner table. Dressed in a light gray summer suit and pale blue shirt without a tie, he looked every bit the *GQ* man. Only difference was he was not as young as he looked and was not a gentleman in the *GQ* mode. Just a very clever and hardened ex-Marine who knew the ins and outs of Washington's intelligence organizations. A dangerous guy who knew a lot about the dark side of town and who could use information to his advantage as a situation dictated. Leslie knew she had to be very careful before giving out too much free information.

She picked her way through the room, avoiding several harried waiters with trays. Steve rose to greet her and gave her a friendly kiss on the cheek.

"Great to see you, Leslie. Been a long time between dates."

"Yes, Steve, it has been a while, but I'd prefer not to consider this a 'date' but rather a business lunch." Leslie wanted to lay out the ground rules at the outset and avoid any misunderstanding later.

"Whatever you want to call it, Les. It's still good to see you."

She was quite aware of his seeming light-hearted approach. Very conciliatory and friendly. She was determined not to be caught off guard by his usually deceptive manner. He always had a reason for what he did.

"When you called I wasn't sure what you were after, Steve. Maybe you can fill me in while I look over this menu."

"Sure. I'm in no hurry. I'm having the roast beef with horseradish and havarti on French bread. I was thinking about it all the way over here."

"Okay, I'll do the same with an iced coffee."

The moment of silence that followed reflected the tension they each felt. It was going to have to be resolved if each was going to accomplish what they had come for.

Steve broke the silence and Leslie could see that this was not going to be an easy relationship to close down.

"Well, Les, I only wanted to see where our relationship stood. I'm still very involved with you and want to keep us going. Nothing more complicated than that."

"Steve, you knew we were cooling down the last few times we got together. The message should have been clear. There never was much romance between us to begin with, so the relationship wasn't going anywhere. I think you knew that."

The waitress interrupted them, took their orders, left a basket of rolls and butter and left.

"Can't we just stay friends, Steve, and leave it at that? There isn't any future for us beyond that and I'm not interested in a deeper relationship without romance. I don't want to hurt you, Steve, but I know you and doubt that you ever had any serious design on me. Let's let it lie and just be friends."

"I guess I'm not surprised, Leslie. I'm not stupid. I can live with friendship if you can. I hope you'll forgive an occasional lustful glance from an old friend." He grinned. "I'm only kidding. Let's leave it at that and have lunch. Tell me what's going on with you."

Leslie felt much relieved but reminded herself not to drop her guard. She knew him too well. He didn't take any kind of rejection easily, so this most personal rebuff wouldn't go down without some additional work on her part. She was glad she'd dressed as conservatively as possible. Maybe a change in subject, she hoped, would ease the tension.

"I'm into a story, Steve, that's a bit of a mystery tale. I thought you might be able to help me piece it together. There are a lot of missing pieces that need to be filled in. I'd like your take on what I've got so far."

"Great. Try me."

"Just remember, Steve, this is all conjecture, but I think it could amount to something big. I'm just trying to see if it has legs."

"Okay, Les, get on with it. I'm all ears."

"Well, in simplest terms, I'm suspicious that someone high up in Washington circles is covering up a serious health problem. Why it's important to cover it up is one missing piece, but we could speculate that the individual's worth would be diminished if his or her health problem became public. Who the sick person is, is another piece to fill in. These two pieces obviously are tied together. If I knew the 'who' I think I'd know the 'why'. That's the mystery I'm working on."

She hadn't told him much, but it was clear to Berk that the carefully constructed cloak of secrecy he and Sidney and he had thrown over the President's problem was beginning to unravel. Where had it broken down? He was both stunned and fascinated. It had seemed to be very securely tied down.

What loose end had been left untied?

"That's very interesting, Leslie. What's the basis of this suspicion? If I knew some more background, I might be able to help."

Leslie had thought this through before the meeting.

She had decided not to give too much background away. Certainly not the tie to the plane crash and Al's involvement with the aviator cardiologist. Just stick to the Washington bigwig illness cover-up story and let it flow from there.

"Just based on a tip I got. When I checked the tipster's credentials that left me with good reason to follow up on it."

Berk could tell when smoke was being blown in his face. He suspected Leslie knew a lot more but was going to hold back for reasons not clear at this time. He would have to gradually get her to reveal the background and eventually the leak that had placed her on the trail of the President. The failure of security bothered him. He couldn't see where they'd made any serious mistake. He'd have to gain her confidence and get her to open up.

"That's not much to go on but I'd like a few days to work through some scenarios. Then we could get together and discuss the possibilities. Okay? Now, friend, let's eat our lunch and talk about any other aspect of this mystery you care to let me in on."

They turned their attention to the food, but each was sure the other was under control. Leslie was sure she could fend off Steve's advances and still get some valuable insight from him. He was sure he could get his former lover to reveal the identity of her informant and divulge a lot more information.

CHAPTER TWENTY-TWO

Hospital security at St. Anne's was housed in the basement of a very old, gray, stone-faced building. The age of the building, however, was no indication of the sophistication of the surveillance equipment. Like many security operations in Washington, the person in charge was a former government security worker. Donald Eagerton was a former FBI agent who lived on his St. Anne's salary plus a government pension. Not a bad combination.

Al wondered if Eagerton had weighed as much when he was an agent for J. Edgar Hoover. Doubtful. The red-faced, beefy, bald head of security for St. Anne's unwedged himself from his desk chair with some difficulty to greet the visitor. He'd be a large man even if he lost 100 pounds.

All in all, though, he was a friendly guy with a warm smile.

"Nice to meet you, Dr. Seibolt. Have a seat and we'll get you some coffee. How do you like it?"

"Black will do just fine."

The order went into his telephone intercom. "Two black, Mary. Thanks. Now tell me how I can be of help to you."

Al replayed the story of his partner's death and the facts that led him to wonder about a health-related issue and a cover-up. As he told it, the story began to sound more and more plausible even though it was all sheer conjecture. The former FBI agent listened intently and seemed genuinely interested.

"That's not a bad bit of detective work for a doctor.

At the agency we'd call that a 'Perry Mason.' Fascinating in concept but totally lacking in any hard evidence. Of course, that's when Mason finds the receipt for the key to the locker which contains the bag with the chemical formula the former company president is hiding from the new company owner who just got murdered. Trouble is, Mason isn't doing it anymore except in reruns."

Al tried to gauge the response. Was it good humor or just downright cynicism? If the latter, it could indicate a lack of respect for the amateur sleuth's role and a disinclination to be too helpful.

"That's a fair analysis. I wish I had some concrete evidence. However, all I'm trying to do at this point is follow a lead that could begin to put some flesh on the very lean skeleton I've concocted. Frankly, if this lead fades, I'm left with a blank slate and may have to fold up my tent and return home. I've already been away from my practice longer than I had intended. All I'm asking for is your help in sorting out this one lead."

The head of hospital security leaned forward as the two cups of coffee were placed on his desk. He handed one cup to Alan and leaned back precariously in his chair. "Well, I'd like to help, so let's see what I can do for you in terms of an explanation for those unexplained minutes of x- ray time. I have my logbook here that will tell me who was on duty on the night in question. We keep two guards in house every night between 8pm and 8am. That's a 12-hour shift during which they travel a preset route through the hospital, punching time clocks as they go. We could use four to cover a place this big, but two is all the bean counters say the hospital can afford. All of our security guards are former FBI agents, like myself, and very experienced in matters of building security. Let's see."

He leafed through the hardcover ledger-style book. "Well, it looks like Ed Beldon and Gene Murray were on duty on the night in question. Both have been here over ten years and are as good as any on my staff. They'll both be here in a few minutes to sign out for their shift. Now, tell me what part of North Carolina you live in. I was born near Asheville."

CHAPTER TWENTY-THREE

The two guards were already out of uniform and each carried a gym bag. They appeared to be in their late 50's or early 60's and could have been two guys on their way to a gym for a swim or maybe a game of handball. Each was beefy and built very squat. Al mused that there seemed to be a mold that turned out retired FBI agents. The three in this room were almost clones of each other. He also thought that he would not like to meet the two guards in a dark alley.

There was more than a hint of potential violence just below the surface. When they entered Eagerton's tight office, they had sized up Al in a casual but not disinterested manner.

Two cops sizing up an unknown quantity. Everyone was a potentially dangerous adversary.

Eagerton maintained the air of informality that he had used with Al. "Ed. Gene. This is Dr. Alan Seibolt, and he has a few questions he'd like to ask you. I've been over some interesting ground with him. Have a seat and let me get you two some coffee."

The two sat down in the remaining chairs and continued their noncommittal silence. Eagerton went to the door and asked for two more coffees.

"Okay, Doc, ask away." Eagerton opened the door for questioning.

"I appreciate your time, fellas, so I'll be brief and to the point. I'm trying to determine if a cardiac catheterization procedure was done in this hospital without any record of it. There's reason to believe that something unusual took place in the cath lab on Tuesday evening, August 23, but there is no record of any procedure. There are unexplained minutes of x-ray usage in the lab on that particular evening, which is an indication of activity in the lab. I understand that you were the security detail that evening and morning, so I wonder if you can recall any out of the ordinary occurrence during that period of time?"

"So, you think someone came into the lab and did a procedure on the sly? Is that it in a nutshell, Doc?" Ed Beldon showed his skepticism in a wry smile. His partner remained silent and stone-faced.

Beldon continued, "That would be quite a trick. But now that you raise the point, the lab is in a pretty quiet part of the hospital. The building is pretty closed down after 6 in the evening, so you could work there on the QT if you knew how to get in and out without being seen and if you knew how to work the equipment and could clean up professionally. A lot of if's. We also check the area every three to four hours, so the timing would have to be pretty good too."

Al picked up on the routine checking procedure.

"Did the area check out OK that evening?" He wanted to see the log but didn't want to show any signs of distrust in the security pair. Eagerton took care of that for him.

"Well, let's check the log and clear up that issue." With that he reached behind him and pulled a large loose-leaf binder off the top of the file cabinet behind his chair. He thumbed his way through the thick log-book until he found the page he was looking for.

"Now, let's see. September 10. Here we go. Looks like a routine night. The cath lab was checked three times, once at 8:30 in the evening, again at 3:00 and 8:00 in the morning. Nothing out of the ordinary."

Al pickup up on the timing discrepancy but tried to minimize his curiosity to the guards.

"That's a six and a half hour stretch with no security visit. Is that usual?"

Again, Beldon was quick to respond. "We're good, but not per-fect. We don't hit the clocks on a perfect schedule. I think you'll find that a stretch that long isn't unusual. With just two guys, the time between checks can be that long sometimes. Gene, that was your beat that night. Did you see anything out of the ordinary?"

The silent partner looked as if someone had just awakened him from a very deep sleep. He rubbed his eyes with his left hand and scratched the back of his head with his right. He appeared to be deep in thought.

"Can't say as I do. It was a routine night. I haven't had anything but routine nights for over a year."

Al saw an opportunity to check the logbook now and took it. Gene Murray's statement implied it was a very innocent log so no one should be concerned about his interest in the book.

"Could I have a look at the log book, Mr. Eagerton?" "Sure, be my guest." Eagerton turned the big ledger around for him to inspect.

Al tried to seem as casual as possible. He wanted to see if that long stretch of uncovered time was unusual for that particular site. Again, he didn't want to look too suspicious. As he became familiar with the ledger, he could see that the cath lab was always visited at intervals no longer than 6 hours apart, but 6 hours was not that unusual. Some sites regularly had gaps as long as eight hours, but the cath lab was not one of them. The delay that night did not jump out. On the other hand, the security person could make the stop and not see anything if he didn't want to. Al looked up into the smiling face of Don Eagerton.

"Satisfied, Doc?"

"Yes, I think so. You've been very helpful and so have your two security guards."

"Does that mean you're through here?" Murray spoke up for the first time without being prompted.

Careful, Al thought. There might be something going on here and I don't want to give them any indication of my suspicions.

"Yes, I think that wraps it up for me. Thanks again to all of you."

He didn't want to seem anxious to leave, so he rose slowly and put out his hand to the two guards. They shook his hand with steely firm grips. Eagerton's handshake was less firm and seemed friendlier. The guards were giving him a subtle warning to bug off. Their handgrips were unmistakably hard and menacing.

As Al faced them for a final good-bye, the look in Murray's eyes was cold and detached. Al felt uneasy under that gaze and was happy to leave the basement of that building.

CHAPTER TWENTY-FOUR

Leslie and Al had arranged to meet for dinner and exchange infor-mation from the day's meetings.

Al was enjoying the variety of good restaurants in the D.C. area and Leslie was an exceptional guide to good eating. That night, they ate at a small French bistro in D.C. It was quiet, with a reasonably priced menu and wine list. They had begun working on a nice bottle of red Bordeaux as soon as the waiter left with their food orders. Leslie wore a sweater and skirt with just a string of pearls. Understated, but in no way concealing her animal vitality and casual confidence. He hadn't found a fault yet and was beginning to think that was because there weren't any to find.

Al's enthusiasm couldn't be contained. "I think I hit pay-dirt at St. Anne's. They have an unexplained use of their cath lab x-ray equipment, which coincides with the time of Jeff's visit to the D.C. area. The cath lab chief and his head tech were puzzled by the finding. The security people could be in on it. I met with them. Two tough- looking security guards who could have assured the necessary privacy during the critical evening hours. I still have to do some work investigating the staff. I can't believe the team was composed of all outsiders. I don't think Jeff would have accepted that. All in all, it was a very productive visit."

Leslie picked up on Al's enthusiasm, "Wow, that is exciting. I think you've uncovered the kind of lead that lends our whole theory credibility. It's what an investigative reporter salivates over. I can't say the same about my meeting with Berk. We fenced a bit and I threw out a few morsels of our suspicion. Berk said he wanted to think about it. I can't read him. Nevertheless, I agreed to meet him tomorrow, at his office, to follow up on the matter. I wish I had something more tangible to show for my effort."

They both were feeling upbeat. The wine created a warm sense of relaxation and the information exchange had done nothing to discourage them.

"Let's look at it this way, Al, so far, nothing has popped up to negate our working hypothesis. I think we've strengthened our initial suspicion, so let's keep moving in the same direction tomorrow. Anyway, here comes our first course so let's put sleuthing aside and enjoy the moment."

Leslie smiled but felt a bit tense when contemplating her meeting with Berk the following afternoon.

CHAPTER TWENTY-FIVE

Leslie had agreed to meet Steve at his office-apartment just outside Georgetown. The building was of pre-World War Two vintage but was in good repair. A four-story, yellow brick building with no character. She and Steve had often used it for a rendezvous during their intense but brief dating period. As she mounted the familiar steps to the second floor, Leslie had misgivings about agreeing to meet at this place that recalled many recent memories. She and Steve had enjoyed a robust sex life, albeit devoid of emotion. With Steve, there had been little inhibition. She wondered what it would be like with Al but sensed that he and she would take a while before they could be free of inhibitions. For reasons she never understood, Steve both scared and relaxed her simultaneously. He scared her with regard to the violent side of his work, about which she knew few details, but relaxed her in their sex life due to their lack of romantic entanglement and his confidence in the physical side of the relationship.

"Why am I thinking about this now? I'm here to get some inside dope on Washington VIP's with heart disease and not to encourage a former sex partner," she thought.

Standing in front of the door, she hesitated to grab the handle. "Get yourself together, Leslie. You settled the relationship with Steve weeks ago so don't give it another thought. All business."

She used her old key and the door opened easily.

Familiar surroundings greeted her. Steve was not there yet, so she walked around the apartment and looked for any changes. The place was still half office and half apartment. The front room, normally a living room, had been converted into an office with a large wooden desk and two upholstered chairs and a sofa. The wall hangings were still–life etchings by Morandi which gave the room an air of elegance, even if they were only fair reproductions. It was an office, but it bore the look of a living room. The lighting was provided by several antique floor lamps. In Steve's line of work the office was best kept simple and disconnected from any identifiable type of security work.

He was a very private operative and the office whispered, "private." There was no space for a secretary because there was no secretary. Steve preferred to work alone and that really meant alone. The back rooms were a conventional bedroom and kitchen. The white walls were beginning to peel in a few spots and the floor slanted a bit. The well-worn oriental rugs needed better pads and the window treatment was folded shades. All in all, an understated sophistication showed through. Wealthy clients would feel at home and less wealthy ones would not be intimidated.

Leslie settled down on the cracking, brown leather sofa and began picking through Berk's accumulated magazines.

The click in the door hardly drew her attention as Berk let himself in.

"Hi, Leslie. I knew you had a key, so I didn't worry about being a few minutes late. Glad to see you made yourself at home."

He hung his sport jacket on the oak coat rack and walked over to Leslie. He gave her a harmless peck on the cheek. "Like a glass of wine? I've got some already open in the fridge, so it's no trouble?"

"Sure, why not? Sounds good to me." "Okay, give me just a minute."

Steve returned from the kitchen with two glasses of red wine. "Here's to good times past," Steve toasted. Leslie raised her glass to meet his. Steve settled in at the opposite end of the sofa and opened his briefcase.

"Let's get started on your mystery. I've been giving it serious thought. I'm still more than a little curious how you got going on this, but that can be saved for a later conversation. Let me show you what I've done. I reviewed my files on the many Mr. Bigs in D.C. and looked for any leads on serious heart disease not already out there in the public domain. I also made a few casual calls to people who usually know this kind of stuff. Best I can do is two senators up for re-election who seem to have been somewhat out of view for the past two months or more. They may be keeping something like that quiet. I've got it all down in these two files for you to study."

Berk had decided that the best strategy was to play this along gently and try to get Leslie to reveal more about her source. The breach of security was critical, and he was determined to find out where the breach had taken place.

This was both professional and personal.

Leslie took the two folders and began scanning them with interest. She was not unaware of Steve's casual move to the middle of the sofa so that he almost touched her right elbow. He made a few motions to items in the folder she began to read. His hand played with strands of her hair and touched the back of her neck. For some reason, she didn't warn him off. All that recall on her way in had actually turned on a low level of excitement and now Steve was building on it.

She wanted to call him off but didn't make the move.

Steve took that as an invitation, gently drew the folder out of her hands and placed it on the coffee table. Without a protest, she let him kiss her softly on the lips. The kissing grew more intense and she could feel herself drifting. A dim voice said, "Don't do it," but the voice grew dimmer and dimmer as she allowed his hand to gently caress her breasts through the thin fabric of her polo shirt. They spoke very little, but the script was familiar to each of them.

Leslie abruptly sat up straight and gently removed his hand from her breast. "Steve, I thought I'd made it clear a few weeks ago that we were no longer going down this road. I meant it then and I mean it now. I thought you were able to accept that. Maybe it was my fault this afternoon for letting my guard down and giving you the impression that I had changed my mind. I haven't."

Berk was surprised that Leslie had drawn back from the sexual precipice when it seemed she was about to go over.

He couldn't let this take his mind off the real reason for his meeting with her.

Leslie knew she couldn't keep a sexual option open and begin a normal relationship like the one she was forging with Al. Her resolve was strong to make the final break with Steve.

"Leslie, I guess I misjudged your resolve. I reluctantly accept your decision. I hope that won't keep us from being friends and staying in contact."

"Steve, I'd like nothing better than continuing our friendship on a different, less heated, basis."

"Okay, that's settled. Now let's get on with the real reason for this meeting."

Leslie felt a wave of relief. She had finally made the break and that took a load off her mind. Now she had to fence with Steve over details of the story she was nurturing and not give away any crucial nuggets.

"Leslie, who else knows about this story you're working on? Anyone at your paper?"

"No, Steve, it's not a story I'm covering. I told you. Just a lead I'm curious about and want to see where it takes me."

Steve didn't let his surprise show. Not a regular story. Then what was her motivation? "Come on, Leslie, level with me and I can be of real help. Keep this all locked up and I'm flying blind. I'll be of little use."

Warning lights flashed dimly in Leslie's brain. She sensed him pumping her for information. She wasn't sure why but her sixth sense said, "Watch it!" She was hesitant to share even innocent information. "That's all I can say, Steve. My snitch wouldn't like it if I blabbed about this. I'm going to have to let it stand at that."

With that, she headed for the bathroom and Steve knew the session was over. He was frustrated that he'd learned nothing about the breach in security that had let Leslie get the scent that something was going on.

Out in the street, Leslie felt good about her resolution of the Steve Berk relationship but realized that she'd gotten very little information out of him regarding the mystery. She'd follow up on the two senators he'd offered information on, but they didn't sound like very hot leads.

CHAPTER TWENTY-SIX

A sultry late afternoon made air conditioning a necessity. Al wondered how this city, built on a swamp, had functioned in the summers before air conditioning came to its rescue.

He couldn't wait to get Lou Rousso's list of St. Anne's lab personnel. He'd arranged to meet the lab's head tech in a bar not likely to be frequented by any lab staff. Two blocks from the White House, in the basement of a fading but still popular hotel, the O'Farrell, was a bar that also served as a regular retreat for the White House press corp. It was still early for that crowd. The old oak bar was lined with stools upholstered with worn red corduroy. The bar rail was well worn and the mirror behind the bar was splattered with lost metal backing. The floor was a dark stained oak with warped slats and a soft cushioned feel. In short, this was a comfortable, heavily used watering hole. Toward the back was a series of booths that could seat up to six.

Al had settled into the one furthest to the rear and was working on his second draft of Bass Ale when Rousso slid in opposite him.

"Any trouble finding this place, Lou?"

"A little, but parking was a bigger trick." Pointing his index finger nowhere in particular, he continued. "You know, some of these faces look familiar to me. That guy over in the corner near the cash register. Have you seen him before?"

Al turned slightly and could see the handsome profile of a TV network substitute anchor. His name escaped him. "I think you've seen him do the TV news, but I can't think of his name."

"Yeah, yeah that's who it is. I knew I'd seen him before. Wait'll my wife hears this. She'll be spending her afternoons here."

"Would you like a drink, Lou?"

"Sure. Same as you're having will be fine."

Al motioned to the bartender for two more and turned back to Lou.

"Did you bring the list?"

"No problem. Here it is. Ten names in all, including the two who have left since the day we're talking about."

"Did they leave for any particular reason?"

"Well, the nurse took maternity leave and the male tech left for no particular reason. I spoke with him but couldn't get him to give me any complaints or any reason.

He'd been in the lab for little over a year and hadn't had any problems. Said he was moving down South but didn't leave a forwarding address. Picked up his final pay check and just left. Darryl Edmonds, a single guy, around thirty. Seemed nice enough. Another thing. He didn't ask for a reference so I'm not sure he was moving to another job.

Just left."

"Strange. Anyone else on the list with any unusual habits or behavior? Anyone who might have been involved in the kind of off-hours use of the lab? I know that's a vague question, but I'm groping for any lead whatsoever."

"You know, since our meeting I've asked myself the same question. Is there anyone on the list I wouldn't trust?

We're a pretty tight group. Get along very well with one possible exception, Peg Carter, one of the nurses. She doesn't mix with the group and seems to have a very separate life. Single girl without a boyfriend. I've never been able to get friendly with her in over three years, and the other nurses keep their distance from her. She'd be the only one I'd question on this score. The others are clean as a whistle, believe me."

Al got up and brought the two beers over from the bar. "Do you have any idea what might have happened that night? I know we've talked once but now you've had some more time to reflect. Is my hypothetical situation plausible? Could the lab have carried out a procedure without leaving any trace except that oversight on the x-ray timer?"

"I hate to admit it, but it's possible. Security isn't tight, but they could've been in on it. The rest isn't such a big deal. You'd want some staff who were familiar with the lab, otherwise there'd be all sorts of small screw-ups left behind."

"So, what you're saying is that an inside job was possible and that someone on this list could have had a hand in it. If you had to bet, you'd put Peg Carter at the head of the list and possibly Darryl Edmunds."

"I'm not accusing anybody of anything, mind you, only playing this game with you, Doc."

"I understand, Lou. I'm not dragging you into this, but I will ask you to keep this under your hat. I think I can learn a bit more if no one thinks they're under suspicion."

Lou gave a nod of agreement and followed that up with reassuring words, "Okay, I understand. You can trust me. I'll keep a lid on it."

Al felt good about the progress he'd made and wanted to make Lou feel that he'd been a real help. He lightened up the mood by showing his friendliest smile and asking, "How about another beer?"

CHAPTER TWENTY-SEVEN

When Leslie left his apartment, Berk had the uneasy feeling that she was holding back a lot of information. He was sure of that.

Her suspicions were too close to the truth to be ignored. He had to know more about her real intentions. How much did she know and was anyone else in on it with her? It was worth a bit of his time and effort to find out.

His surveillance of her apartment from his car had been unproductive. He'd seen her enter her apartment building around 5:30 PM but now, two hours later, she had yet to come out. Several other people had come and gone, but he couldn't place any of them. Parked in a good spot to watch the front door, he was committed to a long evening of sitting and watching and eating a sub in the car for dinner.

It was a typical late September evening in Washington. A bit warm and humid. His window was down, and the radio played softly.

The lights were on in her apartment, and after two more hours of watching, he concluded that there wasn't going to be any action tonight.

The drive back to his office was a simple 10-minute run into Georgetown and out Connecticut Avenue. He'd decided to sleep over in his office rather than go home and watch TV with Terry. Their non-relationship allowed plenty of latitude. He smiled at the thought.

He parked in his reserved space alongside the building, locked the car and headed for the street and the front door to the building. He could sense another presence in the parking lot. Could be an innocent person parking there or it could be something more. Darkness gave the other person an advantage, so he decided to keep walking toward better light. No sense turning and confronting a likely innocent person. He made it to the front door, unlocked it, went in and climbed the stairs rapidly to his second-floor office.

Whoever was out there had let him get inside the building and have the door lock behind him.

He hadn't imagined the presence and knew the front door entrance was easily opened by a professional. He put a light on in his bedroom, keeping the front office dark. He felt silly putting so much stock in a feeling, but the episode with Sidney had put him on edge. He sat down on the office floor in the darkest corner behind one of the two overstuffed chairs, facing the door, and waited. His Beretta was loaded and in his hand. The prey was now the hunter.

The door opened very quietly, and a figure entered. It was no longer just a feeling. The door closed quietly behind him. Berk could see a man briefly silhouetted in the light of the office doorway. He was carrying a gun in his right hand. He could have nailed him right then, but his curiosity was piqued. What was going on? Who was gunning for him? Literally. He wanted this guy to give him some answers. The figure advanced very quietly toward the lit bedroom, moving along the wall in shadow. No sense taking any risk, thought Berk.

"Stop right there and drop your gun."

The figure stopped but there was no clatter on the floor. "I said 'drop it' and I meant it. Don't be foolish."

In that instant, the figure fell to the floor and rolled behind the big chair in the opposite corner.

"You're gunning for the wrong guy, buddy. You won't leave here alive unless you come out and toss that gun into the middle of the floor."

Still no answer. He knew the gunman was planning how he could still get his kill and get away. Not one likely to negotiate. The intruder was still mentally on the offensive, even though Berk was holding the better hand.

Berk had placed the telephone and base on the floor beside him. He picked up the phone and punched a few numbers in without completing the call. He spoke as if into the phone. "Detective Presley, my name is Steve Berk. There's a fellow with a gun in my office, 8773 Connecticut Avenue. I wonder if you could send a squad car over and help break the stalemate we find ourselves in." He paused. "Sure, I'll be patient. Thanks." He hung up.

"Your number's up, so let's relax and wait for the cops to arrive," he said into the darkness.

Berk knew a rush was coming any minute. He wasn't sure from which direction, but this scene was going to end very quickly.

The gunman decided it was best to go after his adversary and not try to make it to the door. The chair was his cover, and he slid it ahead of him toward the voice he'd heard on the phone across the room.

Unfortunately for him, Berk was no ordinary prey. A former Special Ops Marine with more killing experience than any civilian hit man, Berk knew better than to allow his voice to give his position away. By the time the gunman had pushed his chair almost to the middle of the room, near where the telephone conversation had taken place, Berk had crawled along the wall toward the entrance and now was behind the gunman who was faintly lit by the bedroom light. He could now see his target well enough to get off a shot. He aimed for his right shoulder, guessing that would disable him. He hoped to question him about what was going on.

The shot was on target and the gunman screamed as the bullet shattered his shoulder. Berk waited for a response.

"Kick the gun out into the middle of the room or my next shot'll make a cripple out of you."

No response again.

One tough bird. He'd never give in and ask for help. Berk's second shot hit above the right knee and shattered the femur.

"You're not going anywhere now so why not toss the gun out here and say 'uncle.' This can only get worse for you. I just want to know who sent you and why."

"Fuck you, Mack," was the only response. He still had his gun and was obviously not going to surrender.

The shots would bring the cops so there wasn't much time. Berk now reversed the chair movement and pushed his chair into the one partially shielding the gunman. The twice-wounded man would be in no condition to fight but could get off a shot. Berk pushed the two chairs together until the other man was trapped in a corner. His pain was evident in his scream as the chairs pushed him roughly. He dropped the gun. Berk felt confident that he could go hand-to-hand now. He put the light on and walked over to the corner led by the smeared trail of blood. His gun was ready if needed.

The gunman's left-handed knife throw was too wide to hit him, but Berk's training took over, and he reflexively put two slugs into the middle of the man's chest. The hit-man was through. Steve carefully searched his pockets for an ID and found a driver's license in a very slim wallet with little cash. Nothing on his body gave a clue about why he was gunning for Berk. His gun was a very professional, snub-nosed .38 with no markings.

Berk spent the next two hours at police headquarters and returned to his office at dawn to clean it up.

Someone had sent a pro to blow him away. Why? Who sent him? He'd have to work this through very carefully. He had to also consider that there might be a follow-up hit men when this one's contractor learned that the effort was a bust. Sidney's death was now very clearly something other than a routine mugging gone bad. What the hell was going on?

CHAPTER TWENTY-EIGHT

High above the Arizona desert, Ed Covington could watch a beautiful sunrise come up behind the barren hills to the east or in the evening look west and see a spectacular desert sunset. His office and living quarters occupied the entire penthouse level of a 12-story, high-rise building.

The vistas he surveyed stretched for over a hundred miles. He loved the view and enjoyed having breakfast in his office where he could work out on a treadmill while watching the morning news on television. The set up was exceptional and he appreciated it.

Covington Industries was not well known to the public, but it was well known on Wall Street as one of the Fortune 500 companies which enjoyed an enormous amount of federal contract money for a range of products, from rocket thrusters to tank air-conditioning units. Covington was a defense industry giant with great dependence on Washington. In

Covington's case, his relationship with Jack Henderson was central to the success of his multi-billion-dollar empire. They were close personal friends and had been since their college days. His financial backing of Jack's campaigns had been crucial throughout the latter's career. Now, with Sidney gone, Ed Covington was Jack's number one confidant and advisor. For years, Covington Industries had benefited enormously from his friendship with the Senator and now President.

The death of Sidney Curtis had made the President even more dependent on Ed. The threesome had been a very successful team. On the surface, it was Jack's personal appeal, Sidney's sage, uncanny political advice and Ed's money. Jack Henderson valued Ed as a friend and never realized the influential role Ed played in Sidney's counseling. Sidney knew how brutal and clever Ed was and relied on his insights and amoral moves to develop their strategies. It was Ed Covington who had been behind most of the crucial turns in Jack Henderson's career. Jack was not aware of this. Sidney had gotten the credit and Ed Covington couldn't have cared less. His ego needed no boosting. Now it was just a twosome.

Ed acknowledged that it was unfortunate Sidney had to be removed, but Ed's plan called for the absolute minimum number of insiders. He believed very strongly in reducing the chance of any leak, or accidental betrayal of secrets or even possible blackmail. The most effective means of accomplishing this was to reduce the number of people in possession of sensitive information. Through Sidney, Ed had been kept abreast of the cover-up. Now he would have to personally stay on top of it. He would be more directly involved. One priority would be to continue shrinking the circle of potential leakers. For this he had a number of semi-reliable operatives who were totally unaware of his identity.

Most importantly, Jack Henderson would have to maintain the wall of secrecy surrounding his own ailment. Ed was going to keep in very close contact with Jack to assure that he followed the game plan. Jack needn't know about the out- of-White House goings on, but he had to stay otherwise on course.

Recent events were disturbing. Ed was not used to disappointment and had little tolerance for failure. The failed attempt on the life of Steve Berk gnawed at him. He knew this would put Berk on alert and make any subsequent attempt on his life more difficult. Furthermore, Berk would wonder what was going on and could become an annoyance as he poked around for answers.

As Ed and Sidney had agreed, he was keeping Jack Henderson out of this loop. They couldn't afford to leave any trail leading to the White House. Jack would be briefed occasionally, but only in the most oblique manner. Never with direct facts. The election was all that mattered, and nothing could interfere with that. Keeping Jack's health condition a secret was the top priority. Eliminating Sidney had been the first step in assuring no trail back to either Jack or Ed. Now it was time for Steve Berk to go and the initial effort had been botched.

There was no way the deaths of Curtis and Berk could be connected. That would leave only Jennifer Henderson as the remaining potential witness aside from Jack and himself.

Her recent liaison with an old beau was being closely monitored by Covington and was a development which had succeeded better than he had any reason to hope it would. Berk's recording of the hotel tryst was secure in Covington's safe and would be a useful tool for silencing Jennifer if need be. He was sure that Berk had a copy, but that would be secured when he was taken out. At this moment, Jennifer's elimination would be too difficult to pull off and could lead to more investigation than he wanted. However, if an unusual opportunity presented, it might be worth the risk. He preferred to get the election behind them before proceeding down that path. As a witness, Jack was probably going to be taken care of by natural causes, so there was little reason to think beyond removal of the three primary witnesses.

The nurse and technician from the hospital episode were slated for elimination. Definitive closure on that episode was on track, now that some time had elapsed since the two workers had left their positions.

There was always a lot of risk in a high-stakes game, but Covington had been a risk-taker all his life. That had netted him an enormous personal fortune and seemed to be a natural way of life for him. Several gambles early in his life had gotten him the necessary working capital to begin buying companies and amassing the empire he now owned and controlled. At times the risky business seemed an end unto itself. He enjoyed being the master planner and hardly cared who was cut down as his plans proceeded inexorably to their successful completion. His almost constant wheeling and dealing had made marriage unnecessary. The gratification he received from business conquests was a surrogate for marriage and family. His emotional makeup was better suited for the former than the latter.

CHAPTER TWENTY-NINE

Tracking down the recently departed lab tech was no easy task, but Leslie's reporter skills proved highly effective. The address was in an Atlanta suburb. Al decided to call, confirm Darryl Edmunds' address, and see if he was willing to discuss the matter at hand. The phone number Leslie had found was for an apartment building's front desk. The person on duty knew Darryl and indicated that he was not answering the intercom. Faking his identity as Darryl's uncle who was planning a visit in the near future, Al was able to engage the operator in a quick overview of Darryl's situation. She was friendly and seemed to know Darryl more than just casually.

The apartment was a one-bedroom affair which went for $1400 a month. Not so steep considering the extensive outdoor activity facilities. No, Darryl did not have a job yet. That gave Al reason to pause. How did he rent the apartment without any current means of support? The answer came back before he even asked the question. Darryl had bought it rather than rented it. So, a job was less relevant. Going price, $180,000. And he bought it with a rather small mortgage. A nice guy who didn't make any trouble for anyone. Single. And reasonably attractive.

That was all she could say. Had to run. Another call was coming in.

Well, that was helpful. And a red flag. Darryl had left a modest paying job, then bought a fairly upscale condominium before securing another job. And bought it with a large down payment. Had to be a source of money somewhere. His parents were alive, according to his last employment record, so he hadn't collected some big insurance claim on their lives. A quick check showed his parents to be of average means and not likely to fund a very large cash outlay. So, another red flag. The trail was warm but still wasn't getting them anywhere. Darryl would have to be questioned. The nurse, Peg Carter, was more immediately accessible but now there was even greater reason to be careful in questioning her. There was increasing reason to believe something bad happened in that lab and that staff members were involved.

Peg Carter was home but was unwilling to talk to anyone about anything. She was adamant, and Al was unwilling to spill the beans about the cath lab theory. There was no sense trying to get her to be cooperative. She was one resolute woman. Al felt this was consistent with their theory. She had something to hide.

That left Darryl Edmunds and a trip to Atlanta if Darryl could be contacted.

CHAPTER THIRTY

The death of the White House Chief of Staff had briefly shocked the nation's capitol. His cold-blooded murder on the street was seen as a tragic but random event. The President felt the loss very deeply. Sidney had been his closest friend in addition to a most trusted advisor. True grief was hidden beneath his stoic exterior as he went through the formal burial and memorial services. There'd be a new Chief of Staff, but this would not replace the loss of a close friend.

For Jennifer, the loss was not as deeply felt. Sidney and she had jousted a lot over their respective influence with Jack. Nevertheless, she'd known him for over a decade and seen him through the trauma of his wife's death.

Steve Berk felt the loss of a business associate. More importantly, the manner of his death had been disquieting.

He'd witnessed an assassination that had set him on edge. Its implications for him were subsequently magnified by the attempt on his life in his office.

The Presidential re-election campaign was on track.

Sidney Curtis had been replaced with Jon Bliss, a long-time friend of Jack Henderson's and most recently an executive with a Washington-based TV and radio conglomerate with over 100 stations principally in the South and Midwest. Politically, the appointment was an overture to the conservatives in the party and not likely to cause any waves with the repressed moderate wing of the party.

Jack Henderson continued to run strong in the polls in spite of a limited travel schedule. All Jon Bliss knew was that the strategy called for a working president who campaigned by being presidential, in the White House. There were a few scheduled trips out of Washington, but they were widely spaced and wouldn't begin until October. There was no arguing with success. A schedule of White House appointments with leaders of Congress, governors, labor leaders, business leaders, highly visible celebrities and any suddenly newsworthy individual, was every bit as effective in putting the President in the public's eye and mind as running around on the rubber chicken circuit courting local pols. Jennifer's trips were proving quite popular and further kept the pressure off Jack to travel. Everything was running smoothly.

The President allowed Ed Covington to manage the campaign and any potential headaches which could arise from the medical situation. The less the President knew the better. Jack found it difficult to believe that Sidney's death was a simple mugging gone bad. But, on the other hand, there was no record of any kind implicating Ed in that sad affair. He wondered if Ed considered the number of people in-the-know too great for security purposes and had decided to "thin the herd." That was pure speculation on his part and he had no intention of confronting Ed head-on over that suspicion. He could see how deep he was getting into the cover-up by his failure to pursue even a suspicion of wrongdoing.

Steve Berk and Jennifer were the remaining witnesses and he wouldn't be surprised to learn of Berk's death any day now. He knew little about Berk's role in the cover-up other than that Berk had been present during the hospital excursion. Jennifer was another story. Covington knew how close they were, and he would never consider her a candidate for "cleansing." If he did, what recourse would Jack have? Perhaps he was being naive. His hand was not as strong as he thought. Jennifer was at risk, even though she knew little. There was no way he could contain that danger. The lesson he'd taken from Watergate was to limit direct involvement and limit the number of witnesses. The President stays outside, completely. If possible.

Jennifer had been somewhat remote since he'd developed the heart problem. She was visibly concerned, but they'd had very little contact. For both, this was a major change in their relationship. For him, there were no alternatives, but for her, there were plenty of options. They needed to talk. He wasn't sure to what end, but he owed it to her to discuss his concerns. He wanted to create a satisfying solution to their intimacy problem and this would have to begin with a conversation.

CHAPTER THIRTY-ONE

Darryl Edmunds could not be reached by phone in Atlanta. When Al called, the condo manager said his car was in its usual spot but there was no answer at his apartment.

Al was becoming suspicious that all was not well with Darryl. His suggestion that someone look in the apartment was not well-received.

Leslie made the next call an hour later and met with a very different response. The security person was very charming and eager to have conversation. Leslie hung up immediately and turned to Al.

"Something's wrong. I'm betting they found something in that apartment and cops are on site."

"Why do you say that?"

"Well, sometimes you get the impression that the person you're talking to is stretching out the conversation in order for the police to trace the call. That's my reporter's instinct. Something is not right with Darryl Edmunds."

"Now what?" was all Al could offer.

"Best I can suggest is that we drive to a remote pay phone and try again. Let them trace it to this city, it won't lead to us."

"Okay, Les, let's go. I'm growing uneasy about this piece of the puzzle."

They parked downtown and walked to a rare pay phone in a large department store. The not unexpected Indian summer heat was oppressive, and the store's air-conditioning was welcome. The call was answered promptly, and the same genial voice came on.

Leslie cut right to the chase. "Sweetheart, let me talk to the nearest police officer to save us time. Tracing this call won't be worth the effort and I need to know what was found in the apartment."

A short pause then a male voice came on. "Please identify yourself, ma'am. This is Sheriff Edgar Rooney of the Atlanta Police Department."

"Sheriff, I can't do that, but I can be of help to you if you tell me what's going on."

"Look, whoever you are, I need some ID before I release any info."

"Don't be pigheaded. I can read about it in the paper tomorrow and never say a word to you." She paused. "Just tell me what you found."

"A dead man with his throat cut. Now if you know anything that has any bearing on this murder, you better clue me in."

"Sheriff, if the man is Darryl Edmunds, his death may relate to a complex situation in Washington D.C. He recently worked in D.C. I can't say anymore at this time, but I will pass on other relevant information as I uncover it. Was it Edmunds?"

"Yes. It's him. And it looks like a professional job. I sure wish you'd identify yourself, so we could talk a bit more openly."

"I'd like nothing better, Sheriff, but at this point, I need to weigh what little evidence I have before going public. I'll be in touch." She hung up. "Let's get out of here before the D.C. police surround the damn store."

The drive back was somber. Both were deep in thought. Another piece of the puzzle identified, but whom did it point to?

Leslie spoke as she drove. "Well, that settles the cath lab issue. Something big and secret did take place in that laboratory, just as the x-ray timer indicated. And it had to be very big for a murder cover-up. Three murders. Jeff Oldham, Sidney Curtis and now Darryl Edmunds. There certainly has to be a connection. I keep coming back to Steve Berk and his high level of interest in the story I said I was looking into. I know we're on to something big and dangerous. I like it, but I don't."

Al was a bit less sanguine. "We're assuming Jeff's death was murder. We don't have a shred of corroborating evidence. With Edmunds gone, our potential witness list is down to the nurse who won't talk to anyone. It's certainly not enough for us to take to the police."

"Who's talking police? We solve the mystery and I have a killer of a story. This is a bombshell of enormous proportion. Whatever it is."

Al was a bit taken aback by Leslie's cold analysis of what was at stake. "Okay, okay. I agree for now. Let's think about the next angle to pursue. I've been thinking that both of those cath lab personnel had to receive payment for their work. If we could get some lead on where the payment came from, we'd have something to go after. Now, how do we get to see their bank records and deposits for the past few weeks?"

"That might be a good lead, Al, unless the cover-up people are clever enough to cover their tracks with cash payments. That's my fear, but it's worth a try. Maybe Edmund's bank in Atlanta could help us if we convince them we're trying to settle his estate. Let me work this angle."

Al was quick to see an opening, "And while you're at it, it sure would be interesting to know who Nurse Carter has been calling the past few weeks. If she's frightened by our inquiry, I wouldn't be surprised if she called her payoff man with the news that someone was sniffing around.

A tap on her phone and a call again to get her agitated might pry something loose. I also think she may be in great danger of following in Darryl's footsteps. If she would talk to us she could be warned."

"Not bad thinking, Doc. I think I know someone who can do the phone trick. I also think we should try to contact her again to warn her of the danger she might be facing."

CHAPTER THIRTY-TWO

L eslie was early at Berk's apartment. He wasn't there yet, so she let herself in with the key she'd never returned. Her plan was simple.

First get him to agree to do the tap and then clarify, once again, the termination of their not- so-romantic relationship. He'd be willing to drop the intimacy in exchange for the information she would have to surrender to get him interested in doing the telephone tap.

There was no telling how long she'd have to wait, so she decided to put the time to good use. There were still a few items of hers in the apartment that should be removed. There was the usual stuff a part-time girlfriend might leave behind in anticipation of a return visit. The closet in the bedroom still contained a few pieces of her clothing. She laid these out on the bed and found a light, zippered travel bag in the closet to carry the stuff home. But the bag was not empty. When she opened it, a DVD fell to the floor.

Curiosity got the best of her and she examined it. It bore a very recent date but was otherwise unlabelled. Still mildly curious, she put it in the disc player. A recording came on and it clearly was not a commercial recording. A woman was seated on a bed facing a man in his undershorts.

As the tape continued it became clear that this was some kind of homemade recording, and not a very good one at that. The camera angle never changed, and the sex was fairly pedestrian stuff. She watched it with passing interest until the woman turned slightly and could be seen in profile. Leslie's attention suddenly was riveted on the screen. Washington's most recognizable woman was seen on camera putting her brassiere back on as if she was dressing in her own bedroom.

Leslie was stunned. Jennifer Henderson on video disc with an unidentified lover. She checked the date on the tape and saw that it was dated only 6 days ago. What was going on? Why did Steve have this tape? Who was the "director" of this production?

Leslie put the disc into its case and started to return it to the travel bag, but on impulse, put it in her pocketbook instead and returned the travel bag to the closet. She put her clothing into two reusable grocery bags and then sat down and tried to put the tape into some perspective. It was obviously a "spy" tape. Berk had to be the spy. That was his game. What was Jennifer Henderson doing in a strange room, screwing around with some unidentified guy? Everyone in Washington knew the Hendersons as a loving couple. They were very big in popular magazines and were even seen together, occasionally, on late night TV interview shows. This made no sense.

But what the hell was going on? How did Steve Berk figure in this? Sidney Curtis shot to death on a Washington Street. A cath lab tech found murdered in Atlanta. That mysterious unexplained cath lab adventure. Berk's interest in her story. What about the death of Jeff Oldham, Al's friend? Something very dark was going on. She could feel it but couldn't see it. What was the link between these bizarre events? Jennifer Henderson, Sidney Curtis, and something cardiac?

Of course, it had to be a Washington big-wig. The concealed illness. Of course, the President. That's it. Jack Henderson himself. He's the link here. He ties it all together, and Berk is the secret operator who does the dirty work, such as spying and recording. No wonder he was so interested in Leslie's story. It all made sense now. Her heart was pounding with excitement. The moment of discovery. Of clarity. It was exhilarating and scary now that the implication began to emerge. And she had gone to Berk looking for help in unraveling the matter. Ouch. Now here she was in his apartment expecting to exchange information for a telephone tap. What a misread.

The stairs creaked, and she knew it was too late to get out. She'd have to play it cool and figure a way out without giving any hint about what she knew.

Berk unlocked the door and smiled when he saw her sitting on the sofa. "Let yourself in, I see. Old key came in handy? Been here long?"

"No, just a few minutes before you. I wanted to pick up the clothes I left here during our previous life."

Walking toward the bedroom, Steve smiled at her again. "Oh well, did you find what you needed?"

"No problem. I put my clothes in a few bags I found in the closet and that's it."

"Were those the bags in my closet?"

"Yes, but they didn't seem to be anything you'd treasure, unless they were destined for the flea market hall of fame. Somehow I doubt that."

Leslie wanted to keep the mood light, but Steve's reference to his closet had an ominous tone.

From inside the bedroom, Steve continued the conversation, but Leslie could sense he was talking and thinking at the same time. His words were coming out a bit slower and she could tell he was distracted while trying to sound quite natural. Unease began to set in.

Berk returned, still smiling. "Like a drink?"

"Sure, how about a beer? Something cold."

"Coming up. I'll get a mug out of the freezer."

"Steve, I can't stay long, so let's get down to business."

"OK, let's. What were you doing in the closet? Don't bullshit me, 'cause I'm not in the mood. You rummaged in the closet and tripped a number of my signals. Spill it out."

His smile had vanished and been replaced by a cold, blank expression. Leslie could sense danger. He was no simple investigator. He was known to be very dangerous when he sensed a threat. Leslie tried to imagine an avenue to safety. Flight was very much on her mind.

"Steve, I just wanted to be sure I got everything. You know I used to use that closet. It was all very innocent."

"That's fine, then you won't mind if I look in the bags and your handbag."

She now realized that taking the disc had been impulsive and unwise. Berk would know it was gone and that would imperil her. She didn't need the actual disc, only the information she had gleaned from it.

"Of course not, Steve, the bags are next to the chair over there." She pointed to the bags of clothing next to the stuffed chair near the bedroom. But her eyes were on the door to the apartment. She was gauging the distance and whether or not she could make a dash through the door before Berk could catch her and find the disc in her pocketbook.

As soon as he reached into the first bag, Leslie was at the door and out through it before Steve could grab her.

Racing down the single flight of stairs to the street, she knew it was going to be close. As she passed through the doorway and into the safety of the street, he caught her and grabbed her purse. As he yanked it, Leslie was spun around and the strap broke. She continued racing into the daylight and realized that Berk had given up the chase once she was in the street. She looked back and saw him take the disc from her purse. He glared at her and the look was menacing.

She continued down the street to her car, checking frequently to be sure he wasn't in pursuit.

Luckily, the spare key hidden under her car bumper was still there. Just minutes later she pulled into a public parking lot to gather her thoughts and catch her breath.

She'd never been so frightened.

She knew a lot now, and he knew she knew something he didn't want her to know. That really scared her. It was sufficiently important to bring a sense of terror to Leslie. She needed Al and needed him for more than just consoling.

She had a lot of news to share but she really wanted protection. Her dress was soaked with perspiration and even some urine she had lost involuntarily. She couldn't stop shaking, but she drove away in spite of her legs feeling heavy as lead and her heart racing wildly.

Ten minutes later some semblance of bodily control was restored. She no longer had her cellphone, but she had an old phone at home that she could reactivate.

CHAPTER THIRTY-THREE

Leslie called Al from home. Her adrenaline surge was leveling out and she felt the fatigue commonly experienced by people who just missed having a major trauma. They agreed to meet at a park in Alexandria, across the river from Washington.

The cloudless sky and warm temperature filled the park with joggers, bikers and power walkers. Everything seemed right except that Leslie felt an uncontrollable urge to cry. She was still trembling when Al arrived. He could feel the tension in her as she spoke. They huddled together, and Leslie had a purging cry. It seemed to bring her back to some semblance of normal.

The disc plus Al's information about the clandestine catheter lab episode put everything into place. The President was the missing piece they'd been after. They had no proof of anything, though, only a damn interesting story.

Al wanted to settle Leslie down some more before diving back into the case. "Let's walk a bit, Leslie." He offered his hand and she quickly accepted the offer.

"I'm scared, Al. Berk is dangerous, and I think he'll come after me."

"I can't believe he's the whole operation though, Leslie. Don't you agree?"

"I don't know. They'd want to keep this whole thing very small."

Al could see her gaining control of herself. She was now beginning to immerse herself in the story once again.

"I'm trying to conceive of any way to see this get resolved, even a hard-to-imagine solution. Al, what do you think Jennifer's role is in this crazy escapade?"

"Well, Berk has a crime to keep covered up, namely an airplane he probably sabotaged. The President has a secret illness and a job to keep. The only one who seems to be a wild card is Jennifer Henderson. She surely knows about her husband's illness and the plan to keep a lid on that until after the election. She even seems to be acting out. I can't see her involved in the killings. She's in danger even if she knows only a part of the truth. They, whoever they are, probably see her as the same wild card we do. Maybe she'll play ball to stay alive."

Leslie asked, "What about the recording? Won't Berk use it to keep her in line? And who knows if there aren't other incidents that are on disc. This mess is like a Hydra, Al. You think you're getting a handle on some part of it and suddenly it sprouts more complicated pieces."

"I agree, Les, but Jennifer Henderson may want shelter from the coming storm. Maybe she'll take some risks. The disc or discs and the eventual scandal would kill the President's reelection bid, so they may be as unusable as nuclear weapons. Powerful stuff in theory to control her but too powerful to be a tactical weapon at this stage in the reelection campaign or even later."

"If we got her attention, Al, she might offer us some useful insider information and help establish her as only a minor player in the affair. We just don't know what part she plays. One thing is certain, once the story is out, we're safe. Until then, we're a giant threat."

CHAPTER THIRTY-FOUR

Peggy Carter's small two-room bungalow sat in a decaying neighborhood and did its part to maintain the run- down appearance of the area. She was hoping to sell it, combine the money with her new-found nest egg to buy a condo in Florida to start all over again.

She carried her groceries into the house and set them on the kitchen counter. She never knew what hit her. Before she could unload the groceries, a blow to her left temple shattered her skull and ended her life. The groceries scattered all over the kitchen floor. Her scant jewelry was pocketed along with anything else of value that could easily be carried away. The intruder wanted to give the scene the appearance of a robbery that had been interrupted by the occupant, which necessitated a blow to her head. Maybe murder was not the intent and the blow harder than planned. Maybe the robber was inexperienced. The police would be a long time figuring this one out, if they even cared to spend the time on a routine burglary and homicide in a neighborhood not unaccustomed to violence. The killer had done his job and was long gone when a neighbor came over in response to the incessant barking of Peg Carter's dog.

Leslie and Al noted the story in the *Post* and had no doubt that robbery was not the motive. The murder only further confirmed what they knew all too well. The witness list was getting shorter, and in fact, only Steve Berk and the Hendersons remained on it, unless you added Leslie Nugent's and Al Seibolt's names.

Ed Covington was not yet aware of the last two names. Steve Berk was only too aware that a second force connected to the White House cover-up was operative out there and that he was on its list. He was determined to stay alive and his loyalty to the White House was secondary. Sidney's death and the attempt on his own life were pretty clear evidence that Berk was no longer the preferred operative for maintaining security for this operation. In fact, he was on the prospective victim list. The appearance of the man he'd killed in his apartment now made a lot of sense.

What role to assign to his reporter friend was less clear. He didn't know how much she knew, but that last episode with the disc convinced him that she now knew he was mixed up in something involving the First Lady and that his interest in her story was not just a ploy to bed her down.

He had to assume that she had viewed the recording. It was also reasonable to assume that she would try to fit the Jennifer Henderson escapade into the story she had tried to bounce off him. Knowing Leslie, he didn't doubt that her imagination would make the connections needed to solve her riddle. He didn't see her connecting him to the killings, but the killers would be interested in her once they learned how much she knew or suspected. Maybe that could be traded for some time to figure his way out of this. Now who would be interested in that information? It frustrated him that some other force was at work and he couldn't identify it.

For the first time in his life he was the quarry and the hunter was very good at concealing his/her identity.

Berk wondered how the hunter out there knew the role of Peggy Carter. The only people who could have known, beside himself, were

Sidney, the doctor, maybe the President, and the lab tech. He discounted the President as being preoccupied during the procedure, and the doctor who was in their company up until his fatal flight. That left the lab tech and Sidney. To get the information from the lab tech, one would have to know his identity and involvement. That led to circular reasoning. That left Sidney as the source of information, but to whom did he give that information?

Some other force was out there that he was unable to identify. He was sure now that it had eliminated Sidney Curtis and Peggy Carter and must have had some contact with Sidney to get information out of him regarding the cast of characters in the cath lab episode. It was now trying to eliminate Steve Berk. No doubt about it. This force didn't like any witnesses left alive.

CHAPTER THIRTY-FIVE

"**M**rs. Henderson is unable to take personal calls at this time but I will be pleased to give her a message on your behalf."

The First Lady's expected first line of defense was in operation. Leslie had expected this response, but she only wanted to get a message through to Jennifer Henderson.

"That's fine, just give her this message with my phone number. Tell her that her very recent evening activities outside the White House have not gone unnoticed."

"Is that the entire message?"

"Yes. Give her this cellphone number and ask her to call at noon today. I'll be awaiting the call."

Now it was just a matter of time.

Al and Leslie continued to brainstorm the possibilities. Al's motel room was the only place they considered safe and only Al had been going out for food. Leslie was tense and fearful that Steve Berk would have her usual haunts staked out. Considering her state of nerves, she and Al hadn't even made an effort to lighten things up by sharing any intimacy.

Her cellphone rang promptly at noon and Jennifer Henderson was on the line.

"Hello, this is Jennifer Henderson. With whom am I speaking?"

"I'm Leslie Nugent, Mrs. Henderson, a reporter with the *Daily Sentinel*. We've never met. I have some information that I'd like to discuss with you in private. It's very personal, so I think it should be off the record and very confidential, for your sake, not mine."

"I'm not sure what you're talking about, but I would like to hear more. The telephone may not be the best means of communication if the matter is that personal. Could we meet somewhere?"

Leslie paused. Sure, the First Lady was interested.

The bait hadn't been all that obscure in its meaning.

Leslie had expected a positive response and was ready with a meeting place. "How about my attorney's office on 17th near Avenue G. Peter Gallant. He's away for the week and his office should offer privacy as well as being convenient.

Your security people could check it out and assure themselves of its safety and privacy. It's the office of Schiff and Gallant."

Jennifer Henderson sounded cool but quite willing to have the meeting. "It sounds fine, but I'll have to call you back before I can commit."

Twenty minutes later, the call came from the First Lady's secretary with an affirmative for 3 PM. The two of them would meet alone.

The early fall Washington heat wave continued. Every air conditioner in the District ran on high. On the positive side, traffic was light. As Al drove, they discussed strategies for the encounter. Henderson was bound to be very cautious.

"She probably had her staff investigate you thoroughly, Leslie, so she knows who you are. She may even know that you know Steve Berk. If she does, that could be dicey. Best approach will be to show a strong lead card right away and get her attention. She may just leak some important information that offers us a few outs. Remember, our objective is to see if she can help us work through this maze, get the story out and get us out and in the clear so we can get on with our lives."

"Al, I'm less committed to the story now and more interested in just resuming my normal life and letting our relationship take its course. This mess has gotten way out of control. It's far more than I bargained for."

"I'm glad to hear that, Leslie. The story was beginning to crowd me out of your life. Let's keep working with the leads we uncover, but also maintain some much- needed perspective."

They embraced and clung tightly to each other, indicating their mutual agreement on this score.

The area around 17th and Avenue G was a mixture of boutique hotels, foreign restaurants, small clothing shops and office buildings. The building they entered was one of many four- or five-story office buildings built before World War II along this stretch of Avenue G. It was in a fair state of repair and shared a similar lack of distinction with the rest of the neighborhood.

The waiting room for the law offices of Schiff and Gallant had only a few occupants. Leslie had warned the staff that she'd be using Peter Gallant's office and that the person meeting her was the First Lady. She told them to expect security people. They'd been stunned by the news and their cooperation was extraordinary.

Jennifer had arrived early and was waiting in the office when Leslie came in. Leslie was impressed with the older woman's poise and composure. She had to be suspicious but gave no indication of unease. The two women sat on facing love seats separated by a low mahogany coffee table with an empty pottery bowl in the middle.

Leslie spoke first. "I'm glad you were able to make this meeting on such short notice. I assure you my information is important and well worth your time. And please, call me Leslie."

"Leslie, I was able to read through your cryptic message, so I guess it is important. I'm curious to know your role in this."

"It isn't easy for me to be precise, because I don't know some important pieces of the story I've been assembling. Let me start at the end and work back to the beginning, which is where you could be most helpful."

"I'm a good listener. Give it a try."

"Okay, let me start by telling you that I've seen a video of you having sex with a man other than your husband. The disc was dated a week ago. I also want you to know that the disc is not in my possession, so don't think this is some form of blackmail. All I'm after is information. Someone else is interested in making such a recording and holding onto it. The reason why is unknown to me, although it isn't hard to make a logical guess. More important is where this all fits in with that story I alluded to. I think it does fit and that's why I asked to meet with you." She paused and could see the concern on Jennifer's face.

Her expression was deadly serious.

"I don't know what story you're assembling, so maybe when I know a bit more I can comment on the video you've seen and where it fits in."

"Fair enough. Here's what I know. A number of people are dead, and their deaths seem to all tie back to your husband. A cardiologist from North Carolina and two technicians from a cardiac catheterization laboratory in town are dead. What they all have in common is the possible connection to a Washington VIP with a cardiac condition who's trying to conceal that information from public scrutiny. I have reason to believe your husband is that VIP and that a cover-up of that illness is the reason for those deaths. I don't know if your husband has any direct connection with the killings and I'm willing to give him the benefit of a doubt. How your extra-marital sexual activity figures in this is unclear and is really none of my personal business. It may be entirely unrelated, but as a reporter developing a big story, I can't feign a lack of interest. I think it's being used by someone or will be used somehow to keep the bigger secret safe. In addition, the White House Chief of Staff has been murdered. That may figure in as well. Am I warm? I'm sure there's a lot I don't know but that's it for starters. Now, you tell me, what's going on?"

Jennifer Henderson stared down at the worn oriental carpet and began to shake her head from side to side. Her composure wasn't shattered, but she was clearly shaken. The room was very quiet. Wheels were turning furiously in the heads of the two women as they each pondered their next move. Jennifer didn't know who else knew about her meetings with Howard Westlake, but she now knew that others outside of White House security did. This reporter as much as told her so. That disc was the work of someone very well- informed. It had to involve White House security, so she could be sure someone close to her husband was involved. The question wasn't how much to confess about her sex life, but rather how it tied into this more sinister cover-up that she hadn't even been aware of. Sure, she knew Sidney and her husband had been keeping a lid on his illness until after the election, but that was their doing.

Now she knew for the first time that the doctor who examined her husband had been conveniently eliminated. It was apparent that she was very close to a dangerous scheme, and she had best begin putting some distance between herself and the likely suspicions that would arise if the plot was uncovered. Her own self-interest was uppermost in her mind. She decided that the less revealed the better. This young reporter was certainly not going to be her confidant.

"Look, I'm not going to deny what you've seen on that disc but that's my own business. I'm more concerned that you see some connection between my private life and a very serious accusation. I'm willing to work with you but only if you agree to keep this thing quiet until I can convince you that my involvement is inconsequential and at most, passive. I can't promise you answers to questions about actions I have no knowledge of, but I might be willing to help you unravel the mystery to assure you of my non- involvement."

Leslie was surprised at the seeming sincerity of the response. It was a carefully crafted response created on very short notice. She believed what she was hearing but warning voices told her that there were other players out there who would go to any extreme to prevent just what she was agreeing to do. At this point she didn't want to compromise the gentle confessor role she'd offered Jennifer, so she decided to call it a day and regroup with Al to plot the next move. It appeared that Jennifer Henderson might cooperate and that was a big step. From the reporter's perspective, an inside informant of her stature was huge.

Leslie knew this meeting was about over. "Okay, let's both agree to keep a lid on this until we can substantiate it with reasonable certainty. I know you're well aware of the rules of reporting from your earlier days on network, so I trust you know just what I mean. I'll respect your privacy but only as long as you stay on the level with me. Mrs. Henderson, something criminal is going on and the President is involved at some level. I just can't determine what his role is. Or what your role may be. I was hoping you could offer something on that score. It looks like you want to take some time before offering any information that might be of value in sorting this out. I understand your cautious approach."

"Leslie, I think you understand the difficult position I'm in. I'm obviously more concerned about the potential scandal than you are, so you'll have to give me some breathing room to figure things out for myself." Jennifer rose and walked to the door. Leslie followed her out into the hall where two Secret Service men were waiting. The two women parted with a smile and a handshake.

CHAPTER THIRTY-SIX

The Congress Motel was an off-the-beaten path, sixteen- unit motel near Bethesda. Al had decided to change location and began using cash instead of credit cards in case they were being followed. The room was like a thousand others.

The stale odor of cigarette smoke was unmistakable. The single large window overlooking the parking lot was light-tight with a drawstring drape. It would do for a very temporary base.

When Leslie recounted the meeting to Al the two of them were stunned by Jennifer Henderson's failure to deny any part of the story Leslie had disclosed to her. She hadn't confirmed anything, but she had given the story an element of credence.

"That's the encouragement we needed, Al, but it's not confirmation of the actual deeds and who did what. She may not know. We have to consider that possibility."

Leslie was her old self again and not preoccupied with Steve Berk.

"Look, Leslie, this is big and probably well beyond our amateur sleuthing skills, all due respect to your reporting know-how. You've already put your life at risk with Steve Berk. Too much is at stake for us to think we can follow this through to closure. I think we have enough now to get some professionals involved."

"Like who? With what? We don't have one piece of hard evidence against anyone and the story is too incredible to buy on our word alone. We need more time and we need Jennifer Henderson on our side."

"Great. The First Lady is going to give us her husband and a mess of high-up conspirators. That doesn't seem likely. I think we know what happened. Jeff Oldham was a pawn in a deadly cover-up. He was just unlucky. Maybe my interest is satisfied now. Remember, I came here to find out what really happened to Jeff. I don't need prosecutorial proof. The rest is up to history, reporters, and parties with far larger stakes than I have in seeing the cover-up exposed."

"Al, this is a huge story for me and it's also what brought us together. Stay with me a while longer and try to see it through. Give it a few days more. We haven't had time to discuss it, but I think we both feel that there could be a future for us. I finally feel my life coming together and I like the feeling."

Al was moved by Leslie's plea. He believed, much as she did, that they each had felt the beginning of a real relationship.

"I guess I'd have a hard time leaving you in the lurch with all that's going on around us. But let's keep the risk to a minimum. Now let's take a break and release some of this tension."

"I thought you'd never ask, Doctor Seibolt."

CHAPTER THIRTY-SEVEN

The sunset was turning the distant desert sand red.

Downtown Tucson was bathed in the same stunning fiery light. In his shirtsleeves and blue cashmere V-neck vest, Covington was every bit the relaxed billionaire in a setting of casual elegance. The coded report on his desk told him that the activity in D.C. was still undercover but that Steve Berk had managed to survive the attempted assassination. Since a little before the failed hit, Berk had been under surveillance by Covington's D.C. operatives. Subsequently, something had happened at Berk's apartment which involved an unidentified woman. Berk had seemingly recovered something from the woman that could have been a video disc. Obviously, she could figure in the plot in some way. Covington didn't like the prospect of some mystery woman popping up in the story. He was determined to put a wrap on it before the weekend, before any more twists and turns could further complicate the matter. Decisive moves were his stock-in- trade and this episode was crying out for closure. The lid needed tightening.

True to his business instincts and goals, Covington had no intention of losing his most valuable business connection, namely the President of the United States.

Their close ties were the most mutually beneficial arrangement an industrialist of his dimension could possibly develop and sustain. He estimated that his White House connection was worth at least five to eight billion a year in defense contracts that might otherwise have gone to his competitors. He had carefully cultivated his relationship with Jack Henderson and it had literally "paid off."

The President would continue to be kept out of the loop. Jack would understand the value of unquestioned distance from the steps necessary to assure his reelection. The President must be free to comment from a position of near ignorance on this matter.

Berk was to be eliminated without any hitch the next time. That would leave Jennifer and the two security people at the hospital where Jack's procedure had been carried out. For the time being, the security men could be left untouched. Their knowledge was very limited, and they could be taken out at a later date if any possibility of a connection was raised. He considered them well-paid thugs who understood the need for silence and the certain retribution that would follow any deviation from that understanding. The deaths of the two lab workers would assure the silence of the security men when that information came to light. Jennifer was the puzzle. Berk's video disc might be sufficient threat to keep her quiet. Any video disc would have to be secured as part of the Berk elimination plan.

The mystery woman was of no consequence once the disc was safely in his hands. On the other hand, why had she tried to make off with it? This question would not go away. He made a mental note to reflect further on this dimly connected piece of the plot.

The election was less than a month away and there could be no complications. Jack's reelection seemed assured.

What happened after that was of less consequence. The Vice-President would be easily convinced to continue in Jack's footsteps. After all, Ed and Jack had chosen him with Sidney's concurrence. A quiet pre-election interim was the objective and he would now assure that with a brief phone call.

CHAPTER THIRTY-EIGHT

Steve Berk's precautions in his office were aimed at deterring any intruder and protecting his back at all times. He still had no idea where the threat was coming from. That scrape with the hit man had been disconcerting. It had the feel of a mob hit and that could mean almost anything.

Despite his unease, he drifted into a deep sleep.

His well-locked and fortified office would have received very high marks from any security company. It allowed him to sleep in relative security. However, the well-locked and sealed door didn't prevent the small transparent plastic tubing from sliding underneath the door into the office. The gas it carried was odorless but highly lethal. The CIA had developed the deadly gas for just such an application. It was based on a German pharmaceutical company's formula that had been tested sparingly but successfully in the death camps in the final days of World War II. Given a longer war it would have become the predominant mode of execution for Jews, Gypsies, and others caught in the Nazi net of destruction. It was the most lethal formula yet developed by that very inventive industry.

The tubing had to be very narrow gauge to slide through the very limited space under the door. As a consequence, it took over an hour for sufficient gas to spread through the rooms and assure the sleeping death of Steve Berk. During his sleep, he gradually slid into a drug-induced coma. The drug was a powerful anesthetic. The next phase ushered in cardiac rhythm irregularity and eventually fatal ventricular fibrillation. Once the coma was established, it was all but over.

The building had been under surveillance to determine the pattern of Berk's comings and goings. They knew he slept there frequently, so it was just a matter of time before he was inside, and they were ordered to move.

The front door was hinged from inside to prevent its removal from the outside. The coded door locks were too troublesome to deal with. All this had been known to the team that now proceeded to cut through the door with a high- speed but quiet sabre saw to create a small space for a man to crawl through and enter the room. Some noise from the saw was unavoidable, but this was a mixed-use building with Berk the only tenant who chose to live in his office from time-to-time.

The man who crawled in through the hole in the door was masked and breathing oxygen from a small tank and gear not unlike that used by scuba divers. Once inside, he removed the door from its hinges. Two men in gas masks entered the office. They quickly replaced the door with a very reasonable look-alike, allowing very little gas to escape.

At this hour of the night, there would be no tenants on site. The gas would largely dissipate in an hour or two, but to assure its safe elimination they opened a window and fresh air began to replace the toxic atmosphere.

Berk was dead. He had slept right into the hereafter.

The men quickly searched the office and the adjoining bedroom. The disc was not difficult to find. The safe in the floor under the carpet was no challenge to these professionals. Orders were to disturb nothing else and so they left. The original door locks were carefully transplanted into the new door as were the original hinges. The team assigned to the door was quite adept. Berk would eventually be found, and his cause of death would be undetermined. There would be no way to detect the gas. The break-in would not be detected. They took the original door away with them.

CHAPTER THIRTY-NINE

It was only a few minutes before midnight when the call came to Covington. Berk was dead. The disc had been found and was secured. It would be in his hands by noon.

He hung up.

Now he wasn't sure he wanted to be with his "date" in the other room. An adrenaline surge had his mind spinning through a series of steps to take next based on this report. Nevertheless, he turned his attention to the woman waiting for him. She was a senior sales executive with a potential supplier of helicopter motor parts that he bought by the thousands. She had come down from the home office in Denver rather than trust this major contract to the regional salesman. She was eager for the contract and ready to work for it.

He walked into the living room and could feel himself begin to respond to the sales pitch coming at him from across the room. She was unbuttoning her light brown silk blouse and he could see that she was going to make an effective opening argument for the contract. He guessed her age at mid-forties. He wondered if she was married. There was no ring but what difference would it make if she were.

Many of the women whom he enjoyed up here were married and in some ways that was how he preferred it. No entanglement sought and none offered. In addition, he liked the idea that their husbands would be subject to a tough comparison. That appealed to his competitive nature. Back to those very generous breasts peeking out from behind the blouse. He'd hold out for a much stronger bid, although as he approached the bidder, he had to admit this was a strong opener. Berk and the disc were now very remote in his mind.

The rep from Denver was high on the three cocktails she'd downed earlier. She seemed eager to get down to business. This was the kind of selling she liked to do. A win-win for both parties. Two hours later, she was fast asleep in his large bed. The contract was hers. She would also come away with some daring moves to try out on her husband back in Denver.

CHAPTER FORTY

Reading the newspapers in a local diner, Leslie and Al were stunned to learn of Steve Berk's death. The obituary was brief, with no details to suggest any dark and dangerous business he'd been involved in. The story recounted his military exploits and the successful private investigator business that he ran by himself. In short, nothing new and nothing to shed any light on their quest.

Leslie was feeling her normal self and Al drank her in.

Dressed very casually in jeans and a fine print shirt with her hair pulled back and loosely tied with a rubber band, she was not unaware of her effect on Al. He was having a similar effect on her. This randy feeling going between them seemed out of place in the context of the serious and even dangerous matter they were involved in. Yet, it was a fact and needed to be reckoned with.

Although Berk's death was a shock to Leslie, it was no surprise to her. She knew that he often played with fire. Getting burned was always a risk in his line of work. She felt safer with Berk gone but a bit uneasy due to not knowing how his death had come about. They couldn't accept the police theory of sheer coincidence. Would this put some new and unknown assailant on their trail? The police had received an anonymous call about suspicious activity in Berk's building, had found a locked door leading to his office apartment. They broke in and found him dead in bed.

The coroner had found very mild coronary artery disease and could draw no conclusions about cause of death. The cause was stated as a cardiac arrhythmia although there was no way to prove it or refute it.

There was no mention of a burglary. The locked door implied no forced entry and there was no sign of a struggle, no sign the place was ransacked. The police knew about Berk's line of work but had no basis to assume there was some clandestine plot that lay beyond their reach.

Leslie and Al felt that they had now hit a stone wall.

There were no hints about what direction to follow. Leslie was puzzled, but her wheels were still turning.

She asked the obvious, "With Curtis and Berk gone, where is direction coming from for this cover-up? At first, we assumed it was Curtis running the show. Then we assumed Berk took over. Maybe we were wrong all along. Direction is coming from somewhere and it doesn't seem likely that it's coming from the couple in the White House. Who's left? Someone ordered all those hits and hasn't left a trail. It's got to be someone with a serious stake in the cover-up. I haven't the foggiest idea."

There was no call back from Jennifer Henderson.

CHAPTER FORTY-ONE

The bar in the Wembly Hotel was busy even at the late hour but it still had an aura of discreet privacy. People spoke in hushed tones, consistent with the tenor of the barroom.

Wearing a dark grey slack suit and clear glasses, Jennifer Henderson had found her way unrecognized to a table on the outer edge of the large dimly lit room. She ordered a very dry martini. Her manner sent out vibes to any curious male that she had an appointment and wouldn't welcome company. Minutes later, Howard Westlake sat down opposite her and briefly gave her hand a squeeze. The waitress appeared as if on cue and took his order for a gin and tonic.

"You sounded different on the phone, Jenn. Is something wrong?"

Jennifer had decided not to get Howard involved any deeper in the matter troubling her. That was for both their sakes. "Yes and no, Howard. Obviously, my being here now and our recent time together are potentially explosive. I know we've been careful, but now I know we've not been careful enough. Several people know what's transpired between us, and that's highly flammable. I wanted to see you in person and tell you we have to stay apart for the time being. Believe me, it's for the best. You'll have to trust my judgment."

"I do, Jenn, and I will. It won't be easy but if it's important, I'll accept it."

"Howard, I think I know how you feel about me. You've been very thoughtful and haven't pried into my personal life. For that alone, I'm deeply grateful. I can't explain my situation to you in any detail, so I think the best thing for you is to resume your life as if we'd never met in Houston."

"It's your call, Jenn, but I have to tell you this is hard to swallow. I didn't have any illusion about our relationship being long-term, but I probably kidded myself into imagining some kind of more satisfying resolution. It's hard not to want more of an explanation, but I'll be a good soldier and let you give the orders. I know your situation is terribly complex, so I guess I'll have to give you the benefit of a doubt. I think I love you, so letting go like this is damn painful. I'll do what you ask, but don't expect me to walk away as if this never happened."

"Howard, I wish I could be more revealing about my circumstances, but that just isn't possible. Just know that I'm not walking away any happier than you are. I don't know what the future holds for us. Let's leave it at that."

"Alright, Jenn, let's finish our drinks and then we can dissolve into the shadows."

He squeezed her hand again and she squeezed his in return. He smiled, and she gave him a serious look that said she was not about to drop him out of her life completely.

CHAPTER FORTY-TWO

The White House announced a last-minute campaign trip to Arizona for the First Lady two days after Steve Berk's death. Arizona didn't seem to be a state in jeopardy for the election, but the First lady was going to meet with several large campaign donors, the ostensible reason for the trip. Arizona was fertile ground for fund-raising, considering its large number of affluent retirees from the North. Jennifer was always popular with the gray-haired set, particularly with the women. With the men, her appeal was obvious.

Jennifer had visited Ed Covington's luxurious penthouse several times before with Jack. She knew that Ed was the single largest supporter of Jack's campaigns, past and present. The reason for this requested visit to Arizona was, however, not specified in his call to the White House. Nevertheless, the trip was scheduled as he requested and that made it abundantly clear how influential Covington was. No one else could command such a visit.

In her single days, Jennifer and Ed had dated briefly before her attention had turned to Jack. Although they had never advanced to intimacy, she knew he was attracted to her and he had said as much on several occasions. During their social interactions since her marriage, Ed had been discrete, but his eyes were frequently on her and gave an unmistakable signal.

Why Ed had never married was unclear. There was no question about his sexual preference for women, but he appeared to prefer more casual relationships and got his high from the power plays he frequently engaged in as part of his business. He rarely lost at that game and when he did, the winner would eventually pay a far larger price than he realized at the time of triumph.

As Jenn entered the suite, Ed's butler ushered her into the living area and offered her a seat on the sofa facing the window wall and the blazing Arizona sunset. At her left hand was a bloody Mary, already poured and perfectly spiced to her taste. Ed was a master of detail and undoubtedly had made the drink himself.

In preparation for their meeting, Jennifer had speculated on the reason for the trip. She knew that this was no ordinary fund-raising trip. Hardly. The campaign was awash with money and now, with Jack conducting a very limited travel campaign, expenses were greatly reduced. So, did Ed know about the sex video, the death of the cardiologist, and the cover-up in general? She suspected he was involved, but how far did his involvement go? Jack confided in him, but the President had a firewall around himself that limited his knowledge of what was going on.

This wall was no accident and it served a useful purpose for the President. It was one reason why his choice of confidants was so important. He had to trust them blindly at times to act in his best interest.

Not knowing the reason for this meeting left her uneasy. Was Ed going to hit on her? She laughed inwardly at the sophomoric expression.

She doubted that, considering his relationship with Jack, but the thought crossed her mind.

Ed was very attractive. He was ruggedly handsome and very attentive. In their early scouting relationship, she had found him very sexy, though they hadn't explored each other's desires in any depth. A close friend of Jennifer's had dated him seriously for several months and her tales of that romance confirmed what she thought: Ed was every bit as successful with women as he was in business. Her friend had been devastated by their break-up.

Jennifer had dressed with little attention to any particular agenda, since there was none. But her dress was a bit shorter than her traveling secretary had suggested.

Jennifer picked her own clothes and she was sure her secretary would have raised both eyebrows at her choice of undergarments.

Sitting in the plush softness of the velvet sofa, sipping her bloody Mary and watching the sun set over the parched desert, she felt relaxed and pleased with herself. This lifestyle wasn't half bad. She smiled inwardly as she felt the warmth of the drink overtake her.

"Que sera, sera," she whispered to herself as Ed entered the room and crossed over to her with a big smile on his sun-tanned face. As usual, he was dressed in very casual but expensive southwestern attire. He sat down opposite her, across the large wooden coffee table, and he relaxed into the soft leather armchair.

"Jennifer, thanks for coming on such short notice. I know your schedule is very tight. I needed to see you and felt it was best to do it under cover of the campaign."

"Ed, you know the White House doesn't ask questions when you call. You called and here I am. Simple as that."

"Like rubbing a magic lamp, Jenn? Out pops the genie. Do I get three wishes?"

The innuendo was crude, but she chose to fence with him rather than encourage his verbal forays.

"Depends on the wishes, Ed. You have more latitude than anyone else, but even you must know there are boundaries."

"Yes, we'll get to that in a minute, but first tell me how you've been."

A sense of unease had crept into the conversation, albeit subtly. Jennifer could feel the serious undertone in all this banter.

"I've been just great, Ed. Campaign's going great. Looks like a no-sweat November third. You should know. You've been involved as much as, if not more than, any staff. I know you know all about Jack's medical problem. We've managed to keep that under wraps, so it should be smooth sailing, here on in."

Jennifer was being as superficial as possible, not knowing what Ed was after and knowing his penchant for details and control.

It didn't take long for Ed to get to the point of the visit. "I've got an interesting video, Jennifer. I think you know what I'm talking about. You also must know my one major concern is the maintenance of security with regard to Jack's problem. There has got to be an absolute sealed door on this matter. I'm worried that you're making waves that could come back to haunt us all. I think I know why you've begun to explore alternate sources of, let me say, satisfaction. Nevertheless, it creates a vulnerability that, for now, can't be allowed to continue."

"Stop. Right there, Ed. I don't want to see this mess unravel either. We could get caught in a very nasty cover- up. Our goals are more similar than you could ever know. Maybe my reasons are different, but I want this election to go smoothly and I don't want that disc to be a liability either. Keep the damn disc. My wandering is over. And not because you have the disc. I think we can find some common ground on which we can agree to work and meet our individual needs. I don't need a lecture or a threat from you."

He liked her direct and tough approach. This was no pussycat. It only enhanced her appeal to him. She was defiant but not on very firm ground.

He leaned toward her and spoke in a more tender manner. "We understand each other, Jennifer. You also know I always had a warm regard for you. That could serve our mutual needs if we explored the possibility of a closer relationship."

His intentions couldn't have been more clear. Jennifer decided that it was best to keep him wondering about the possibility of a closer relationship.

She got up and walked over to the glass wall. His eyes followed her movement very closely. For all his money and success, she realized he was just another guy where women and sex were concerned. She bent forward slightly with one foot on the bottom railing in front of the window. Her back was to him, but she could feel his eyes riveted on her. The setting sun sent a strong light through her skirt. She remained in that pose for a minute or so.

As she returned to her chair to pick up her purse, she casually commented, "Nice view at this hour." Her brazen performance surprised even her.

Ed smiled broadly, but he was not going to rush what he considered inevitable. His one thought was simply, "This woman will be mine, and she'll enjoy every moment, including the initial resistance."

"I like you, Ed, and I guess you know that. But don't take too much for granted. I may have strayed with an old friend, but I've ended that brief adventure. It was impulsive, and it was wrong. I was just reacting poorly to Jack's situation. Don't think I'm an easy mark because of the disc. And, oh yes, about the disc itself. It may be too hot to handle and can only be used once. If I were you, I wouldn't put too much reliance on it."

Covington smiled. He liked her straight-from-the-hip style. Her retort only made her more attractive to him.

She continued, "Just remember, Ed, I'm not going to lead anyone into this mess and have it go public. We may have different motives, but our goals are the same. We both want Jack's illness to remain a secret."

She returned to her hotel and left for Washington the next day on the Presidential plane. On her flight, she reexamined her situation and her relationship with Ed.

They each apparently saw the other as a threat. He believed he was in control, but she could see the weakness in the hand he held. The elimination of him and the threat he posed now had become a matter for serious consideration.

CHAPTER FORTY-THREE

Leslie and Al parted painfully at Reagan Airport. Al's practice obligation could wait no longer, and Leslie had a job to maintain. Their future together was promising, but the events that drew them together had run their course.

For Leslie, the White House story lacked the necessary corroboration to go forward. Their suspicions were sufficient to satisfy Al, but Leslie was frustrated that it led to a dead end in terms of a real blockbuster publication.

Their last night together had been a mixture of sorrow and hope. If they were intended to be together in a deeper sense, time would tell. For the first time, "love" had been professed as the mutual feeling between them. The physical distance being placed between them was a serious obstacle to overcome, but they agreed to keep the fire burning until some positive resolution came into sight. They had little choice in view of the feelings they now felt toward each other.

As Al's plane taxied to takeoff position, Leslie was driving over the Memorial Bridge into Washington. She was convinced that the key to this story had to be the First Lady. Somehow, she would have to find that key to unlock Jennifer Henderson's role in the affair. The disc convinced her that Jennifer was vulnerable. Someone beside Steve Berk and herself had to know what was on that disc and now probably had it in his or her possession. That person might exercise considerable control over Jennifer. That person's role in the affair was more obscure, much less the person's identity. But she could work on that. After all she was a reporter, and this was her killer story.

Berk's death bothered her a lot. The police didn't seem interested and accepted the coroner's report without any question. There had to be more to it than that. It was too coincidental that Steve should die of natural causes a few days after her encounter with him over the disc. That was a place to start, Steve's death. At least that was amenable to investigation. Her car headed for the D.C. police station that had handled the matter.

BOOK THREE

STYMIED

CHAPTER ONE

The police headquarters building looked older than its years on the outside and was even more worn and tired on the inside. The department just didn't have any money to spend on the ambiance of the station house and wouldn't have spent it if it did. The walls hadn't seen fresh paint since the days of Eisenhower and some of the bulletins taped on the walls were of the same vintage as the paint. The only way something came off the wall was if someone needed it and had no way to make a copy. The "wall original" usually sufficed for department purposes and usually carried with it some of the original wall paint.

Captain John McDonald was the D.C. police detective with senior responsibility for the Berk investigation.

Leslie had dealt with him on several occasions in the past and had always found him very business-like and straightforward.

That afternoon McDonald was his usual no-nonsense self.

A 20-year man on the force, he had risen through the ranks and was considered a certainty to make Chief in the next round of promotions. At 50, he was ruddy faced with a full head of red hair turning grey. His brow was wrinkled even when he slept. His large head was square-shaped and his face pleasant-looking. Weight was his problem, but his clothes fit him well and concealed a lot of excess tonnage.

He invited Leslie inside his office. "You heard it all on TV, Miss Nugent. No shit, pardon my French, it was a simple case of dead in bed with no evidence of foul play." He leaned back in his chair with one file on his desk and a deadpan expression on his face. The chair groaned as he leaned back and stressed its springs.

"Can I see the file? Just to satisfy my curiosity?"

"Not usually, but in this case, for a curious woman, I'll make an exception. Here. Look it over."

He turned the file around so she could read it.

Leslie carefully thumbed the thin document from beginning to end. One thing did catch her attention: the reference to a reported attempt on his life a few days before he died. She had not heard about that. It made his death even less likely to have been a natural event.

She decided to test the Captain on that score. "Don't you think it's a bit unusual that there was an attempt on Berk's life a few days before you found him dead in the sack? Seems like too much of a coincidence."

"Well, we did give that a second glance, but there was nothing to go on. And I mean nothing. He was found dead in his bed without a mark on him. There was no evidence of foul play. Give us credit, we do investigate these matters."

"Still, sounds like something should connect those two events, his death and the recent prior attempt. Anyway, I have one more question. Did you find any suspicious material in his office, any weapons, any pictures, tapes, videos, DVDs or books?" She tried to slip the video disc question in casually.

"Nope. But in view of the natural cause of his death, the search was very cursory. After all, his wife is the owner of his possessions now, and we would need a search warrant to go through them. We're not likely to go after one and not likely to get one if we did. Look, I knew the man and his line of work. There was always lots of potential for bad things to happen. There was no evidence of a struggle. Just Berk lying on his back, in bed, very dead without a mark on him. We did take blood to test for possible poisoning, but there was nothing there. A lot of coincidence to swallow, but we can't tie his death to the previous attempt on his life."

Leslie got up to leave. "Well, I guess that's it then. You've been very helpful. I appreciate the opportunity to see that report. Thanks for your time, Captain McDonald."

Leslie left the office and ran the gauntlet of leering eyes right out to the street.

CHAPTER TWO

The row houses on Avenue D were in very good repair and the sparse trees lining the street added a faintly pleasant, pseudo-suburban touch. Nevertheless, this was part of an inner-city neighborhood riddled with crime and unemployment. Errol Jensen's family and his immediate neighbors had worked hard to keep their street alive while the surrounding neighborhood was dying. They had succeeded in their limited objective. Their street was a model for others in the area but precious few tried to emulate it, or if they did, they usually failed in the attempt.

Errol brought home a good paycheck from his job in the White House. His wife, Emily, an English teacher at the local high school, also contributed a significant share of the family support. As a result, the Jensens were able to keep their three children in parochial school and out of trouble. Errol was a no-nonsense father who knew how close they lived to a precipice. Just as in his job at the White House, he was eternally vigilant as a parent. His children could attest to that. He or his wife knew where they were and what they were doing at all hours. Somehow this didn't suffocate them; they felt secure in that knowledge.

The death of Sidney Curtis had stunned Errol. He had admired Curtis and respected his dedication. The matter of the First Lady had been left in his hands since only he and Curtis had any in-depth knowledge of the situation, as far as he knew. Berk's involvement, he assumed, was over now that Curtis was gone. Absent Curtis, Errol continued his close surveillance, keeping thorough notes on her occasional nocturnal outings. They had recently stopped abruptly, so Errol was now getting more sleep during his nighttime shifts.

Sitting over his morning coffee with his wife and kids already out of the house and on their way to school, he was stunned to read about Steve Berk's death. Curtis and now Berk. This was a bit much. He thought back to the strange evening when the President went to a hospital for a clandestine meeting with some Middle-Eastern big wig.

Berk and Curtis had been the major movers on that one, just as they had been on the First Lady's outings. Why was Berk involved in the hospital foray? Was the hospital episode as it was presented? White House security, namely himself, had been kept at a safe distance. Why? And now the two key operatives were gone. Of course, the President was a witness but who was going to ask him about it? Since they had decided on utmost secrecy, Errol was not going to step forward and be the inquiring detective. No way. Yet, something was amiss, and the death of Berk was very disturbing.

White House logs were normally very complete, but Jennifer Henderson's wayward activities were not mentioned in them. Errol Jensen could only wonder what had brought on her recent wandering, but he had no one to talk to with Curtis gone.

The telephone rang, and Errol let it ring three or four times before picking it up.

"Hello, I'm looking for Mr. Errol Jensen."

"Who's calling?" he answered, unwilling to identify himself to an unidentified caller.

"I'm Leslie Nugent, a reporter with the *Daily Sentinel*. I'd like to ask Mr. Jensen a few questions, if he's home."

"Okay, this is Errol Jensen. What's on your mind, Miss Nugent?"

"Thanks Mr. Jensen. I'm sorry to be disturbing you at home. It's pretty important, though, and I can't think of anyone else who could help me the way you could."

"I'm flattered, Miss Nugent, but I can't imagine anything I know that could be of much value to you."

"Well, Mr. Jensen, I'd just like to tell you a short story and then you can see if you have any information which could be of interest to me. Would that be okay?"

Errol was silent for a moment. This would likely be more than a casual listening session. Questions were bound to follow. Normally he would decline letting the reporter gain access to any information he possessed. That morning, however, with Berk's death weighing on him, he was ready to open up a bit more than usual.

"Okay, Miss Nugent. I'm game." He sighed and sat back in his large armchair.

"Well, here goes, Mr. Jensen. You can stop me at any time. This is all off the record and I have to ask you to keep it a secret between the two of us. Are those ground rules okay with you?"

"I think you can trust me, Miss Nugent."

The story sounded more believable to Leslie than even she had thought. This was the first time she'd assembled all the pieces and told it to someone in a single sitting. She and Al had gone over bits and pieces a hundred times, but this was a first for her. When she was done, Errol was silent for a moment on the other end.

"That's quite a story. You probably expect me to say it's the most far-fetched bit of baloney I ever heard, but I'm not going to say that. I can't fill in any details you're missing, but I can tell you that what I do know doesn't contradict anything you're telling me. That's not the same as corroboration, but I don't think I can be of help to you beyond what I just said. I've had two years of law school at night, so I know the difference between corroboration and lack of contradiction."

Leslie was breathing fast. More confirmation. Maybe not as clear and specific as she'd hoped but confirmation of a sort, nevertheless. Her level of excitement grew by the minute. She had struck gold on a hunch and now she needed to firm up her source and get real information to back up her suspicions. How could Errol Jensen be won over to her side? His White House loyalties would have to be redirected. Get him to see that a cover-up was disloyal to the real White House and that he owed his loyalty to the institution, not the occupants.

"Mr. Jensen, we need to talk. There's a lot at stake here, and we need to be together on this. I mean it. We need each other. I've told you a lot, and I need you to level with me. Something evil has been going on, and I don't think you want to be part of a cover-up. Let's put our information together and see if the complete picture is sufficiently compelling to merit further investigation. I think it does, but I need to convince you. I need your backup to confirm important parts of the story and eventually get an editor to buy the package."

"Whoa. Look, Miss Nugent, I'm only a policeman. I'm not an investigator and certainly not an investigator of the White House occupants. I'm there to protect them from any outside mischief, not to spy on them or try or get them in hot water. I certainly don't want to encourage the press to speculate about the kind of intrigue you're trying to ferret out."

"Okay, Mr. Jensen. Can I call you Errol?"

"Yes, that's okay with me. But I'll stick with Miss Nugent, if you don't mind."

"I understand your reservation, but if you were an essential witness who could help unravel the kind of crimes I've been alluding to, I don't think you'd retreat behind that argument. You've got to help me. If there's nothing to substantiate, no damage is done."

Again, there was a pause on Jensen's end. "Okay. I feel like a fool, but I'll give you some help. You'll have to let me decide what's reasonable and what's not. Now, what do you want?"

"Great, Errol. First off, I'd like to know what the President's log indicates he did on August 23. Let's start there. I'm sure that's something you can get. Even if the best you can do is the security log for that day. Get that and give me a call. I'm betting that something on that day will smell fishy."

"All right. I'll do that much. I'm a little troubled myself after hearing your story. But, if I get the slightest hint that I'm being used for some reporter's selfish purpose, I'm gonna dummy up on you and you'll lose a valuable source."

"That's a deal, Errol. Here's my number."

CHAPTER THREE

The logs of White House entry and leaving were easily accessible to Jensen. As Chief of White House security, the actual logs for the current year were kept in his office.

Wednesday, August 23. An entry in the log indicated that late in the day the President and Sidney Curtis along with a Mid-East consultant, had left to rendezvous with a Palestinian leader. Now it all came back. He had been uneasy about the arrangements, since White House security people were to be kept at a significant distance from the actual meeting site. Steve Berk had accompanied the party at the request of Curtis. This was explained as part of a security arrangement agreeable to the Palestinian leader. The President, through Mr. Curtis, had insisted on this unusual arrangement and so Jensen had had no choice but to go along with it. The rendezvous was to take place at St. Anne's Hospital, where the Palestinian was staying as a patient under a false name and false pretenses.

He paused in his reading. It had sounded fishy then and was even more fishy now that he had that reporter's slant on things. The time could certainly have been used for the catheterization procedure she had referred to. He couldn't deny that but couldn't confirm it either. The Palestinian's name was not in the log entry and the Mid-East expert was also unnamed. Could he have been the doctor who did the procedure? It was doubtful that anyone had gotten a good look at the consultant. He hadn't. Still, there were two plausible explanations and the one in the log was no more credible than the one that would fit in with Leslie Nugent's story. He'd give her a call tonight.

CHAPTER FOUR

The Oval Office was quiet that Sunday, and Jack Henderson appreciated the break in normal routine. Sitting at his desk in his robe and slippers, he pondered the future. His reelection in a few weeks was virtually assured. It had never really been in doubt, but the implication of his incapacity had been difficult to gauge at first. The limitation it imposed on his campaign had seemed immense. That was all in the past now. Curtis had done a masterful job working around it and even turning it to an advantage while maintaining utter secrecy.

Ed Covington was a White House guest and was staying in the family wing in one of the guest rooms. Over the past month he'd done this on numerous occasions. He had informally become a one-man kitchen-cabinet. His briefings to the President were valuable but were deliberately lacking in detail where any issue surrounding the careful concealment of the President's health problem was concerned.

Curtis had laid out the campaign strategy with the President and it had made sense. His death had been a terrific blow, but the strategy had remained intact. The only difference had been an aggressive and extensive role assumed by Covington. Considering his background and personality, that was no surprise. The death of Berk had been a surprise, but Ed had kept Jack in the dark on that matter, probably to leave no trail back to the White House.

He suspected that Ed was sealing off the cover-up so there would be no leaks. Only Jennifer and he, himself, were witnesses, and they each had powerful vested interests to keep the cover-up covered up. Furthermore, they each had only skeletal knowledge of what else had transpired.

It had started out so simple. The President was supposed to lay low for a few months until after the election and then reveal his illness after an appropriate interval. Not a huge deal. Admittedly, there was a major deception here, but no one was supposed to get hurt. With Curtis in control, Jack had felt almost justified in the planned course of action. That was how it was with Sidney. He had always exercised just enough control to keep Jack confident that the direction they were headed in was the right one. With Sidney gone, Jack felt as if he'd lost his rudder. Ed was not Sidney. Sure, he was every bit as smart, but you couldn't be sure whose interest he had at heart, and there always was that element of ruthlessness that he occasionally displayed. Sidney and Ed each played to win, but Sidney had recognizable boundaries; Ed had none. Now Ed was his Sidney and Jack was uneasy. He wasn't at all sure what Ed had been doing, ostensibly on his behalf.

Keeping the President away from the cover-up meant keeping him in the dark, and Jack was only now waking up to the realization that there could be blood on his hands. Blood he had never intended to see spilled.

He, the goose who laid the golden eggs, was also the remaining threat to Ed and the steps being taken to reelect the President. Knowing Ed, Jack knew that his mind was turning over these same thoughts.

Somehow, this sordid piece of history would have to be told and he should be the one to tell it. Not now, perhaps, but not too far into the future. He reached for the small hand-held dictation unit. The story began with a swim in the White House pool and ended with a President blowing the whistle on himself and some people very close to him. Two hours later, he put the last of three tapes in an envelope and placed the envelope in the wall safe behind the portrait of Ulysses S. Grant. His mind was beginning to divest itself of a number of matters that had disturbed him over the past few weeks.

CHAPTER FIVE

The following morning, Jennifer stood in the doorway to her husband's room still dressed in her robe and nightgown. "Jack, I need to talk to you about some recent events." She cautiously entered the room and sat on the side of his bed. Jack didn't say a word. He sensed something uneasy in her manner and felt it best to let her speak without any prompting from him.

"I don't know if you're aware of what's been going on with me, but even if you are you need to hear about it from me."

"That sounds a bit ominous, Jennifer, so I guess we really do need to talk. There are some things I want to get off my chest, too."

"I'll get right to it. Jack, I've been foolish and it's eating me up. I love you and I let our recent distance take me away from you without any regard for our relationship. I know it was wrong. It happened but it's over.

I need to get it out and get us back on track. You can't be blamed for your problem, and I can't let it destroy us. We need to help each other, Jack."

She remained in her slightly distant position, waiting for a sign of affection or forgiveness. Jack weighed her vague confession and tried to put it in perspective. He gave no sign that he was going to be supportive.

He thought, "Was it as simple as that? Just forgive and forget? What happened? Whom was she involved with?"

"Look, Jack, I'm here to be your wife. Full-time. The past is past. What I did was brief but foolish. All I can say is that it was a selfish venture and now it's over. I desperately want us to get back on track. I also don't want to give up with regard to your heart condition. I want to understand the medical situation in some detail, including the range of options. We don't need the White House. We do need each other and need to give your medical problem our best shot. I want to be included."

"There's been a lot of water over the dam, Jenn. I believe several people may be dead because of my problem, and I'm trying to come to grips with my role in this. So, right now, I don't want to go into the details of any infidelity. I assume that's what you're alluding to. After all we've been through, that hurts me more than you can know. Christ! I can't believe it. We hit this one rough patch, and you go off the deep end. I'm terribly disappointed, but I don't want to discuss it now. I accept your confession as a sign that you're sincere about putting it in the past. I'm going to leave it at that for the time being."

He paused to let that sink in. Jennifer realized that he'd been totally unaware of her brief affair with Howard Westlake. It made her wonder what else he didn't know about events of the past weeks.

"Right now, I don't even know how much malefaction has taken place in the name of securing my reelection. If and when that comes out, there'll be a mess bigger than Watergate and reputations will be ruined. Are you up to that? Believe me, it'll be awful, and it should be. I'm willing to take my chances, but I may only be a short-timer. You won't escape the tarring, Jennifer, and you'll have much longer to live with it."

Jennifer was feeling numb. "I can't be sure that I'm up to the mess that might result."

"I'm not sure either, Jenn. And, I'm not even sure what damage has been done. Do we remain silent? Forever? Does Ed get out of this without a scratch? I can't believe he isn't behind the whole scheme. I think Sidney and Ed had a close relationship, with Sidney the public face and Ed pulling the strings at a distance. Sidney's death may have been Ed's way of reducing the risk of exposure. Cold- blooded and effective. That's Ed's way. Well, do we come clean sometime or other? There are some big unknowns here."

"Jack, the more I think about the options, the more I see a need to eventually clear the air. But maybe not immediately. Let's get through the election and not create national confusion. We can give our story to the press in due time. That way there's time to mend our own bruises. I'm game for disclosure but would like to see the dust settle first and see the future a bit clearer."

"Jennifer, I dictated some notes on what we're discussing and would like to put them in the hands of someone we can trust to write the story at an appropriate time. Someone possibly at the Post, would be my choice, but I don't have a particular person in mind."

"Let's go slow on this, Jack. Let your reelection pass and then decide on how to let out the news of your illness. After that gets absorbed, we can see where to go with the dark side of the story. I don't think we should drop a bomb and have no control over the potentially damaging reaction."

"You're may be right, Jenn. I'll have to sleep on that. I don't want to act without regard for the reaction that will follow. I keep thinking that if something happened to me the story might go untold. I don't want to leave it all in your lap. Plus, you have even more limited knowledge about it than I do."

"Jack, I've met a bright, young woman on the *Sentinel* who I think would be easier to keep under control than a senior pro at the *Post*. Putting the information you have in the hands of the *Post* may be hard to keep under wraps until some future time. I just think that control is critical at this stage. She could be the storyteller, using your information and possibly do it as a special to the *Post*."

"Let me think about that, Jennifer. I'd like to meet this person and size her up for myself. Why don't you have Edith contact her and set up an informal meeting with me."

"That sounds like a good approach, Jack. I'll get to it today."

They moved close together on the edge of his bed. The contact was reassuring. Healing was beginning.

Jennifer leaned closer and they embraced. Two people very alone in the eye of a storm where it was always most calm. They clung to each other for much-needed reassurance.

CHAPTER SIX

Sitting in the White House coffee room, Errol Jensen was relaxing with two of his young associates from the White House security staff.

"How are you guys doing? I know the pool duty wasn't a plum assignment, but it isn't everyday you get to spend some casual time with the President."

The tall young man with a deep voice and strong southern accent was the spokesman for the inseparable duo.

"That trip has ended, Errol. We haven't been to the pool on assignment for several weeks. I think the President finds swimming too tiring."

"Wait a minute. You mean that cushy early morning dip patrol is over for you guys?"

"Looks that way. Last time we were there, the Prez came out of the pool lookin' awful tired. He didn't finish his laps. He just stopped. We were told to keep this info to ourselves. So far, we have. You're the first and only person we've told, but you're our Chief."

Jensen was stunned. More pieces were fitting into the puzzle. It was unbelievable how the story the reporter told him was gathering momentum.

No "smoking gun," just an incredible bunch of uncanny coincidences coming together to make for a very credible story of White House deceit.

Jensen was growing impatient for five o'clock to roll around. He was eager to leave the White House, make that call to Leslie Nugent and see where she would go with this new information.

Jensen's office was small but orderly. From the small window, he had a good view of the White House driveway and the guardhouse at the entrance. As he had mused many times in the past, the guard was a front-line sacrifice if there ever was an attack on the premises. The little guardhouse could easily be blown away by an attacker. The next line of defense had to be impregnable. The defense force was well- trained and almost invisible. Few visitors to the White House had any idea how thorough the plans were to thwart an attack.

Now, the head of White House security was facing a different kind of threat to the President. It was more subtle and insidious and harder to defend against. The President himself was possibly the biggest threat to the office of the President. The log entry had convinced him that Leslie Nugent may have been on to something very serious and potentially important for the integrity of the Office. Sometimes a scandal was purifying if it was handled in a manner that demonstrated the resilience of the system. Watergate had hurt but the public had to respect the system as it dealt with the mess in an orderly manner. No coup.

No tanks in the streets. One President left and a new one came in. Jensen was totally committed to such an orderly process.

His first call to Leslie Nugent reached her office answering machine, so he hung up and decided to go to a nearby pub for a couple of beers. He sat alone in a booth at the rear.

At this hour, the pub was nearly deserted. The booth was a quiet and secure place to have a phone conversation. No one would be close enough to hear his half of the conversation. He tried her again fifteen minutes later and she answered on the second ring.

"Hello, Miss Nugent. This is Errol Jensen."

"Oh, hello, Errol. I'm so glad you decided to call back. I was thinking about this call all day long. Tell me the news."

"Well, the log was easy to research, and it's sort of consistent with your theory. I also recall that day, since the activity in question was quite unusual and disquieting. A small contingent did leave the White House and went to rendezvous, presumably with a Palestinian envoy at a local hospital. The log entry has several vague bits of information. An intermediary accompanied the White House entourage and he is not named in the entry. An unidentified person accompanying the President and his Chief of Staff is very unusual and potentially very dangerous. Nevertheless, that's what happened. They returned several hours later, minus the intermediary. That's all I can offer you."

"That's terrific, Errol. Do you think you could identify the intermediary if I showed you a photograph?"

"Probably. Unless he wore a disguise, which I don't think he did."

"I'll come by with a photo and see what you think. Do you see how it all fits into the puzzle? It may not be the 'smoking gun,' but it makes my rendition of the whole story much stronger."

"I agree. I've given your theory a lot of thought today and I haven't found any holes in it."

Jensen was reluctant to bring up the matter of the swimming pool incident. The President had told his security detail to keep it secret and so he had to respect that wish.

"But now I have some live news for you, Errol. The White House called and asked me to come by tomorrow for a brief appointment with

the President. There weren't any details given, but it must have some re-
lation to this matter. I may be wrong, but my intuition says it's connected,
somehow."

Jensen was determined to keep the reporter's imagination as subdued as possible and keep her focused on facts and facts alone. "I guess
that's possible, but don't get too excited. It may be something far less significant, though I must agree that the coincidence makes you wonder. Will
you stop in and see me after the visit to let me know what transpired? I'm
more than a little curious myself. And, Miss Nugent, please be careful.
Neither of us knows what's going on, but the stakes in this game are often
a lot higher than many players realize. Just be careful."

CHAPTER SEVEN

The President's appointment secretary, Margaret Avila, was under strict orders to let Covington know of any changes in the President's schedule. The addition of the *Sentinel* reporter to the next day's schedule would be brought promptly to Covington's attention.

The telephone in Ed Covington's office gave a gentle ring. He put his newspaper down, noted who the caller was on the screen and picked up the receiver.

"Hello, Margaret. What do you have for me?"

The news had him shaking his head affirmatively. "I see. The meeting is tomorrow at three." Covington hung up and called Jennifer.

"Jennifer, Jack is meeting a reporter tomorrow. Do you have any idea what the meeting is about?"

Jennifer was caught off-guard. She decided to offer up as little as possible.

"I recommended the reporter. I think Jack wants to size her up as a person to document events in his last term in office." With that, she waited for Ed's response.

Covington was not easily put off. He could sense Jennifer's hesitation in her answer. "Is that the full story, Jenn? What are you not telling me? There's more to this than a simple interview, isn't there?"

"Look, Ed, I'm not very close to Jack's mindset at this time. He may have a more complex agenda for the meeting. I just don't know."

"Okay, Jenn. We'll leave it at that." He hung up and left Jennifer wondering what she had let the reporter in for.

Jennifer's ambivalence was troubling her. On one hand, she wanted reconciliation with Jack and that meant agreeing with his strategy for clearing the air. On the other hand, she liked her life without the clutter of a scandal. In that regard, she was on Ed's side. Now she may have just thrown a young reporter to the wolves. So, she wasn't the much-admired First Lady of the media, but the public didn't have to know that.

Covington next made a local call on a disposable cellphone. "Mr. Anthony, a member of my staff will meet you at your office tonight where the details of an assignment will be delivered."

Covington wondered if the reporter coming to see Jack could be the same woman who had given up the tape to Berk in their street tussle. It was a stretch, but something told him there was more activity buzzing around him and the President than was immediately apparent. His instinct was to compress what he did know into a workable scenario.

The number of parties involved in this affair seemed to shrink and expand. His intuition told him the number was small, but that the dots could be connected. Now there was a young woman reporter recommended by Jennifer to the President possibly as a potential whistle blower. Berk had struggled with a young woman in the street outside his office/apartment. They could be the same person. How much did she know about this operation? She knew Berk and she knew Jennifer. She could know a lot. She had to be contained. Was she working alone? Was anyone else aware of the operation? Five people had been silenced and a sixth wouldn't draw much attention, if it were done with care.

Trouble was Jennifer now knew he was aware of the reporter's involvement. Just another strike against Jennifer. Her position was becoming untenable.

CHAPTER EIGHT

L eslie was firing on all cylinders. Al was coming up from North Carolina for the weekend, and the White House had asked her to drop in for a brief visit with the President.

Not only was that unusual, but the caller wouldn't give her a clue as to what it was about. She could only guess that it had something to do with the mystery she was trying to unravel. The President's wife was the only White House connection she could imagine between herself and the President. It was all very mysterious. She looked forward to the weekend with Al to try and figure out what was going on.

Her plan was to drive to the White House for the three o'clock appointment, have the meeting with the President and then drive to Reagan Airport to pick up Al. The timing wasn't bad.

As she entered the White House and gave her coat and handbag to the security officer in the vestibule, Jensen came forward to meet her and explain the rules of the House for guests.

Leslie tried to calm her nerves with a little humor. "Guess the guy saw my legs at one of the press conferences and wants to get a better look at what they're carrying."

The Head of White House security was not in a humorous mood. "I'm surprised the agenda is such a secret," was his more serious response. "Now, these are the rules of the House."

After a brief wait in the hallway outside the Oval Office, the door opened and a very well-dressed, gray-haired woman came out. She introduced herself as the President's special assistant and ushered Leslie into the imposing room.

It was not an unfamiliar setting. She'd seen it in the movies and on "West Wing" many times. The President, seated at his desk, stood up to greet her. The assistant left the room and it was just she and the President.

The introductory chit-chat was pleasant and light- hearted. She was put at ease by the President's very warm and friendly manner. She marveled at how gracious he was and how he made her feel like an old friend in just a few minutes of easy chatter. The silken manner explained, in part, his political success. She also saw him as fit and healthy with no external sign of failing health.

"First, I'd like to know a bit about you, Ms. Nugent. My wife recommended that I meet you and, of course, that counts for a lot. Nevertheless, I'd feel more comfortable if I knew you a bit better myself. So, Leslie, tell me about yourself. Where are you from? What do your parents do? Any siblings? And what do they do? I don't see a tell-tale ring on your left hand, so I assume you're single. How'd you get into reporting and what's your beat, so to speak? Tell me who you are. Et cetera, et cetera."

She gave him an abridged bio of Leslie Nugent. It was very straightforward. She omitted nothing of importance except her recent snooping into his very private affairs.

She suspected his wife had omitted that aspect too.

"That's helpful. Now, I'm sure you're wondering why I asked to see you, Leslie. Well, it's not easy to explain so I'll just simplify a bit. I hope that will suffice."

"Certainly, sir. It's your call. I hope I can be of help in doing whatever it is you're going to ask of me." Leslie felt the perspiration soaking through the underarms of her pale blue shift. No antiperspirant was made for this situation, she thought.

"I have a story I want you to tell and I'm going to ask two things of you. You're getting quite an exclusive, so the restrictions will be acceptable. First of all, tell it. Second, don't tell it until at least one month after I'm gone. And I mean 'gone.' Do you understand what I'm saying?"

Leslie's throat was too dry to answer, so she nodded emphatically.

Jack Henderson felt it best not to reveal the details of the story he had put on tape. He was going to trust this young reporter with a dynamite story and assume that she could pull it off at the appropriate moment. He wouldn't be around to know how it played out anyway. He could have given the tapes to his trusted estate attorney, but he feared that someone wanting to obstruct publication of the tapes would have an opportunity to wage a legal battle at that juncture. Lawyers would be lawyers. No, this was best. Give it directly to the press and assure its publication. Just ensure a period of delay, long enough to spare the country the scandal of a seated President being involved in a major cover-up.

"This briefcase contains three audio tapes which tell a story as far as I have been privy to certain events. Mind you, it's likely not the full story, since I have relied on others implicitly. I'm asking you to swear that you will keep the briefcase in a safe location. There's a bit of 'cloak and dagger' here. To assure no premature publication, I had to enlist the help of the CIA. The briefcase is locked. Any attempt to break into it will trigger a destructive release of strong acid inside the case that will destroy the tapes. The key to the case already has been given to a trusted attorney with instructions to give you the key on demand, no sooner than one month after my death. He knows who you are and will contact you after the one-month interval, so there's no need for you to know his name. He knows nothing about the contents of the case, so he shouldn't have any hesitation about following my instructions nor should anyone have any basis for preventing him. Those are my terms. I think they're clear. There's no other condition to be discussed. I'm sorry for all this mystery, but it obviously matters a great deal to me. Are we in total agreement?"

Leslie was still struggling with a dry throat, but she was now able to speak. "I do, sir. I do implicitly and will comply fully. I don't know why you're trusting me with this mission, but I accept the terms as spelled out. I think I know a bit about what may be on the tapes and I assure you the story means a lot to me. I won't disappoint you."

"Okay. Here's the briefcase. It's locked now. I wish you good luck. There's going to be quite a stir when the story comes out, so you'll be in the eye of a hurricane."

He offered his hand to her. Leslie shook the hand of the 43rd President of the United States in the Oval Office. Her head was swimming, but she knew that the meeting was over. The assistant who had let her in now appeared as if on cue and led her out of the room and down the corridor to the door through which she had entered the building. They exchanged parting pleasantries and Leslie found herself outside the White House on a cool and cloudy mid-October afternoon. She took a deep breath and tried to calm down.

CHAPTER NINE

Jensen was waiting for her as soon as she emerged outside. "Was it what you expected," he asked in a friendly voice.

"I think it was. I can't be absolutely sure but there's every reason to think so. We met alone, and he gave me this briefcase to stow away for the time being, without taking a peek. A bit mysterious, if I must say so."

"Look, Leslie, I don't want to scare you, but you're getting pretty deep into some mischief people in power may want to keep quiet. That could be dangerous. If your story is as good as you think it is, several people have already died and now you're taking the whistle blower's seat. I'd be mighty careful from here on out. Remember, I'd like to help in any way I can. Keep my cellphone number handy."

"That's comforting, Errol. I mean it. One final thing. The President didn't go into any details or even paint the picture in broad brush strokes. Nevertheless, I got the feeling that he may know even less than I do about what's been going on around him. That seems odd. Now I've got to hustle out to Reagan to pick up my guy." She gave him a firm and friendly handshake and headed for her car with briefcase in hand.

The President sat alone in the Oval Office. He'd asked to be undisturbed. The brief session had been draining for him. His mortality weighed heavily on him, but it also gave him license to act more decisively than ever before in his life. Re-election was a certainty, but it was also a certainty that a full second term was not in the cards. His cardiac limitations would become apparent once the election was over. He couldn't fulfill the obligations of the office and that meant giving it up.

The best course was to become Jack Henderson, private citizen, and seek the best medical care available. So now, the only question was what to do about the upcoming election. So much had been done in the name of winning that prize. Even now he wasn't sure that he knew the full extent of the campaign to re-elect.

His marriage was on shaky ground. He'd never dreamed that it was so fragile. He never considered that his health could drive such a wedge between him and Jennifer. The world was closing in, and it was time to face the truth.

Suddenly it occurred to him that his simple transfer to the young reporter may not be so secret. The actual content of the meeting may not be known but some would question the need for such privacy unless something of consequence was discussed. Jennifer knew about the meeting, so others could too. The girl could be in serious danger.

He spoke into the intercom to his assistant's office. "Mary, get Errol Jensen. Tell him I want to see him, now. It's urgent."

A sweat had broken out on his forehead and he could feel his heart beating faster and more forcefully than usual. He tried to calm himself down. This was no time to have an attack of shortness of breath.

Jensen moved rapidly up the back stairs of the White House. He wanted to run but his training restrained him. Quickly and calmly was the White House way. Never give away the full extent of any emergency. There were precious few secrets, even in the White House, so if you were going to head off a panic you had to be calm in the face of danger and emergencies. The floor was calm, and he slowed as he approached the side door to the Oval Office. He entered without knocking.

The President was on the floor beside his desk. He could tell from his color that he was probably dead, but Jensen checked his carotid artery pulse to be sure. There was no pulse and he was not breathing. Trained in basic life support, Jensen could see that the President's pupils were fixed and dilated, a sign that the brain was far gone. He was very dead. A stream of bubbly, pink fluid ran from his mouth and formed a small puddle along-side his head.

Jensen promptly started chest compression knowing full well that it would be futile. His call for emergency assistance was answered promptly by a team of White House staff who took over the resuscitation effort.

Jensen pressed the intercom button and initiated the series of steps that would now dominate the nation's attention for the next few weeks. In the back of his mind, he recalled the conversation with Leslie Nugent. She was probably the last person to see the President alive. She had spoken about a briefcase the President had given her and that it might have a bearing on the matter they had discussed. The danger light flashed in his mind again. She might be carrying some very threatening infor-mation. Even though he was not privy to any conditions the President may have attached to the release of the information, with the President gone, the possibility of its imminent release only heightened his sense of concern for her. He wanted to warn her of his concerns.

How could he escape this scene with so much to do? He felt he had to at least call her. All he wanted Leslie to do was lay low until he could help her plan a safe path out of the potential danger he saw her in.

CHAPTER TEN

The ride out to Reagan Airport was no more than a twenty-minute jaunt without rush hour traffic. Leslie drove into the short-term parking lot and prepared to lock the car when she realized that the briefcase might be more safely kept in her possession than locked in the car. That was her best judgment, so she took the briefcase and headed toward the terminal.

The two men who had followed her since she'd left the White House had to make a decision. She had parked in the lot for arrivals, so it was likely that she would return with more people. They'd been alerted to look for a briefcase in her possession and they could see she was carrying one. That was the assignment: take the briefcase from her by force if necessary. They were trying to decide when it would be best to make their move.

Before they could decide, Leslie had run across the frontage road, just in front of a bus, and into the terminal. They chose to follow closely behind, but now were confronted with a crowded airport terminal.

"We've lost her. Let's separate and search the waiting areas one at a time. If either of us sights her, call on the cellphone."

After 10 minutes or so, one of the tails spotted her moving 10 yards ahead of him. All he could see were the tops of heads. He made his call, and they both observed her from a distance. Suddenly, she stopped and was in the arms of a man.

In the crowded waiting area with so many people greeting arrivals, it was not difficult to reach down and pick up the briefcase standing on the floor next to the embracing couple. The two men, with the briefcase, slipped unnoticed into the crowd and left the airport.

CHAPTER ELEVEN

A few miles away, the car carrying the two men and the briefcase carefully threaded its way through traffic on the way to an assigned drop point.

"That was close, but somehow it went off smoothly. I thought we'd lost her there for a while."

"Getting that briefcase was what I was worried about, but it just stood there asking to be picked up."

The driver breathed a sigh of relief. "This turned out to be a piece of cake. I can't wait to get that paycheck and take my chick away to Hawaii."

"Yeah, I know what you mean, Bruno. It's good pay for a few minute's work."

"Do you know what made this briefcase so valuable?" asked the man behind the wheel.

"No idea, Bruno, and I'd just as soon not know." "What's it say on the tag?"

"The ID tag on the briefcase has some doctor's name on it. A guy. Does that make any sense?"

"What the hell are you talking about, Larry?" The car pulled off the road into a rest stop.

The driver reached for the briefcase. "Gimme that fuckin' case."

The driver looked at the tags and confirmed his partner's observation.

"What the hell does this mean? She was carrying a briefcase when she went into the terminal. Maybe she uses his briefcase. They looked pretty friendly."

"I don't know, Larry, that doesn't sound right. I don't like this. I think maybe we got the wrong briefcase."

"How could that be? She was the right girl and the briefcase was right next to her. There wasn't any other briefcase, Bruno."

"Remember, we lost her for a few minutes. We were lucky to pick her out of the crowd and we couldn't see if she had that briefcase until we got very close. Larry, I think we screwed up."

"Maybe. Wait a minute. Let's look inside it. Maybe the answer's inside. Open it up, Larry."

The case was not locked and opened easily. The contents couldn't have been more uninteresting or less mysterious. Some man's overnight clothes and a small toilet articles kit. It was more like a small overnight case than a briefcase. No secret compartments were evident. They didn't have any prize to deliver and both agreed there would be hell to pay. Their employer could be very nasty when the outcome was less than he expected.

"That briefcase must be back at the airport, Bruno, and I ain't goin' back for it."

"We wouldn't know where to look anyway, so there's no sense goin' back. But who the hell is the guy and where will we find him and the girl with her briefcase?"

"You jerk, you just looked in his briefcase and said there was a name tag. What does it say?"

"Al Seibolt, a doctor, from some place in North Carolina. That's no help."

"Is there anything inside that might give us a clue? Like an address book? Look around inside, Bruno."

"Hey, here's an address book just like you guessed. Let me see if it has any local addresses in it."

After a brief moment of page turning, he shouted out, "I've got it! Here's an address in Virginia, not too far from here and it's a chick's address, Leslie. Maybe she's the one he was rubbing up against at the airport. Let's pay her a visit and see if she has a briefcase with her."

"Yeah, that's the thing to do. Give me the address." The car reentered the traffic and headed toward the nearest Potomac River crossing and back out to Virginia.

CHAPTER TWELVE

As Al and Leslie prepared to leave the airport, it was apparent that his overnight case was gone.

"Damn it. I should have been more careful. I've been ripped off here. Leslie, my overnight case is gone." Al's head wouldn't stop shaking from side to side. Leslie tried to restore their earlier mood.

"Well, we can report it to the airport police, in case someone picked it up by mistake. Anyway, it wasn't as important as my briefcase, so let's keep it in perspective and not let it ruin our weekend together. I'm just happy to be with you. Case or no case. We'll buy you another toothbrush, and you can sleep in the buff at my place."

Still shaking his head in disbelief, Al began to smile and get back in the mood he was in just before he discovered the loss.

"So, where's your case and what's so special about it?" "I stashed it in a locker just before I got to your gate. Let's pick it up and I'll tell you all about it in the car on the way to my apartment."

The TV screens in the airport were now carrying reports of the President's death within his White House office. No cause was given but there was no suspicion of foul play.

Leslie was stunned along with everyone in the airport. "I just saw the man, Al, and he seemed fine. It was less than an hour ago. I can't believe it."

"Tell me all about it when we get to the car."

CHAPTER THIRTEEN

Ed Covington sat in on a very tense and somber White House meeting, helping to work out the details of the Vice President's swearing in. The President's death had stunned the staff. Covington marveled at how well they had kept his heart ailment a secret. The cover-up had been severely tested over the past few hours and no breaks in security were evident. Jennifer had taken the news very hard in spite of her knowledge of Jack's situation. Her feelings for her husband had never changed, even though she had acted at times in her own self-interest. At that moment, she was by herself in the Presidential quarters.

A staffer handed a message to Covington. He recognized the code name of the sender and immediately excused himself. He went upstairs to the guest quarters where he'd been living on and off for the past several weeks.

Careful not to use the White House telephones, he used his own cellphone and dialed his local contact. The story that came back to him was not to his liking and he made that abundantly clear. His contact could feel the icy chill in his voice and it made him shiver. He knew the man's low tolerance for failure. The people responsible would eventually be made to pay a high price for their failure.

"I want that briefcase and I want it soon. Put out an all-points to your organization in D.C. and Virginia to find that couple and recover the case. I've told the front gate guard here at the White House to give you her car's license plate number. I don't care what it takes. The couple is expendable. Now, do something right and call me back in an hour with a report."

He hung up and sat facing the portrait of Andrew Jackson. He wasn't seeing anything, though, as his mind turned over the matter of the tapes and the holder of the tapes. Something clicked, and he smiled. He dialed a number on the White House phone.

"Nancy, I want to speak to the Chief of Police for the District." He paused. "It's urgent. I want him right now."

The secretary for the Oval Office was in a state of near shock over the events of the past few hours but was working non-stop as messages crisscrossed over her message-laden desk. Confusion reigned, but she was bearing up under it.

Chief of Police McKenna was on the phone in less than a minute and Covington filled him in.

"Thanks for your very prompt call back, Chief. I'm sure you can appreciate the stress level in the White House at this time. I wanted to get an urgent message to you, so we can coordinate our efforts on a matter of utmost urgency and secrecy. It involves the woman who was the last person to see the President alive. I have good reason to believe that she took a valuable briefcase with her from the Oval Office when she left."

The Chief interrupted, "Was the President alive when she left?"

"We don't know, but the nature of their encounter is top secret, so we don't know what transpired or how the briefcase came into her possession. We do know she didn't enter with one but did leave with one. The briefcase has not been recovered. I need your police on the case, but they must treat the briefcase and its contents as classified and top secret. We want it back intact. National security may be involved. I can give you her license plate number and her home address. The briefcase is a brown leather, hard-frame attaché case with the presidential seal on the flat top surface. That's how the guard described it as she left."

Covington promised to get back to him as new information came in. "Oh, yes, one last thing, Chief. We'd prefer to maintain a very low profile on this to avoid any embarrassment for the staff at this terrible moment of grief. Please keep all communication secret and communicate with me directly if you have any questions about the briefcase and its return to the White House. I appreciate your discretion."

Covington hung up. This was a calculated gamble. He was betting the police would do a better job of man-hunting than those mindless apes of his out in the field. In either case, neither the police nor his men were likely to cross paths. This way, he had two independent search teams working for him.

CHAPTER FOURTEEN

Errol Jensen was concerned about Leslie. The more he thought about the events she had described, the more he worried about the cover-up continuing in full force now that the President was gone. Leslie was a surrogate for the President if the briefcase held what he thought it did.

There was no way the contents of that case were going to be revealed to the public if the cover-up leader had anything to say about it.

Back in his office, Jensen called Leslie on her cellphone.

"Hello, this is Leslie, in her car. Who wants to speak to her?"

"Leslie, this is Errol Jensen, at the White House. We need to talk. I'm concerned about your safety and want to be sure you're taking all necessary precautions."

"The President was so concerned about the contents of the brief-case and the story I was to tell. Forgive me, Errol, but did he die of natural causes?"

"All indications are that it was acute heart failure. That's not the issue. My concern is that the briefcase he gave you is now dynamite with a lit fuse. The cover-up mastermind must know about it and will stop at nothing to retrieve and destroy it. You're in serious danger. I want to see you get the story out and live to read it."

"What are you suggesting?"

"First of all, don't go home. They must have it staked out."

"Second, get to your nearest police station and call me from there. Where are you, anyway?"

"We're in Virginia just ten minutes from my apartment."

"Okay, just do as I told you. The local police can serve as your protection until we can get the briefcase into responsible hands."

"Okay, Errol. My friend, Al, would like a word with you."

"Hello, Mr. Jensen. I just thought you should know that my brief-case was stolen in broad daylight at the airport when Leslie met me. I don't know if there's any connection, but it sounds a bit too coincidental to be a coincidence."

"I agree. And that probably has the thief or thieves in deep doo-doo with their boss. They must have mistaken your case for Leslie's. They look like fools and that will only intensify their effort to get that briefcase you're carrying. Someone has killed many times to sustain the cover-up. They won't stop now. Remember, the tapes may name names and that could be fatal to someone. Hey, I've got a call that I have to take so just do as we agreed."

"Okay, Mr. Jensen, Leslie and I are heading for the nearest police station and we'll call you from there. Thanks for the warning."

Jensen had a call on his special phone from the D.C. police. This was a cellular system installed to avoid interception or interruption. The calls were rare and usually meant something big was going down.

"Hello. Jensen here."

"Errol, this is Chief McKenna. I just want to keep you posted on an unusual call I got from your place a few minutes ago. I don't know if you know about some briefcase that left the White House a few hours ago. A Mr. Covington called me, on the promise of utmost security, to ask the D.C. police to help recover the briefcase. I'm only supposed to discuss the matter with him and him alone. I'm also supposed to return the case to him alone. Seemed more than a bit odd. That's not how we've done business with the White House in the past. Anyway, I've alerted all precincts in D.C. and nearby Virginia, but I wanted to be sure you were in the loop, on an unofficial basis, of course. I know you would do the same for me and have in the past. I'm just returning a favor."

"Chief, I do appreciate the call. Now I have to make a call right away, so I've got to run. Thanks again. I'll get back to you."

Jensen quickly dialed Leslie's car phone and hoped that the couple hadn't found the safe haven he'd steered them to. The phone was picked up on the second ring. He breathed easier.

"Leslie, this is Errol again. Cancel my advice and don't check into any police station. Do you read me?"

"I do, Errol, but what's going on?"

"Look, something fishy is going on at the White House, and I don't like what it looks like. Do you know Ed Covington?"

"Not personally but I certainly know him by reputation. Close friend of the President and his wife and very involved in the reelection campaign. What does he have to do with this?"

"Well, Covington is running a one-man 'get the briefcase' operation and has enlisted the D.C. and Virginia police in the effort. It sounds like he has a very special interest in what's in the briefcase and that scares me. The police are working for the White House on the assumption that the briefcase is top secret and needs to be returned to him. For the time being, the police are not our friends where the briefcase is concerned. Now listen closely. Avoid the police and get away from your car. They must be looking for the car and watching your apartment."

Leslie's voice had a tinge of panic as she began to digest what she had just heard, "What do you think we should do? I'm starting to feel very uneasy about this whole White House mess. I just want to unload these tapes and get on with a normal life."

Errol could sense her feeling of weariness with the whole episode as well as a sense of panic. His police training didn't allow for any letup at this point. This was the climax, and he was determined to see it through to a successful completion.

"Look, Leslie, you have to ditch your car and do it quickly. Park it somewhere very crowded, public and legal, so it may not be detected easily. Then, call me and I'll pick up you and Al. For the moment, I'm not a player in this game so we should be able to stash the tapes somewhere safe until we can figure out what to do with them."

"Okay, Errol, that sounds like a good plan. We'll call you in a few minutes once we've ditched the car. And thanks for the heads-up."

CHAPTER FIFTEEN

Covington went to the family quarters to see how Jennifer was doing. He found her in the Presidential suite, sitting in her bedroom and staring out a window.

"How are you doing, Jenn?"

"About as well as any widow of several hours, I guess. It hasn't been easy. Even though he'd been ailing, I loved Jack and never wanted to see him go. It's not going to be easy to get used to. And I don't mean giving up the White House and all that goes with it." Her eyes began to fill with tears.

"I know, Jenn. Jack was my closest friend and I'll miss him too. Just remember, I'm here for you if you need me."

"Ed, just one thing I need to ask. What happened to the reporter and the tapes I told you about?"

"I'm taking care of that, Jennifer, so don't give it another thought. I'm doing the necessary damage control." Jennifer could sense his disinclination to discuss the matter in any detail. She let him think his explanation was sufficient for her.

"Okay, Ed, it's in your hands."

After Covington left, Jennifer felt an intense sense of guilt over the danger in which she may have placed the reporter. She could imagine what Ed's "damage control" meant. With Jack's death, her concern about herself and her reputation had begun to recede in her mind. She hadn't done anything criminal and her extra-marital activities had been a brief, foolish reaction to her husband's debility. She regretted her actions, but now regretted her deal with Ed even more. She'd never be a free person as long as he held the video disc over her. And now she helped hang a sword over the head of that young reporter. This was just an indication of what a cover-up could lead to. She was determined to end it, no matter what the personal cost. She picked up the telephone and dialed Errol Jensen's office.

"Hello, this is Errol Jensen."

"Mr. Jensen, this is Jennifer Henderson. I need a favor from you."

"Anything within my power, Mrs. Henderson. And please accept my condolences. Your husband was a fine man."

"Thank you, Errol. I have to ask you something. Did you meet the young woman reporter who met with my husband shortly before he died?"

"Yes, I did, Mrs. Henderson." The security chief was immediately on guard. He was not going to volunteer any information at this point. He'd play dumb and be a good listener. He didn't know what her relationship with Covington was on this matter. Just listen, he told himself.

"Please keep this quiet, Errol. I have reason to believe she's in danger, and I want to help her avoid it. I need your help."

"I'm at your service, Mrs. Henderson. What can I do?" He still didn't know if he could trust her.

"I'm not sure, but I'd be comforted knowing she was with you. Whatever her intentions are. Do you see what I'm aiming at?"

"I'm beginning to, Mrs. Henderson, but it's still a bit foggy on my end. Do you want me to go out and find her and bring her to the White House to be safe?" Jensen was trying to see where she stood in this increasingly complex matter. His offer was a baited hook.

Jennifer could see that the security chief was unaware of the danger within the White House. For Covington, recovery of the briefcase and tapes would be a godsend.

Trouble was she was unsure about the fate of the reporter, even without the tapes.

"No, Errol, just find her and get her to safety. I have reason to believe the briefcase she received from the President is a source of danger for her. It may contain very sensitive information. As a starter, I would be comforted if the information was in your hands. People may want to prevent that information from ever being made public. That's why I think she's in danger."

After hanging up, Jensen realized he would have to get involved directly. He now believed Jennifer Henderson was acting in a forthright and selfless manner.

His first call was to the DC police Chief.

"Chief McKenna, this is Errol Jensen. I understand all about your role in recovering the special briefcase. I just want to alert you to the fact that the people in possession of the case are not in any way guilty of any criminal act. It's important that your officers not approach them as other than innocent citizens. If you need any confirmation, I suggest you contact the First Lady. Second thing, the case should not be returned to anyone but me. I don't believe any person with a top-security clearance has contacted you about the briefcase, so it should be considered a security item and returned to the Office of White House Security. I know this may contravene what you've been given to understand. I hope you'll trust me and follow this more usual channel. Sorry I'm so long-winded."

The police chief sounded a little exasperated but trusted Jensen. "This is getting more complicated than I like. Now I have two contradictory requests from the White House. I assume there's a reason why you guys aren't together on this, but I don't want to know any more than I do already. I'll go along with your request. You're White House security as far as I'm concerned, and the other request came from a more political source, if you will. I sure hope you're not sending me out on a limb."

"Chief, that's all I can ask. I'm glad you trust me. You're not being used by me for anything other than a legitimate security mission. Let's stay in close contact on this one."

"Okay, Errol, I'll do what's necessary from my end."

"Thanks again, Chief." Jensen sat back in relief. At least the police would be working toward a good outcome for this messy affair.

Now, he wondered, who else is out there looking for that briefcase?

He next waited for a call from the couple to place themselves in his hands for safekeeping.

CHAPTER SIXTEEN

The network at Covington's disposal had not identified the couple nor their car. The two operatives who had picked up the wrong briefcase were heading to an address in Virginia on the hunch that the woman in the address book was the one they'd seen in the airport. They arrived at Leslie's apartment and no one answered the bell when they rang. To make sure the apartment was empty, they jimmied the lock and confirmed that the woman was not there. They decided to wait across the street in case she returned in the next hour or so.

Al and Leslie had abandoned their car only a few miles from her apartment in a shopping mall parking lot.

Temptation was great to make for her apartment in a taxi and wait there, but Errol had been emphatic about not doing just that. They obediently ducked into a convenient bar and grill in the mall and called the White House security chief.

Jensen was relieved to hear the voice of the reporter.

She told him where they were and waited for instructions. She never felt more vulnerable.

"Look, Leslie. Stay where you are, and I'll be by for you in about half an hour. Rush hour traffic being what it is, I can't get there any faster. Just stay put, and I'll be there. The Shamrock Bar and Grill in the Potomac Shopping Center. Here's my cellphone number, just in case."

"We'll be waiting here, Errol. We're not moving from this place."

A mall security guard spotted the license plate on their car. He knew he could earn a few extra bucks by calling it in to the unlisted number he'd been given by his brother-in-law. The network operated in just such an unstructured manner. An "army" of informants spread all over the D.C. area with a single number to call. It usually worked. This time it worked like a charm. The information was relayed to the men in the car in front of Leslie's apartment, and they took off for the mall just minutes away. They confirmed the car's license plate and set out to search the mall on foot, seeking the couple they'd seen in the airport. They split up inside, aware of the advantage they held. The couple wouldn't know them, but they knew the couple's identity.

Traffic out of Washington was snarled in the usual afternoon rush hour jam. Jensen could do nothing but tap away on his dashboard as he crawled along at a pace just about that of a leisurely stroll. He hoped his friends were safely tucked away as they waited for his delayed arrival.

The two gunmen had split the mall evenly between them and agreed to meet back at the main entrance in 30 minutes. If either spotted the quarry, he would call the other on the cellphone and not attempt a capture on his own. The mall was relatively empty at this late-afternoon hour. The search would not be difficult.

Al and Leslie sat in a booth in the back of the Shamrock and nursed their beers very slowly. They reflected on how they ever had gotten into this situation. The attaché case they were transporting was obviously the "hot potato" someone was keen on recovering.

"I'd love to hear those tapes, Al, so at least we'd know what we were risking our lives for."

Leslie was more than a little anxious to hear the tapes. Her reporter's nose for news told her the tapes held a blockbuster story. After all they'd been through, it was only right that this prize should fall into their hands.

"You know, Al, I always thought there was more to this story than a simple White House cover-up. There are too many killings and it doesn't make sense for a sick President to start such a vicious cover-up. It would make more sense for someone like Covington, with a big economic interest, to want the reelection to go smoothly. He seems to have a big stake in the entire affair and could finance any scheme he wanted to put in place. It makes you believe there is a shadow government."

The gunman seated himself at the bar and scanned the interior in the big mirror facing him. The couple several booths down were clearly the pair he was after. The briefcase on the bench alongside the woman was the cincher. He casually ordered a beer and took out his cellphone. "Got 'em in the Shamrock Bar on the ground level. Meet me just outside the Shamrock."

"Why waste a good beer?" he thought and began to drain the big glass.

The couple in the booth was seemingly oblivious to the net that was closing around them.

The gunman was suddenly surprised to see the couple get up and prepare to leave. He started to follow them.

"Hey, buddy, that'll be three-fifty for the beer." The man behind the bar didn't want to be stiffed.

The gunman was caught by surprise as the couple exited through the door. He struggled with his billfold and threw ten dollars on the bar and ran to the door. The couple moved with some speed toward the up escalator. His partner was not yet in sight. He took off in pursuit.

"I thought that guy was paying a lot of attention to us in the mirror." Al was now certain that they were being tracked. They had to get away from the guy on their tail and not go so far that Errol wouldn't be able to find them.

"Leslie, we have to confuse this guy and do it now. Let's split up and join up again here at the top of the down escalator in a minute or two. I'll take the briefcase and draw him away. I'll try to lead him away and lose him. Then I'll double back for you in a minute or two. Just disappear in the opposite direction from me and then double back. Do it now. There's no time to discuss it."

Al broke away to his left and after a moment's hesitation, Leslie darted away to the right. The gunman saw them split up and stopped for a moment. Then he took off after the one with the briefcase.

The mall was sparsely populated, and Al was able to run with a small crowd between him and the man on his tail. His goal was to duck into a store, see the tail run by and double back to pick up Leslie. By then, the commotion had caught the attention of mall security guards. They converged on the area of the chase and one arrived in time to see the gunman running into various stores as he sought to find the elusive figure he was chasing. The security guard called for him to stop and identify himself. In response, the gunman drew his gun and dropped the guard with a single shot. The gunfire touched off pandemonium in the mall. The gunman wasn't sure which way to go, but he wasn't giving up with the briefcase so near at hand.

Al was hiding in the Gap, using racks of clothing as cover but now he was getting anxious about Leslie. He said he'd get back to her in a few minutes and here he was crawling along behind racks of jeans. He had to make a break for it and get to those stairs to his left where he'd left Leslie.

He made his move and it proved to be just the wrong moment. As he ran out the left side door, the gunman caught sight of him 30 yards down the mall. He fired a round at Al, but the bullet missed, ricocheting off the hard stone floor, smashing into the window of Sharper Image. Instinctively, as he ran, Al used the briefcase as a shield behind his head. That maneuver was lifesaving as the next round struck the briefcase. It didn't pass all the way through, probably saving his life.

By then, mall security officers were arriving in force and the gunman was forced to flee for his own safety. He made it to a side door leading to the parking garage and managed to dissolve into the stream of people heading to their cars in haste. He kept an eye out for his partner and hoped he had made it to the car and would wait for him just outside the garage exit.

Errol Jensen was about to enter the mall when he saw people fleeing through several entrances. He immediately sensed what was taking place. He identified himself to the nearest security guard and was filled in on the essential facts. Someone with a gun was chasing a guy and had already shot and wounded one security guard. There was no mention of a girl and a briefcase. Errol assumed she was in the mall but not in immediate danger. Police arrived in large numbers and the mall was sealed off. The gunmen would now be preoccupied with their own escape, he thought, and not likely to continue their pursuit.

Leslie came running out of the crowd and rushed up to Errol. Panic was in her eyes, but she was unscathed. "Thank God you're here. Tell me this is over."

Finally, the police brought out a man with a briefcase.

Leslie screamed out his name and the police brought him over. Errol cleared up any confusion in their minds, and Al was released along with the briefcase. The three of them headed for Errol's car and a chance to calm down and restore their equilibrium.

The two gunmen slowly drove away in the confusion and were not stopped by the police.

CHAPTER SEVENTEEN

Leslie explained the briefcase's doomsday device. The bullet that had entered the case had set off the acid destruction of the tapes just as the President had explained to her. The President's attempt to reveal what had been going on for the past two months was all for naught. There would be no amazing revelation and no blockbuster story for Leslie.

Errol drove them to their car and told them to lay low until word got out that the briefcase and its contents were destroyed. That would comfort whoever had been making the big play to get hold of it. When Errol had explained the machinations of Ed Covington, they all agreed that Covington had tipped his hand by being so eager to get control of the tapes.

Al had to comfort Leslie as she went into a deep funk over the lost opportunity she'd had in her hand. Now they were back to speculating about events without a shred of hard evidence. It was beginning to look as if the story might never be told, even though most of the pieces in the puzzle fit so well together. Al tried to get Leslie to focus on their personal matters, but she was disconsolate. He understood how much the story meant to her, so he could see that she would have to grieve a bit before coming back to him with her buoyant attitude and optimistic view of their life together. He was patient and understanding. They would have to re-group and see if the story could be salvaged.

CHAPTER EIGHTEEN

Covington felt an enormous weight had been lifted off his back. The cover-up was intact and secure. Now Jack's illness could be revealed as a surprise to everyone, including him. It was sudden death in a man with a heart condition that Jack and Sidney had chosen to keep quiet until after the election. Doc Benson had personal knowledge about the condition, but he was bound by patient confidentiality not to reveal what Jack told him not to.

That left Jennifer. Sure, the President's wife knew he was ill. Yes, but she also went along with her husband's wishes.

In essence, there was a tightly-held secret about the President's health and the President and Sidney Curtis had orchestrated a careful re-election campaign to keep the secret and get Jack re-elected. Yes, it was dishonest with regard to the public, but there was nothing criminal about it. And besides, the two perpetrators were now gone. Ed liked the way this had played out.

Of course, the election would go on as scheduled and the Vice President would have a tough time convincing people he was "the man" with only three weeks left to campaign. He, however, was now the President and would be running for re-election even after a very brief few weeks in office.

Covington thought his chances were good in spite of the much-abridged campaign. He wasn't an unknown after all. Ed was still the trusted insider, and his ideas would carry a lot of weight.

The First Lady could be very helpful. The grieving widow out on the trail would ask the public to give the respected new candidate a chance to continue her husband's much-admired policies. He was sure Jennifer would be very winsome in a mostly black wardrobe. She might do it out of guilt or even just respect to Jack. In any event, she would be a campaign asset. After the election, she could quietly slide into her new and hardly visible life as ex-First Lady. She'd have no desire to bring up the old issue once ensconced in her new comfortable lifestyle. Maybe she'd even settle down with Howard Westlake.

Wouldn't that be a neat knot on the package, thought Ed. Howard had played his part to perfection. The old flame had agreed to see if Jennifer still carried any semblance of a torch for him. The meeting in Houston had come off better than he and Ed had hoped. She had taken the bait and it was only a matter of time before she swallowed it completely and allowed Berk to gather the images that would keep her under control while the cover-up played out. Sidney had never been let in on Ed's secret.

Westlake saw his career take off as the Washington station's network moved him out of Houston and up to Washington as promised. This had allowed him to pursue his re-ignited relationship with Jennifer. Westlake had been given the promotion in exchange for following a simple script. Ed was the silent majority shareholder in the network corporation. He and Howard had known each other since their days as predatory bachelors in the late 80's.

They had been squash buddies and even traded girlfriends.

When Howard had briefly dated Jennifer, Ed thought she would eventually be cut loose, allowing him to swoop in and scoop her up. When she and Howard did part company, however, she met Jack and soon thereafter they became engaged. She haunted him still.

The reporter had no hard evidence of anything. Somehow, she had pieced most of it together, but she never could come up with a smoking gun. In this case, Jennifer Henderson was the only serious loose end, and even she had no hard evidence of what had transpired. So, she was best left alone. For Ed, the book was closed, and things couldn't have worked out any better.

CHAPTER NINETEEN

The election was over, and the former Vice President had won a close race. Florida had been decisive. He'd been able to distance himself from the White House effort to conceal the President's illness. Covington had been invaluable in helping him steer that course and was now his closest confidant and the person guiding him through the early days of the transition.

Jennifer and Howard had resumed their relationship but were keeping a low profile as a couple while interest in the former First Lady remained high. Their public image was that of an old friend who was comforting the recent widow. Rumors of a romance were muted out of respect for Jennifer's still-fresh loss.

Leslie and Al were now set on a course toward making a commitment to each other. They were commuting every weekend to one or the other's home. Leslie was trying to put the big story behind her, but even as she denied any smoldering interest in it to Al, she inwardly harbored an intense desire to pursue it to completion. For the moment, however, all leads had dried up.

BOOK FOUR

TOWARD A CONCLUSION

CHAPTER ONE

C herry blossoms were only a few weeks away from bursting in Washington. Spring was in the air. In Tucson, this was a delightful time of year before the intense summer heat settled in. Ed Covington had returned home to catch up on a myriad of business matters. The meeting of his executive staff that morning indicated smooth sailing with the current administration. He'd stay in Tucson for a few days, then return to Washington to help the newly-elected President prepare the defense appropriation bill. That was what it was all about for Covington Industries, and he couldn't have positioned himself better.

That evening's date was a woman he had met the day before at the bar in his favorite restaurant. They'd struck up a casual conversation and seemed very compatible. She indicated she was an attorney for a firm in Baltimore and had come out to Tucson to negotiate the settlement of a contract dispute between two competitive mining companies in the region. Even in a business suit, she was striking. Her wedding ring was the come-on for him. Mid-forties, a rock climber and the pilot of a twin-engine plane, she was a very enticing package. There was no come-on signal, so when he invited her to his place for dinner and she accepted, he took that as an indication that she was confident she could take care of herself. He wouldn't have been surprised to learn that she was a black belt in karate.

Dinner was prepared by his cook, but he let the staff off for the evening and would serve the dinner himself. This was a common scenario, so the staff saw to it that everything he would need was readily available.

At nine o'clock sharp, Maureen rang his doorbell and he let her in. She was the same knockout he remembered from the bar, only now she was not in her business suit. Her long floral skirt and orange silk blouse were very Arizonian. After drinks in the living room, he served a flawless dinner of lobster tails with an assortment of local steamed vegetables. They brought their melon and sherbet desserts back into the living room and continued the wide-ranging conversation.

"That was a lovely dinner, Ed. I don't think I ever had better prepared lobster tails. You must tell your cook I said so."

"I certainly will. He'll be flattered even if he is accustomed to compliments."

Talk continued for another thirty minutes or so and then they found their way into his bedroom. He undressed and got into bed while she went into the bathroom. He turned the lights down and waited for her to emerge. He was beginning to feel quite aroused. The bathroom door opened, and she stood naked in the doorway for a moment to let him see what he was getting.

"Turn over onto your stomach, Ed. I have a surprise for you."

He rolled over in anticipation.

Before he knew what had happened, his arms were behind him and his wrists were tightly bound together. A noose leading from the bound wrists was placed around his neck.

This made struggling very uncomfortable since the noose tightened if he used his arms.

"What's going on, Maureen? If this is some form of sex game, it's not one I care to play."

"Ed, this is no game. So just shut up and listen to me. You have a disc I want, and I intend to get it from you. You're in no position to bargain. And don't try to buy me off. I'm only after the disc and any copies you may have made."

"Who sent you? You set me up very nicely, so whoever you're working for knows a bit about me. Tell me who's doing this?"

"Relax, Ed. You're not going to learn anything from me. Mmmm. Nice ass. I think we could have had fun." She ran her gloved index finger very slowly down between his buttocks and pressed briefly on his anal opening. She let him squirm a little to show him how uncomfortable it would be to try an escape maneuver. "Now, the disc. Tell me where it is, and I'll be out of here in no time."

"Okay. The safe is in the closet in this room. The wall is a sliding panel at the left end. Push on it on the right side at your eye level and it'll slide into the back wall. The combination is 15 34 32."

"Thanks, Ed. I'm glad you decided to be cooperative. This doesn't have to be unpleasant." She went to the closet, made the panel slide and easily opened the safe.

One disc was inside. She left several bundles of cash and a number of bearer bonds untouched, closed the safe, and slid the panel back into place. She returned to the bedside and stood naked in front of him. Under different circumstances, this could have been very seductive.

"Thanks for making that easy. This could have gotten messy. Now I'm going to release the noose around your neck. I have a knife in my purse."

For a moment, she was out of his field of vision. He anticipated the release of the noose and was trying to conjure a strategy to gain the upper hand. He felt the needle prick in his left buttock and was about to protest when she spoke from behind him.

"Don't worry, Ed, it's just a sedative to put you to sleep for a few hours while I take leave of you. It'll discourage you from taking any steps to intercept me. Now let me release that noose."

She cut the noose free from the bindings on his wrists.

He began to feel the effect of the injection and could barely roll over.

She returned to the bathroom, put on a wig, and removed her makeup. The transformation made her look 20 years older. A bland dress helped with the striking image change. She next released his bound hands. As she was about to leave, she hesitated and took out her cellphone.

A few good pictures would be extra insurance against any retaliation, even though that risk was very small. She positioned the sleeping form so that his male equipment, albeit limp, was plainly visible. For a last inspired shot, she turned him onto his stomach, put a condom on her index finger and shoved it into his anus. A picture with his face toward the camera was all she needed.

She exited the building, ignoring the surveillance cameras in the lobby. She was heading out of state in a car driven and owned by an elderly male companion. It was unlikely any pursuer would stop a couple in a nondescript car, especially after she disguised herself to look many years older. The cover over the license plate was removed once they were beyond the view of the surveillance cameras. The disc was placed in a FedEx drop box in a previously addressed mailer. This job was over. When Covington woke up and cleared the cobwebs, it would just be a bad dream.

Even though he could only think of one person who knew of the disc, there was no way to make a firm connection to that woman in Washington.

CHAPTER TWO

Al and Leslie sat in the kitchen, still in their robes, drinking their morning coffee. The bright morning sun poured in and gave the scene a pleasant glow.

"Al, I want you to humor me. Please. I want to go over the story once more. Sometimes things take on a different light after you've set it aside for a while. Just humor me. Okay?"

"Les, I'm not the skeptic I was when this whole mess began to unfold. I just felt we were in over our heads, and bodies were beginning to pile up around us. I didn't want to lose you in exchange for any newspaper story. So, I'm game. Let's give it one more go."

Leslie jumped up and went to her desk. She returned with a yellow pad and a pencil. "Okay, let's tally up the casualties. There's Jeff, Sidney Curtis, Steve Berk, Darryl Edmonds and Peg Carter. And, of course, the President. So, who's left? Jennifer Henderson and some other force. That's who. The last two left standing. So, who is the other force? I think Covington tipped his hand when he went after the briefcase so aggressively. I think he's the other force, and I believe he had plenty to gain by seeing Jack through to reelection. Jack was his best source of Washington influence. He couldn't do any better than the sitting President. I don't think that's much of a stretch."

"That's good deductive logic, Leslie, but we still don't know where the disc or discs resided as of last week. Maybe we should trace the discs and see where that leads us."

"Okay, Berk certainly had a disc or discs and was killed. No discs were found, so the killers must have taken them from his office. Only two players were in the disc hunt at that point, if you accept my theory about Covington. Jennifer knew there was at least one disc, because I told her when we met. Covington may have been aware of the disc from Sidney and may have heard about Berk's scuffle with me outside of his apartment. Let's just assume Covington knew there was a disc and that Berk had it. The disc was Berk's ticket to the morgue but who sent him there? Jennifer Henderson or Ed Covington?"

"Yeah, it's quite a story, Leslie, but we're no closer to seeing it in print if we can't nail down some proof. Your suspicion about Covington is a nice bit of logic, but there isn't a shred of proof linking him to any of this. I think we can write off the disc as either atmospheric pollution or landfill debris somewhere. I feel bad, Leslie, because I see this haunting us into our old age."

CHAPTER THREE

The chairman of the board of the network that owned the station Westlake now worked for had acceded to the requested promotion. He had never asked why the favor was being asked by the majority stockholder in the corporation. He did as requested, and that closed his book on the matter. Westlake had moved up to the station in Washington and proved more than competent.

Now, many months after the President's death, Howard and Jennifer were beginning to be seen together on the Washington social scene. She had no idea that her initial meeting with Howard in Houston had been a setup and had led to the threatening video. Howard was totally unaware of the recording. Jennifer watched the disc sent from Tucson. It confirmed that she now possessed the troublesome disc.

She promptly destroyed it. As a high school teenager, Jennifer Vincent, as she was known before her marriage, had been a very popular student. Cheerleader, beauty queen, class president and steady girlfriend of an all-state football running back, Jennifer had everything a girl could want. Those who were close to her, however, knew how competitive she was and that she had a dark side that she fought to keep under control. She was aware of her inclination to win at all costs. The race for class president had pitted Jennifer against her number one female rival in the class. A well-timed rumor questioning her rival's sexual preference was enough to tip the vote in Jennifer's favor.

In college, her major in communications brought her into frequent contact with the department head, a fiftyish professor with a wife and three children. Jennifer made herself very available and earned honors with late afternoon romps at an out-of-the-way motel several miles off-campus.

The professor's marriage was saved only by Jennifer's graduation and her move to a television station job very far away.

Her rise to prominent TV on-camera reporter was helped along by her willingness to do whatever it took at critical junctures to take the next step up. Success made her cocky. One of her mentors eventually convinced her that she had the "goods" and didn't need to trade sex for advancement. That took hold and indeed her career progressed with skill on-camera being rewarded rather than skill between the sheets. Then, along came Jack Henderson and a somewhat inebriated fling that turned out to be the real thing.

When she had learned that there was a threatening disc, she knew it had to be destroyed. She had taken an uncharacteristic risk and gambled that Covington had the disc out in Tucson or at least knew where it was. An acquaintance from her TV reporter days owed her big for a story Jennifer had uncovered, which had been sufficient to get a charge of aggravated assault against the woman dropped. Now Jennifer had called in the debt. The source was a very attractive call girl named Eve Burton and she was willing to plan a seduction leading to a robbery out in Tucson. Jennifer had no doubt that the woman was up to the challenge and could be trusted to leave no traceable footprints back to her. The plan was well conceived and came off without a hitch. The disc had been destroyed and her tormentor was no longer in a position to threaten her.

Now the road ahead looked clear and smooth. Life with Howard could proceed unimpeded.

Oh, yes, there was one loose end. The reporter. Could she be a problem? She'd sit on that for a while.

CHAPTER FOUR

An invitation to George Roux's mid-winter party was almost as difficult a ticket to obtain as one to the Kennedy Center Honors. His Georgetown home was classic Georgian style, built just before the colonies declared their independence. The furnishings were antique classics and the carpets from Turkey were priceless. George had earned his first fortune in the newspaper business and had grown it exponentially with aggressive moves in the cable television industry. Now he was a dollar-a-year-man as chairman of the board of the largest TV station in Washington.

Leslie was the guest of invitee Harry Goldstein, owner of the *Sentinel*. Harry and George were old friends who had traveled together on vacations until Harry's wife had become ill with ovarian cancer and died within a year of diagnosis. As her boss, Harry had asked Leslie to come along as his companion and she had been only too happy to oblige.

While Harry mingled with old cronies from the Washington newspaper elite, Leslie wandered about in the crowded quarters, carrying her vodka martini.

Howard Westlake and Jennifer Henderson were standing in a crowded study amidst a group of gossip columnists who flocked to them as the leading Washington celebrity pair akin to a twosome of Hollywood stars soon to announce something of modest significance. Leslie decided not to try to crack the outer rim of reporters and get within a few feet of the handsome couple. Instead, she gradually made her way to the dining room where George Roux himself talked with several political reporters about the recent election. The conversations were pretty standard stuff until they got around to how his network had covered the election.

George, as usual, was sincerely interested in the views of the press and public. "Well, I'd like to hear your take on our coverage. Even though I was openly a supporter of the vice-president, I hope we came across as objective."

A reporter snuck in a challenging question as George paused to sip his scotch. "How much input did you have with your programming people?"

"Not too much. Howard Westlake is a fine navigator in these waters and I trust his judgment implicitly."

"That raises another question, Mr. Roux. How did you select Westlake for his job as programming director? Many of us were surprised at the selection since he came out of left field. Mind you, I think he's doing a fine job. It's just that his selection caught us by surprise."

"Okay, I'm happy to let you in on how I work. There's no big mystery here. You know the network is a publicly held corporation. Well, the majority shareholder is an old business friend and he recommended Howard in the warmest terms possible. Since we were actively recruiting for the position, it was rather simple to interview Howard and select him when he turned out to be free of any warts that would rule him out. He was short on top-dog experience, but the recommendation made it clear that he could grow into the position rather rapidly and he proved to be a diamond in the rough. I think you'll agree that he has proven to be just that. Does that answer your question?"

Leslie's curiosity got the best of her and she blurted out a follow-up question. All eyes turned to her.

"Mr. Roux, who was the influential talent scout?"

"I don't see why that's important, but it needn't be a secret. Ed Covington was my contact. Ed is indeed the majority shareholder in the corporation. And now, I must get back to my other guests. Thank you all for your interest. Enjoy the evening and try those duck-filled ravioli. They're stupendous."

With that, the crowd parted and let him leave while the reporters started to search for those raviolis.

Leslie felt queasy. The old story was again nagging at her. Howard Westlake, the recent First Lady's principal squeeze, had been more than recommended for his job in Washington by her husband's close advisor, a man Leslie suspected of a major role in the cover-up. Coincidence? She needed some night air and stepped out on the patio just off the study.

Her head was spinning. The next day, Al would be flying up for a short weekend stay. He had hoped she'd put the story out of her mind, but now it had jumped up, front and center. Was she overreaching? Was this all innocent and disconnected? If not, how did it possibly connect?

Once again, she was back to imagining a connection and then setting out to see if there was any possible way to bring it to life. She had named this process "Pinocchio plotting" after the wooden puppet that became a real boy. It felt good to be back in the chase. Her instinct told her that something important had just come to light. Being there had been serendipitous, but that's how careers could be made in journalism.

CHAPTER FIVE

The drive to her apartment from Reagan International Airport was slow going in the late afternoon traffic, but Leslie's non-stop presentation to Al of the new information kept it from becoming boring. Her seven-year-old Honda Civic was showing its age, but Leslie couldn't afford to put it out of its misery. She continued to dwell on her new angle as she drove, so Al kept his eye on the road like a driving instructor but without the dual controls. Al was hearing this news about Westlake for the first time, so he asked questions as she went along.

They knew very little about Howard Westlake and even the standard sources told them little of interest. How he was connected to Ed Covington was a missing link they needed to fill in. Leslie's search of newspaper archives had turned up some routine stuff. She related this to Al once they got settled in her apartment and relaxed with a beer for each of them.

"In the 80's, he'd been a TV newsman in Washington with a pleasing on-camera presence. Next, he turned up in Houston doing programming and then came the big break that brought him back to Washington. Pretty ho-hum stuff as far as that went."

The big breakthrough came when Leslie contacted an old colleague of hers who was in the TV marketing game. He was a bit older and was more a contemporary of Westlake's. He had known Howard casually during that first D.C. period and offered some juicy material. First, he knew that Howard and Jennifer had been a hot twosome for nearly a year when she was a rising star doing evening news spots on TV. Second, among Howard's close friends was an out-of-town business man from Tucson who spent a lot of time in D.C. lobbying senators and congressmen. He was none other than Ed Covington. They were a pretty tight twosome until Howard hooked up with Jennifer. That put a damper on their Butch Cassidy and Sundance Kid routine. Then, abruptly, Jennifer and Howard split and in no time, she was hooked up with Jack Henderson and on her way to the White House. "And that's it," Leslie finished.

Al stretched out on the sofa in the small living area. Leslie was determined to keep him engaged and not let sleep overtake him. She needed his intuitive reading of the situation. She worked best when she had someone to bounce ideas off and Al was a great sounding board. The story line had her riding high.

"C'mon, Al, give me some reaction."

"Okay. Now we know that Jennifer and Howard had a romantic connection way in the past. What's more, Ed Covington was well aware of this. Then, years later, Jennifer, now the First Lady, has a brief affair with someone whose identity we do not know. This is brought about by her husband's incapacity. The brief affair ends up yielding a radioactive video. How fortuitous for Covington. That's his lever for keeping Jennifer from ever spilling the beans about her husband's illness. Everyone else who knows about the President's illness is eliminated."

"Al, that's great. Don't you see? The affair was with Westlake, her old boyfriend. It had to be him. So now the question is, how did his transfer figure into this? The affair wouldn't have happened unless he was in Washington and the man who wanted to get something on Jennifer had him sent there. You used the term 'fortuitous' but I'm thinking it wasn't. It was all part of a plan to entrap the frustrated Jennifer Henderson. Ed Covington used Howard Westlake to snare her. It was a gamble, but he had nothing to lose. It paid off."

"Leslie, I think you nailed it. And now the two of them are having a real romance that grew out of a deceitful plan that she's unaware of." Al continued, impatiently, "Now will you let me show you how to use a sofa for something other than a cat nap?"

"Not yet, Al. We need to come up with a way to get Jennifer Henderson to be our star witness. Westlake doesn't know enough to pull the house down."

Sitting up and trying to keep his mind alert, Al marched off to the refrigerator for a second beer in the hope that a brew in hand would allow him to at least look attentive.

"Look, Al, what do you think her reaction would be if I told her about her boyfriend's initial deceit and the role of Covington in the whole affair? Would that be enough to get her to throw in the towel and try to put the mess behind her? I guess it might still depend on where the video is."

"I'm just not sure, Leslie. Throwing a monkey wrench into their lives could just wind up destroying their relationship with no guarantee of a decisive outcome. I think there has to be a gentler way."

CHAPTER SIX

The local theatre group in Tucson was doing a series of plays by Sam Shepard, and that night's performance was a fundraiser sponsored by Ed Covington. He was trying to be the social dynamo most people in the area had come to expect at these events. His generosity to the community was legendary and tonight was typical of the way he contributed. Covington, however, had yet to recover from the indignity he'd experienced at the hands of the seductive thief. What had transpired had not been revealed to anyone, but his pride had been badly injured. Revenge was on his mind constantly. It darkened his mood even at the gala theater event. He couldn't stop obsessing. There was only one person to whom the video was so important, and that was Jennifer Henderson. There was no question in his mind that she had been behind the theft. Now the question was how to make her pay. Being bested by a woman was unthinkable to him, but the manner in which he'd been humbled was an affront to his manhood.

He knew most of the invited guests personally and tried to be lighthearted at the reception. It took a mighty effort to conceal the dark mood he was stewing in. The next morning, he would put together a plan to savagely avenge his bruised ego.

CHAPTER SEVEN

Howard Westlake had begun sleeping over at Jennifer's apartment in Georgetown. The press had gotten used to the twosome and was paying less and less attention to them.

Jennifer was trying to plan her future. A youngish, well-to-do widow with a very attractive persona, she envisioned herself back on camera but had yet to approach any station in the area. A network role was pecking away at her brain. She was living in the eye of a storm but was oblivious to the clouds around her.

Leslie Nugent was determined to get Jennifer Henderson to help complete the story of the cover-up. Covington had correctly targeted Jennifer as the person who had bested him. And Howard Westlake harbored a secret that could end his relationship with Jennifer. Those clouds could drop a lot of rain on the former First Lady's parade.

Leslie and Al agreed that she would go to Howard Westlake and get him to firm up her suspicion about Covington's role in Westlake's move, promotion and courtship of Jennifer Henderson. Threat of exposure might make him a good target for her and could then open the door to Jennifer. That was how she saw it playing out. She imagined Westlake confessing and then Jennifer wanting to bring down Covington after hearing about his role in Howard's reawakened involvement with her. It was worth a try. Otherwise, she might as well bury the story and that was not going to happen.

CHAPTER EIGHT

Howard and Jennifer were enjoying a quiet evening in her Georgetown brownstone. It was unusual for the two of them to be unscheduled on the same evening, so they were taking maximum advantage of the occasion. They'd ordered in a large assortment of dim sum from their favorite Chinese restaurant and now, with the dinner table cleared, were relaxing on the big sofa in the TV room, watching a Masterpiece Theatre production long ago saved on their digital recorder. They were lying on the sofa with some big pillows propping them up to watch the TV screen. Both were in their bedclothes under soft microfiber robes.

"You know, Jenn, we may actually make an inroad into our backlog of recordings tonight. Sometimes I wonder why I bother recording these programs, since we never have any time to watch them."

"Howard, we need to make an effort to have more relaxed evenings like this. And I don't mean so we can watch more TV. It just feels right."

Howard's cellphone ring was an unwelcome intrusion.

"Should I take it or let voice mail handle it?" was Howard's initial response.

"Oh, just take it. It's easier to answer the phone than let messages accumulate that have to be answered anyway."

"This is Howard Westlake. Who's calling?" Howard listened for a few moments with a growing intensity apparent on his face. Jennifer began to take an interest as she saw his reaction.

He broke the silence with a brief response. "Yes, I understand. I wish you were more explicit."

More silence.

"Okay. Tomorrow morning at 9:30. College Coffee House.

You'll be wearing a yellow windbreaker and black jeans." He replaced the receiver.

"A reporter wants to speak with me. She sounded a bit mysterious. Wouldn't tell me what it was about but did say I'd be interested."

"Did you get a name?"

"No. She said I'd learn all about her and why she wanted to talk to me when we meet tomorrow."

"So, you didn't even get the name of the rag she works for? No name, no employer, and no hint about the subject to be covered. You're not a very good newsman, Howard. A woman would have sleuthed it out better than that."

"Well, she wasn't giving out hints or any hard information. Only thing I know is that she is a 'she' and owns a yellow windbreaker and black jeans. I didn't draw a total blank."

"Nearest thing to one, Howard. Okay, give me a call after your meeting and let me know more, I mean something. Anything about the get-together."

"Okay. Okay. Expect a call."

CHAPTER NINE

The Coffee House crowd was beginning to thin out when Howard arrived. Leslie was not difficult to identify. She was seated at a small corner table with a white ceramic coffee mug in front of her. There were no other objects on the table and a thin leather briefcase was hanging off the back of her chair. She rose to greet him as he approached. She evidently recognized him. He couldn't say the same for her.

"Hi, I'm Leslie Nugent, I work for the *Sentinel*."

Leslie was disarming. Her good looks and friendly smile had helped her thaw many a cool reception. Howard Westlake was already thawed out by the time he settled into the chair opposite her.

"Okay, Ms. Nugent. You have my attention and my curiosity is aroused. Why on earth does a reporter from the *Sentinel* want to meet with the program director of a local TV station? And with a certain degree of cloak and dagger secrecy, I might add." Howard was trying to match her charm with a dose of his own.

"Well, Mr. Westlake, this is a bit complicated. I'm working on a very touchy story and can't tell you a lot about it. I do know a bit about you and have come to realize that you play a part in my story. As a consequence, I need to have you corroborate some details and help me flesh out an important portion of it. Why don't we leave it at that and let me tell you what I know and what I suspect?"

Howard's expression had taken on a serious cast. "Well, I guess you're going to have to do most of the talking to get this conversation rolling since I haven't the foggiest idea what it is you're talking about."

"No problem," was Leslie's quick response. She began laying it out. "I know you're currently quite close to Jennifer Henderson. I know you came to Washington to be the program director for a major local TV station a little less than a year ago. I also know you were close to Jennifer over ten years ago right here in Washington, just before she hooked up with Jack Henderson. Now for the information you won't find in *People* magazine. You were recommended for your position by Ed Covington, a major industrialist and confidant of Jack Henderson. He's also the principal shareholder of the company that owns your station, so his recommendation is more than a suggestion. Now, none of this is particularly interesting. What is interesting is this part. You first reconnected with Jennifer when she did a campaign swing through Texas. You then pursued her back in Washington. You agreed to do this at the urging of your old friend, fellow bachelor and skirt chaser, Ed Covington."

Leslie continued, "This was made especially attractive by a promised promotion to Program Director in Washington. You still found Jennifer very attractive, so that made it very easy to agree to Ed's proposal. Ed needed you to return to Washington to continue your pursuit of Jennifer. I'm betting he never told you why he wanted you to do it. The promise of the promotion was enough to stifle your curiosity. Once back in Washington you kept him informed about your progress with Jennifer. And that's it."

"That's quite a story, Ms. Nugent. The last part must be pure speculation. The part about Ed is pure fantasy."

Leslie was not deterred by his denial. "I didn't expect you to roll over and confirm everything. May I call you Howard?" He nodded assent. "Howard, you have no idea what a mess you stepped into when you let Ed steer you to Jennifer and back to Washington. It's better that you don't know. All I'm looking for is your corroboration of the link to Covington. If you find that hard to give, imagine Jennifer's reaction when I relate the same information to her. Look, I have no desire to damage your relationship with her. Even if that relationship was begun under false pretenses, it seems to have caught fire and evolved into the real thing. I have no need to disturb an honest relationship. I only want to define Ed Covington's role in a much bigger story and this piece involving you will begin to reel him in."

Westlake had begun to perspire as he tried to figure out what his next move should be. "Limit the damage," he kept telling himself. Break this off and buy time to think about what the hell was going on. There was an ominous tone in what this reporter was telling him. She seemed to know some background regarding his pursuit of Jennifer that he didn't know. That made him uneasy. On top of that, she was implying some larger story involving Ed and who knows where that led. Or if he was involved in that as well. He needed time to sort this all out.

Leslie could see his confusion and knew that this was a watershed moment that shouldn't be lost. She decided to let it all hang out.

"Howard, the President was sick when you met Jennifer in Texas. Ed knew all about it. He was determined to get through the election and that meant keeping a tight lid on the story of Jack's illness. Jennifer, of course, knew all about it and he had to find a way to keep her quiet. You were the solution. She was confused and lonely, married to a suddenly older man. She was easy prey for you and that provided some video material which served to keep her 'in line.' The rest of the cover-up needn't concern you, but it's a story that needs telling. If you'll corroborate what I've just spelled out for you, I'll leave Jennifer out of the tale and let you decide how to handle your relationship with her. I'm asking you as a news-woman to corroborate your role and Ed Covington's role in this portion of a far bigger story."

"Okay. I don't like having this part of my courtship of Jenn as a lurking secret that could destroy our relationship. I'll feel better disclosing it to her myself and working through the consequences. I think she'll han-dle it as I hope she will. So, there's your corroboration. Your surmise was right on target. It happened as you said, and Ed made it very easy for me to go along with his scheme."

"Thanks, Howard. I knew this would be difficult for you but your faith in Jennifer should let you carry this off with a minimum of personal fall-out for the two of you."

Leslie felt an enormous rush of excitement but didn't let it show. She now knew that the whole saga was just as she and Al had imagined it. The journalist's high: an exclusive of enormous public interest. She forced herself to keep Westlake as the focus of her attention.

He rose to leave, and she stood to shake his hand. She needed to give him some parting words of encouragement.

"I know this will be okay. You did the right thing by being truthful and that'll carry the day."

He threaded his way through the haphazard maze of mostly empty tables and chairs and left her standing where they'd shaken hands. She felt a fine tremor of excitement running through her and needed something other than coffee to calm her down. She'd set something in motion and now had to see if it played out as she hoped. Howard Westlake and Jen-nifer Henderson would anguish over what had transpired in the early days of their affair before Jennifer decided to end it. Then, Jennifer would fi-nally be willing to come clean and help take down Ed Covington. That would seal the deal for Leslie.

CHAPTER TEN

Westlake was not a very confident guy. Even when he and Ed were debauching a goodly number of women in D.C., it was Ed who did the creative hitting with Howard along as his sidekick to take care of any inconvenient female companion who threatened to derail Ed's plan of attack. Now Westlake felt the need once again to assume the role of loyal sidekick. He was unsure why he was giving Ed a "heads-up" regarding the reporter's suspicions. Maybe this would allow him to put some serious distance between them. His call to Arizona was answered on the second ring.

Covington maintained his composure, but internally his temper was boiling over. That reporter was now in his sights. She knew too much and wouldn't let go. When the President's taped confession was destroyed, he thought it was over. With Curtis, Berk, and the flying doctor out of the way, and the minor witnesses also eliminated, he should be home free. Jack's taped confession had been unexpected but was now in ashes. The video of Jennifer and Howard was of no value to Jennifer and could only prove to be an embarrassment for her. He assumed she had destroyed it.

Jennifer would have been of no concern if it weren't for the reporter digging in the past. The reporter was the loose end that needed tying. His vengeful focus on Jennifer was misguided. The reporter was the fly in the ointment.

He'd find her and scare her off. That would put an end to her nosing around and making the connections that he was working equally hard to bury. Another killing was the last resort. He didn't want to raise any suspicions on the part of her friends and colleagues who might have been taken into her confidence and knew bits and pieces of the story. He would have to threaten her in a very ominous way and seal her lips with fear. A more violent ending would be a last resort but was not entirely ruled out.

CHAPTER ELEVEN

Leslie's car was parked close to her apartment building, on a quiet, well-lit, tree-lined street. The neighborhood was considered safe, so patrol cars rarely came through. Returning home late from the office was not unusual for Leslie. She didn't like to bring work home, so she wrapped up her assignments in the office and headed home with some good take-out Thai food for dinner. As she parked, another car pulled just ahead of hers and let out a man on the passenger side. The car then proceeded to park further ahead. She thought nothing of it until the man stopped alongside her driver-side car door, swung it open and pushed her forcefully into the passenger seat. He replaced her behind the wheel. A second man got into the back of her car, put his hands on her shoulders, holding her in place, while the man in the driver's seat placed a blindfold over her eyes. The car, with its keyless ignition, started up and began to move out of the parking space back into the light traffic.

It all happened very fast and gave her no time to react. The two men were quiet and powerful. A heavy rope or sash was quickly used to bind her in the passenger seat.

Her arms were immobilized and held against her side. She knew that if she screamed, a gag would likely be inserted in her mouth. She tried to calm herself down. She was aware that she was sitting in a small pool of her own urine.

No words were exchanged, and the car moved along at a normal speed, attracting no attention. They rode on dark streets with little traffic and kept to the right side so as to avoid any prying eyes from taking an interest in Leslie's predicament.

The car eventually turned into an alley between two darkened commercial buildings and stopped. The driver spoke first. "You're being given a warning tonight, Ms. Nugent. Someone wants you to stop prying into a matter relating to the White House. That person says you know what that matter is, and you should drop it cold. Tonight, we're going to give you a taste of what's in store for you if don't take the warning serious. Untie her."

The rope was removed, and she moved her arms to restore good circulation. Before she could react, the driver lifted her legs, and the backseat passenger removed the headrest and lifted her under her arms. She was lofted up and tossed into the back seat. Again, before she could react, her arms were again pinned to her side by a heavy rope and she was placed on her back. The two men handled her with great ease. Any thought of battling her way to freedom was hopeless.

Her skirt was pushed up and her underpants removed. The driver raised her up and pivoted her onto the backseat passenger's lap, facing him. She had no doubt where this was going now. The feel of his erect penis between her legs left no doubt. She prayed that he was wearing a rubber. He entered her roughly and began to slide her up and down on his organ. He was large inside her and he could sense some degree of reflexive response on her part. He smiled faintly and continued to raise her and lower her slowly with his hands on her hips. After one or two minutes he grunted and completed an orgasm. She felt no flood of semen, so she took small comfort in believing he wore a rubber. Was it over?

The answer came quickly. She was pivoted around again and found the same penis up against her anal opening. She started to protest, but a hard slap across her mouth reminded her that they were in total control. She clenched her teeth and tried to retreat within herself to distance herself from the humiliation she had no choice but to endure. This time entry was more difficult and painful, but it was accomplished, and he again began rhythmically moving in and out. Spent from his earlier ejaculation, he didn't climax this time.

She was tossed aside, and the driver spoke once more. "I said that was just a taste. My friend was uncommonly delicate with you. If there's a next time, it won't be so easy. You've been given a message."

The heavy rope tie was removed but not the blindfold. The driver started up the car and said nothing more. The backseat passenger next to her just sat there. He had said nothing the entire trip. Being blindfolded left her unable to describe her assailants. The one who did the penetrations performed like a porn-star stud. He was hard without being stimulated and stayed hard through back-to-back assaults. The use of a rubber suggested normal concerns on his part.

The ride back to her building ended with one last warning. "We know where you live and will pay another call if that someone thinks you didn't get the message. It's my turn next time and I'm not as, what'd I say, 'delicate' as my friend here. You can get out now. We'll park your car nearby. Good night, Leslie."

She got out under her own power, removed the blindfold, and very unsteadily made her way up the stairs leading to her apartment building. Her hand was shaking as she fumbled to insert the key into the outside door. Her car was driven away.

CHAPTER TWELVE

L eslie was frightened. The threat was effective. She had no way to prevent another attack if she continued her investigation. She felt vulnerable, soiled and humiliated all at the same time. While she sat on the edge of her bed, her trembling had eased somewhat but was still evident. She felt helpless and wished Al was with her. She desperately wanted to talk to him, if only by telephone. But first, she needed to shower and change her clothes.

Al tried to console and comfort her over the phone. Her tears finally came in a flood and had a cathartic effect. She related all the details of the rape to him. Somehow, having someone to tell afforded her a degree of relief. Leslie was surprised at her ability to recover from the attack and focus on the situation as it existed before she was mauled by the two thugs. What kind of response was called for, given the recourse to violence that could be expected in return? She and Al were convinced that Covington was behind this latest episode.

Leslie had expected Al to try to convince her to give up on the story. To her surprise, he advised the opposite.

The story had to be told and Covington had to be brought down. Could they do it and weather the virulence of his response? Al said they should spend the weekend working on a solution.

"I'll be up there Friday on the usual 7:32 from Raleigh-Durham. Pick me up at the arrival exit for U.S. Air. I think I can get coverage through Tuesday, so we'll have a long weekend. We need to figure out where we're going with this never-ending nightmare of a story. There has to be closure."

Their usual reunion passion was subdued. Al could sense a change in Leslie's response to his gentle show of affection. He'd been very cautious in approaching her physically. It would take a while for her to really recover from her recent trauma. After dinner, the two of them brainstormed options. They were intent on finding a way to bring Covington to justice and get the story out. Al expressed what they both felt. "Just hitting back at Covington might feel good, but it won't get the story out. We need to get the goods on him and make him pay dearly for what he's been doing."

Leslie agreed. "Somehow we need to break into his local organization and get his contacts to spill the beans. Up until now that network has been off the radar because no one suspected there was such an organized network doing the bidding of a faraway mastermind. We're the only ones who can see what's happening. So far, he's been able to have each killing explained by some unconnected set of circumstances. I bet the people he uses don't even know they're being used in such a coordinated manner. It's difficult to see the big picture when you're only playing a role incident by incident. The police haven't even connected the shootings in the mall to anything more sinister. Maybe it's time for us to bring them in on the larger picture and see if they can offer any assistance along the lines we're thinking. Chief McKenna seemed like a reasonable guy. I'd be willing to try him out on our approach. I'd like to bring Errol Jensen along to give us some credibility. What do you think?"

"Leslie, we'll never know if we don't try. We're at a loss anyway, so there's nothing to lose. Maybe we can spark some enthusiasm in McKenna and have the police ferret out the network Covington has been using. Then we'll need to find the leverage that will allow us to confirm the connection we've known about but have been unable to prove."

"I'm game. My story is important, but the rape has raised the stakes far beyond any story's importance. I need to get even. And just one more thing. Why was I attacked now? It can only mean that Howard Westlake spilled the beans to his pal in Arizona. That's another piece of unfinished business. Westlake is the one who indirectly put the finger on me."

CHAPTER THIRTEEN

Chief McKenna and Errol Jensen met with Leslie and Al at police headquarters. The Chief did not make light of Leslie's concerns.

The story she told was cogent and was happening on his watch, so he felt responsible for not recognizing the connection between the seemingly unconnected events.

Jensen felt a need to contribute more than he had to date. Like McKenna, he felt a portion of the scenario had happened on his watch, and he had let it slide. He spoke up. "All these deaths, the mall episode, and now the rape may involve a large number of thugs. That suggests an organization which may be the link we need to get to the 'mastermind.' Chief, we need some snitches out in the field to come up with some loose organization that exists right here under our noses. The organization carries out the crimes, but the person calling the shots is the object of our interest. If we can get to the local connection, we may get to the person responsible for this incredible cover-up and its attendant crimes of murder and rape."

McKenna was responsive, "Since we have a number of potential links back to an organization, we will assemble any pictures we can get of the people involved and try to get witnesses to come forward with any info related to any of the characters. Sometimes a connection isn't apparent until there's a context to fit it into. We have a big context, and we're looking for people to fill it up. There were two guys at the mall, two guys who attacked Leslie, two guys who managed security at the hospital, one guy who did away with Sidney Curtis, X number of guys involved in Berk's death, and X number of guys involved in the murder of Peg Carter and Darryl Edmunds. Some of these guys may have done double duty. We need pictures from security cameras and descriptions from anyone who saw any of these guys close up. We'll get on this."

Al didn't want to see false hopes raised and offered his overview. "I'm not suggesting we take a different tack, but I don't think there's much new information to be dredged up at this late date. Aside from surveillance tapes being erased, these crimes were probably not witnessed. We're going to need fresh leads and frankly, I'm at loss to suggest any."

The mood in the room reflected Al's despairing summation.

CHAPTER FOURTEEN

Howard Westlake struggled to find the right words to begin his confession to Jennifer. He believed their relationship was strong enough to handle the truth and so that was what he was going to deliver. After dinner and with a drink in hand, he began to unload his tale and emphasize his innocence in any scheme, other than the one to garner a promotion he had found irresistible. He realized his story made him out to be a gullible, guileless person who had been manipulated by Ed for some more devious purpose. There wasn't any other way to describe his role in the affair.

He realized that Jennifer was more deeply involved in the matter concerning her husband and Ed Covington, but he had little insight into the intricacies of that complex affair. His only aim was to unload the burden of guilt he had carried for so long and to preserve his close relationship with Jennifer.

Self-analysis had never been his long suit. Howard could easily recognize his guilt, but deeper reflection unearthed a more fundamental issue.

"Jenn, I'm only now just waking up. Ed owned me all along. I've never been my own man. My role in partnership with Ed as single guys on the loose always served Ed's needs. I was left to play second fiddle."

"Howard, that's long behind you. You're a different guy now. It's been very important for us to get this all out. Secrets between us only are divisive. I'm glad you were able to face up to your role in this tortured story."

Howard couldn't let it go.

"Jenn, I've been an unwitting pawn in setting this state of affairs in motion. A pawn was what I've been. And an emasculated one at that. Somehow, I'm going to make up for the mess I've helped create. I have to."

When he finished telling everything he knew and answering Jennifer's questions, he felt enormous relief. The reporter had been right. It was the best course of action. Now it was up to her to absolve him of any guilt and put this behind them. He only wanted them to go forward without doubts regarding their relationship. Her response gave him the assurance he was seeking.

"I love you, Howard, and that's what matters most. I regret not having leveled with you about all that I know about the effort to conceal Jack's problem. I don't know everything, but what I do know tells me Ed is the likely mastermind behind the strategy. He used us both, Howard, and now you have to sever any ties you may have maintained with him. He's dangerous."

Howard had been unaware of her deep-rooted hatred of Ed and her determination to see Ed pay the price for all the damage he had done. Although she had no hard evidence of Ed's role in any of the deaths surrounding the cover-up, she was as convinced as the *Sentinel* reporter that he had been the force behind the cover-up.

"Jenn, where is that video that shows us being intimate before Jack was out of the picture? If it's in Ed's possession, it's still a threat to us."

"Howard, I'll share a secret with you that I never wanted to let out. Ed had the video and it was a potential threat to me, to us. I arranged to retrieve it and was successful. The tape is destroyed. Ed doesn't know I was the person who arranged to take it from him, but I think he'll pin that on me, since he himself told me of its existence, and I had a very good reason to want it destroyed. Knowing Ed, he's stewing over that and needs to have some measure of revenge. Being bested by a woman won't sit well with him."

CHAPTER FIFTEEN

There was not a sound in the apartment. Al and Leslie were sitting in her living room, but each was deeply immersed in thought about how to get to Covington and bring him down.

"You know, Leslie, I don't think we're going to get this resolved through the police. I appreciate their interest and determination, but I just don't see it nailing Covington."

"Do you have a better idea? Because I'm all out of ideas and beginning to consider giving up."

"I do have one idea, but it's dangerous and not one we can control."

Leslie turned, facing him directly, and asked the right questions. "You said it was dangerous. For whom? Why?"

Al stared at Leslie and shook his head. "The answers are 'for you' and 'because you're in his cross-hairs.'"

"I don't like the direction where this is heading, but I want to hear you out, Al. Let's have it. There's no need to sugarcoat it."

"Okay. The one piece of potentially useful information is the threat those two messenger boys delivered to you in your car. They indicated that they would be back if you pursued the story. I assume their orders originated with Covington and were passed down to them through his network. So, we, or rather you, can probably lure them back with further snooping. Then we nab them and begin to backtrack up the chain of command. Only problem is that you become human bait and we can't be assured that we'll intercept them in time to avoid them making good on their threat. I think that plan is viable, but I reject it because it puts you at risk and it's a risk we can't control with any certainty. We don't even know what it is we're preventing."

Leslie was silent. Al didn't know how she had taken it. The very fact that he had aired such a scheme could give her reason to question how much he actually cared for her. He probably should have kept his mouth shut.

Nevertheless, knowing how much this story and her revenge meant to Leslie, he felt he owed it to her to put it out there.

Her response took him by surprise. She had no reservation and wanted to plan a provocative move that would force Covington's hand.

"Are you sure you want to pursue this highly dangerous path? I don't like it. We'd have to get McKenna to buy into the plan and provide the necessary surveillance. He might even find it too risky to proceed."

CHAPTER SIXTEEN

Surprisingly, the police chief came on board after hearing a brief summary of the proposed scheme. He would provide round-the-clock surveillance once the trap was baited. Leslie, Al, and Chief McKenna discussed the plan in a protected room that was swept daily for listening devices. Leslie would meet with Jennifer Henderson to discuss her reporter's views on the still unconnected deaths which she believed were all related to the late President's illness.

This time, Jennifer Henderson welcomed the *Sentinel* reporter. Her cool facade from the previous visit was totally removed. Jennifer was only too glad to have a person to talk with who was quite knowledgeable in the matter of the White House cover-up.

The two women quickly got down to the obvious intersection in their lives. Leslie related the observations she'd made during those last minutes of the President's life and Jennifer filled her in on what life was like for a widowed former First Lady. They were each waiting to hear what the other had to offer in the way of new developments. Leslie jumped in first and indicated that someone had given her a very threatening warning to "lay off" her pursuit of the cover-up of the President's illness. She didn't know how much Westlake had shared with Jennifer, so she went ahead and told her what she'd told him in the restaurant. Jennifer then related that the story he'd told was indeed the one Leslie had just related. Her anger was directed at Ed and not Howard. Ed was the force behind the scheme, and Howard had been drawn along by the current. He wasn't totally innocent, but his role in the bigger plot was just peripheral.

Leslie didn't know how much further to push, so she began a subtle withdrawal. Jennifer showed her wily sense of the moment and didn't let Leslie leave it at that.

"Why are you here, Leslie? I haven't offered you any new information and you haven't asked me any challenging questions. What am I missing here? You're sticking your neck out for nothing. You said you were warned and yet you're persisting at what put you in jeopardy."

"Okay. Okay. I'm here for a reason. I'm trying to bait the hook for Ed, so we can nab a few of the gorillas who were sent to do his dirty work. We haven't been able to identify anyone in the chain reaching back to Tucson. This is an attempt to do just that. We assumed news of my visit here would get back to him and force some action on his part, which might allow us to trap an ape who can help us begin to trace the connections back to the source."

"That's more than a bit risky, Leslie. Ed is no fool and may even see through your ploy. In that event, he might pull some other stunt to get you off his tail. He's clever and evil, so don't ever underestimate him."

"I don't, and I won't. This story is too big to set aside and right now, Covington is the thread that holds it together. I'm not even looking for justice. I just want to tell the story. Then the chips can fall where they may. I still think that breaking into his network and backtracking to him might work. I doubt that he'll admit anything until it's too late for him to get out of this mess without facing major criminal charges. I'm game to put myself at risk and give it a try."

"So be it, Leslie. I wish you luck and will start the ball rolling. I think Howard understands that being a dupe for Ed is not in Howard's interest, so he will probably not keep Ed up to date on your visit. On the other hand, I'll call Ed and let him know that I am aware of his role in bringing Howard back into my life and that he is a very unsavory and undesirable cupid. I'll tell him that a young reporter is my source."

CHAPTER SEVENTEEN

The surveillance on Leslie was comforting even if it was unapparent. The arrangement was that Mckenna would set it up and Leslie would not know anything about it. That was thought to be the best way to keep the surveillance as concealed at possible. She would not know the men or women watching over her. Leslie was given an alarm device that alerted her protectors in the event of any action against her. She was to go about her normal routine and hope the bait would be taken.

It didn't take long for the trap to be sprung. Walking home from her Metro stop one evening, Leslie was shot twice from a slow passing car. The first shot hit her in the shoulder and the second barely missed her head. The shoulder hit was enough to cause her to lose her balance and fall to the sidewalk. The pain would have been considerable if her fear hadn't dulled it. The car continued to drive to the corner, accelerated and turned down the cross street.

Its license plate was covered with a cloth, and the two men inside wore masks. The surveillance detectives fired several shots at the car to no avail. They quickly got to Leslie and were able to control the bleeding from her shoulder wound with firm pressure. They called an ambulance, and it arrived in less than five minutes.

McKenna was distraught. Al was seething inside but strangely silent. They hadn't thought it would turn out like this. Neither of them believed that the reaction to Leslie's continued snooping would be a brazen drive-by attempted killing. They had underestimated the danger inherent in their hastily constructed scheme.

Al realized how close to tragedy his plan had brought Leslie.

McKenna mobilized his forces to look for the car and ordered them to report any abandoned vehicles and recently stolen cars. It was a long shot, but it was all they had. They had to get lucky.

CHAPTER EIGHTEEN

The car was found abandoned. It had been stolen the day before the shooting. The owner had reported the car missing but could not offer any useful information.

Thorough questioning in the neighborhood where it had been stolen did reveal that some kids had been hanging around the car, although they hadn't been seen doing anything more than that. The police now had a lead, albeit a slight one. The Chief was determined to solve this crime. He felt responsible and it weighed heavily on him.

With the full force of the D.C. police in action, it didn't take long to round up and question many of the neighborhood youths. The net had been cast widely and the police who knew the area and its people best had done much of the screening of possible car thieves. Three youths were plucked out of the crowd and given immunity in exchange for the name of their contact.

Al and Chief McKenna were in daily contact. Al was amazed by how the police had worked from so little to begin building a case. He was anxious to see each step move closer to that day of reckoning Leslie had so desperately sought. He was beginning to formulate his own plan of action.

The contact man for the three youths was a "chop shop" operator with a record of only minor offenses. The cops squeezed, and the contact person yielded up a restaurant owner with no record of convictions. He admitted getting a call from an unidentified source who had contacted him in the past to procure equipment or recruit men for undefined assignments. What the equipment or men were used for was never specified to this man. A man would eventually arrive, make a cash payment and commandeer the equipment and leave. The procurer never knew the stranger and didn't ask any questions. The trail went cold at this point.

No matter how hard the police pressured the people they had caught in their net, they couldn't establish any leads to follow. Whoever was running this operation was clever and kept the involved parties from learning about the next phase. The final perpetrators were unknown to the local snitches who knew everyone in the D.C. area involved in shady dealings. Chief McKenna was as frustrated as Al.

They were being outfoxed by their quarry.

CHAPTER NINETEEN

A window seat on the way back to North Carolina allowed Al to get lost in the rising storm clouds and slip into a deeply introspective mood. What happened to that adventuresome young man who had taken lives and risked his own back in Africa? He'd evolved into a careful, unexceptional, standard-model physician. Even with Leslie and the complex mystery they were trying to unravel, he assumed a passive role and let her take the lead. What began with the loss of his friend and partner was an opportunity to revisit his former self and exercise some of the daring that had excited him years ago. Why had he retreated? Leslie needed more from him.

The ride became bumpy as the clouds turned dark and occasional lightning flashes appeared. For the moment, he was back to reality and put his reflections on hold.

The pilot steered away from the unstable air and a calmer flight resumed. Al finally was coming to grip with his split personality. The bolder self needed to assert itself, not just for Leslie, but for himself as well.

For too long, he'd denied that side of himself and had felt incomplete.

Al was now left with his own plan, and that would not involve the police. It was a straightforward matter of revenge. He would have to proceed against Covington without the benefit of absolute certainty of his guilt. He reasoned that eliminating evil called for extreme measures and he would have to be the instrument to settle the score.

He had seen numerous instances of cruelty and evil during his assignments in Africa. Extreme sanctions were not uncommon. He had participated in several, and on one occasion, he had been both judge and executioner. He had not felt any regret for his actions. He was now going to return to that role.

Al's plan was to do unto Ed what Ed had done to Leslie. He would warn him to cease and desist in his threatening actions. The warning would come with a very credible threat to do personal damage to him. It would be necessary first to convince Ed that he was vulnerable and second, that the threat could and would be carried out. Al's resolve was unshakable.

His research revealed that Ed lived in Tucson, Arizona. That's where he would feel most secure, so that was where the deed would be done. Since there was no evidence linking Ed to the attempt on Leslie's life, the police would have no reason to ascribe a revenge motive to Al. Ironically, Ed's carefully constructed wall of secrecy would make it that much easier for Al to carry out the plan and not become a suspect.

The big challenge would be to carry it out and get away without leaving any tracks.

As he worked through the crucial details, he realized that this scenario would still leave the story untold.

First things first, though. Covington had to be neutralized, so that he realized any further violence against Leslie would rebound to him with unacceptable consequences. Killing him was a poor option, since he still was the only person who could account for all the murders and might someday be made to confess. Leslie's story was still out there waiting for her to tell. For now, Covington's violence had to end. The story would come later.

CHAPTER TWENTY

In the last few days, Al had been very much out of character. Until now, he'd let Leslie run the show, and he came along as her trusty sidekick.

The most recent events had given him an exhilarating sense of involvement. He was on a high and wasn't going to return to his former life until he considered this adventure completed. That meant having the cover-up brought out into the open. Mostly this was for Leslie, but it was also for his satisfaction. He wanted this and needed it.

Reading the morning paper had given him an idea he needed to explore before making the move on Covington. The National Security Administration, NSA, believed all that telephone data they harvested could potentially lead to terrorist groups, as they sifted through it and discovered patterns, which grew into leads. So why not see if there was a pattern in the data which could lead to Covington's connection in the Washington area? Now, how the hell could he get to mine this ultra-secret database? He not only lacked access, he also lacked the skill, even if he was allowed in. He decided to pore through his list of former CIA contacts to see if one or more had migrated to NSA.

Now, the work began. He assembled a list of former CIA colleagues from memory. He could recall about 10-20 whose last names he could recollect and spell. Next, using the DC phone directory, he added phone numbers to the list. Using the Internet, he searched out those whose numbers were not in either source.

He started calling. Not surprisingly, all were surprised to hear from him.

He ended up with six lunch dates but no NSA contacts. Those he could contact were able to fill in his list of missing contact numbers. So, on he labored. Near the end of his call list, he finally made a score.

Andy Silverstone had been a close friend when both were in Africa and he had returned to the States to take a mid-level management job with the CIA. After ten years, he had moved over to the NSA and was now involved with data storage and analysis. He could be the ideal contact person if he was willing to do some sleuthing for a friend. The "if" was a big one. They made a dinner date for the following night.

Andy chose a restaurant in a suburban area in northwest Washington. It was quiet on a mid-weeknight so they could select a table that afforded privacy. The restaurant offered an eclectic menu in an Art Deco setting. It had been operating at the same location for decades yet was not well-known among government workers. It was a good choice for a very private dinner.

"Three kids and the original wife. Sounds more than respectable, Andy."

"I know. It's a long way from central Africa and those messy operations we ran. I'm sorry we lost contact after returning to the States. I do know you became a doctor and a cardiologist to boot."

"Yeah, I went conventional, much as you did. Just never tied the knot, so I'm an outlier where my social life is concerned. I do have a serious gal now, so I may fix up that portion of my resume."

"I was surprised to hear from you after all these years. I assumed you weren't calling because you wanted company for dinner. Give me the pitch, Al."

"You're right, Andy. I'm hoping you'll be intrigued enough to bend some rules and help me put the finishing touch on a very important high-level criminal cover-up. I think it will be best if I keep names out of it for your sake. You're going to have to trust me. I hope you feel you can."

"Let me hear what you've got. Then we can talk about rules, trust, and what I can and cannot do, even if I want to."

"Okay. That's fair. I'm out of my league here chasing down a serious crime, but I think I have a good sense of what it's about. Here's the thumbnail sketch. A high-level official has sustained a serious illness but wants to keep it secret for a while. The process of keeping that secret has resulted in a number of deaths, at least five. The plotting has been extremely clever and directed from a remote location with very few tracks to follow. The story is missing the connection to a local source that carries the dirty work. That's where you come in.

"It occurred to me that there must be a pattern of telephone calls between the mastermind and his minions in the Washington area. If I can trace the calls to some source here, I think I can break down the wall of silence surrounding the local operatives and tie the crimes back to the remote source. I know dates that can be used to limit the actual search effort. I also know the point of origin for the calls that trigger the actions. Are you with me so far?"

"You're offering me an opportunity to throw away my career. Let's pretend this conversation never happened and go our separate ways for another few decades."

"Andy, I understand. Believe me. But I wouldn't be here if I didn't think the stakes were high enough to justify some risk. For the NSA, this could be a major breakthrough. It could demonstrate how all that data the senators are sneering at could actually do some serious crime solving and by inference, detect a terrorist plot."

"Al, you're asking a lot of me. Could I try it out on my boss so I'm not some rogue operative?"

"I guess so. Think of it as a real-life criminal puzzle, which demonstrates the power of the massive database. This is very real high-level criminal activity, which should be brought out into the open. Trust me. The crime is a blockbuster."

"Okay. Okay. Let me talk to my boss. I'll get back to you."

CHAPTER TWENTY-ONE

A phone call from Andy Silverstone set up the next meeting. Andy chose another restaurant far off the beaten path for Washington folk. They chose a late hour to assure anonymity.

Andy was noncommittal at first, but Al could see he was interested and in all likelihood was leaning toward a go- ahead.

"My boss surprised me. He didn't throw me out. Kidding aside, he's interested, but is concerned that it might be too high-level for our organization at this time. He's afraid of any more criticism from Capitol Hill."

"Well, that's a tough one. I'll give you a bit more information, but it can go no further than this restaurant. President Henderson was seriously ill for months before the election. Keeping that secret was the basis for the crimes I mentioned. I don't know if any government figure was involved in the cover-up, but a person of considerable influence was the key operative. I can't say any more. I don't think the facts will embarrass anyone other than the guilty party."

"My boss is a good soul. I think we can proceed on that assurance. Give me a list of dates and locations. I'll see if our logic tree makes any useful connection. It looks for patterns and may find more patterns than you'll find useful."

"Okay. You're on. I've been carrying around that stuff since our first meeting. I had a hunch you'd come around. Here's all the information you'll need."

"Fine, now let's eat and get reacquainted."

It didn't take long. Armed with dates and locations, the algorithms of the search were able to play the odds and find a likely pairing of numbers, which fit the hypothesis. Someone in Tucson called someone in the Washington D.C. area only on the dates given. The Washington-area call recipient was easily identified. The Tucson calls to the Washington, D.C. area originated from a number that could not be traced.

Al was ecstatic. Finally, a breakthrough. Now there was someone to track down. The algorithm further searched out a calling pair from the local party to another local party after the call from Tucson, on the same dates. A chain was being uncovered. That second party was also identified. Jules Anthony was the first party and Miles Brogard was the next in line. Another pairing picked up calls from the White House to the Tucson number.

Al congratulated Andy. "This is stunning. What a tool! I hope we can use this information to close out this investigation. You might have a very big success on your hands to fend off your critics in Congress."

"I hope so, Al. I did a big sell job on my boss to get his agreement to go ahead. I could use the justification."

"As soon as there is any tangible progress, you'll be the first to know. Again, though, Andy, many, many thanks."

CHAPTER TWENTY-TWO

Chief McKenna was equally impressed. They finally had some leads. Al told him as little as possible about the method used to uncover the names and McKenna was wise enough not to press him on this subject. Al had done his homework and had some interesting information about the two suspects.

Jules Anthony was a car dealer with two dealerships in the D.C. area. Before getting into the car business, he was an investor in casinos in Atlantic City where he had made the money to buy into the dealerships. He had no criminal record but had been investigated by the FBI in connection with drug trafficking in Atlantic City.

Miles Brogard was a low-profile businessman with no arrests, but he too had been investigated in regard to drug trafficking. These two were possibly connected, making the phone calls that much more enticing.

317

Mckenna was excited. The tracks were leading somewhere at last. "I think we've struck gold. Problem is that if we approach these suspects, word may work its way back to Tucson and alert our quarry that his fire-wall has been breached. It's hard to tell how he'd react. Based on past history, these two guys would be in danger."

"I agree," said Al, "so maybe we don't use the police to make the initial foray. Let me take the lead and see if I can get enough information to justify putting one or both of them in protective custody while we nail down some hard evidence."

"This isn't your place, Al. It's dangerous work and should be car-ried out by someone with experience in this kind of activity. I'd like to send an undercover cop out to do this assignment. You can brief the per-son about the mission and stay on top of the play."

"I can't argue with you, Chief. But I have been so close to this operation that it's hard to step back any distance. I also think these guys might stonewall whoever you send in, and then we've tipped our hand and gotten nothing in return. I could be a bit more forceful and not be bound by your rules. In any event, I found these guys and think I deserve a chance to question them in my own way."

McKenna reluctantly relented. "This whole operation has been a bit out of control, so I'm willing to give you some leeway here and let you have the first shot at these guys. Remember, we don't have any proof ei-ther of them is involved or what role they played, so don't pull out all the stops. I want to be able to explain our actions without the need for a lot of apologies."

"I read you, Chief. I'm not looking to foul up this lead, I just want to see if I can move us forward from this point."

Al explained all to Leslie and she could sense how he had taken charge of this phase of the story. He was now a man possessed, and she could see the futility of any attempt to dissuade him from going forward with his plan of action. In a way, she was glad. Her shoulder wound was healing nicely and suddenly the prospect of getting her story out in the open was looking brighter than ever.

Al's colleagues back in North Carolina had agreed to cover his practice indefinitely while he finished up a personal matter that had begun back when his close friend and partner was killed in the plane crash.

His plan was to go after Miles Brogard, since he seemed to be further down the chain of command. As he saw it, Covington would contact Jules Anthony, who would then contact Brogard to actually put together a specific plan of action. The plan was usually to eliminate someone Covington had decided was too much of a liability. Anthony's involvement kept Covington far removed from the action people. Brogard and his crew would never be contacted by Covington nor hear his name. This was Al's surmise.

Miles Brogard owned and operated several retail food stores, which catered to a high-end clientele in the Washington area. Tailing him from his home for several days, Al assumed the store in D.C. was probably his office site since he never seemed to visit any of the other stores.

Nothing about his business said, "murder for hire." Al decided to watch him at his presumed office to see if any contacts showed up who might suggest underworld connections. McKenna had paired him with detective Marco Ray to identify people known to the Department as potential "bad actors."

After three days of surveillance out in a car, the duo was bored with a diet of pizza, hero sandwiches, and tall sodas along with an endless drone of indecipherable lyrics on rock radio stations. Al's impatience was taking over.

He was beginning to think that force and threats were necessary to crack Covington's well-constructed wall of secrecy. He wasn't sure exactly how this would work with Brogard, but he had to give it a try.

He would go to Brogard's office armed and carrying a recorder. He was prepared to inflict damage on the suspect, if that offered the prospect of useful information. Al was surprised at his own willingness to engage in a violent interrogation, if it came to that. He was determined to make the most of this opportunity. Detective Ray agreed to stay in the car and be as uninformed as possible about Al's proposed approach.

The store closed at 6 pm, so Al entered at a bit before six and asked to see Mr. Brogard. He was directed to the rear of the store and the last employee began to close up.

Brogard's office door was open, so he walked in without knocking. The office was small, neat, and could have been the office of any retail merchant in the rear of his modest establishment.

Brogard was surprised and started to get up. "Excuse me. This is my private office. You'll have to make an appointment and come back during regular business hours."

"I'm here to talk to you now, Mr. Brogard, and not about your regular business."

Brogard was an undistinguished looking man about 50 with a full head of gray hair and a tired expression on his face. He was about 5' 9", somewhat overweight and dressed in corduroy pants and a blue denim shirt open at the neck. Papers on his desk had the look of invoices and bills.

"Talk about what? I don't think I know you."

"I'll explain myself to you. And don't worry, I'm not here to rob the store."

Brogard sank back into his well-worn desk chair with a puzzled look on his face, which conveyed a sense of unease.

Al sat down in a nearby side chair. "Let me get right to the point, Miles. Is it alright if I call you Miles?"

"Why not? And what will I call you?"

"Carson, will do. Just Carson."

Al's gun was within easy reach, and Miles had no gun on his person that Al could see. If one was in his desk, he would come in a poor second should they end up going for weapons. The recorder was running in Al's jacket pocket.

"Your office phone was called by a phone belonging to Jules Anthony on several days which have special meaning to me. I want to know the circumstances surrounding those calls and what action followed on your part."

Al stopped to let the nature of his visit sink in.

Miles's response was the expected expression of total surprise and denial of any knowledge regarding the inquiry. Al was prepared and intensified his request. "The calls are a matter of fact. What they initiated is what I want to know. I said the dates had special meaning and I meant it. I'm not going to leave here empty-handed. I want that information and I'm willing to push very hard to get it. Don't think stonewalling will protect you." He paused.

"I wish I knew what you're talking about. I'm drawing a complete blank. I don't know a Jules Anthony. You must have me confused with someone else."

"Okay. I guess I haven't made my determination clear enough to you."

Al drew his gun and pointed it at Miles. He walked around the desk and drew a rope from his pocket, which he used to tie Miles into his chair and tie his right wrist to an arm of his chair.

"I warned you not to stonewall me. You're forcing me to go beyond simple questioning."

Al held Miles left hand on the desk, palm down and prepared to deliver a crushing blow to the fingers with the butt of his gun.

"Wait. Wait. Maybe I do recall a Jules Anthony."

Al held the gun in his hand above his head, poised to strike. "Do you, or don't you? Don't fuck with me."

"Okay, okay. I do know him."

"You nearly had a very painful and disabling injury. Now tell me what he told you over the phone."

"Names. He just gave me the names of people I didn't know."

"And?"

"When he gave me a name, he told me what I was to arrange for that person."

"Sidney Curtis. What was the instruction, Miles? And listen closely. I'm not a cop. I'm not after you. I'm after the guy who set the actions in motion. Now, what was ordered on Sidney Curtis?"

"He was to be eliminated, and it had to look like a mugging gone bad."

"And what did you receive for that act?"

"Fifty grand to cover the perp and any other expenses. The balance was mine to keep."

"That's good, Miles. Now I'm going to give you some more names and I want you to tell me what was ordered for each of them. Straight and simple like you just did for Sidney Curtis."

After 20 minutes, the list was completely filled out. The rape of Leslie was included. The only event not included was the death of Jeff Oldham, the very event that started the cascade.

"Okay, Miles, we're through. I'm going to release you with a warning. It won't be in your best interest to pursue me. Just let it rest. Just let it rest. Do you understand?"

"Yeah, I do."

Al untied him and left quickly. Marco Roy picked him up around the corner after seeing him exit.

CHAPTER TWENTY-THREE

Al and Leslie were thrilled to learn that they had been on target all along. Brogard's confirmation was mind-blowing. Now it seemed that Jules Anthony was the last stop before tying Covington in. With Brogard's confession, Anthony would be hard pressed to deny his role in the chain of command. The only question was whether Anthony could implicate Covington by name. The phone call data was convincing but didn't close the loop tightly. It was circumstantial. Jules Anthony could be given a name and a course of action but might never know who issued the order. Once again, it was necessary to dig deeper to see if a link could be found to tie Covington and Anthony together. How and why did Covington develop a "relationship" with Jules Anthony? This would have to be squeezed out of Anthony.

Marco Roy was on time and drove the two of them to an appointment Al had made with Jules Anthony at one of his car dealerships. The secretary informed them that Mr. Anthony had not arrived and had not called to say he would be late.

"That's very unusual for Mr. Anthony. He always calls if he's going to be late."

Al had bad vibes about this situation. "Could you call him to find out if he's coming? That would be helpful."

"Sure. I'll try his cell."

Al settled into a chair and waited.

"There's no response, so I left a message. This is very unusual."

"Could you give me his home address? I think I'll drive out there and see if there's a problem that's delaying him."

She wrote an address on a phone message pad and handed the top page to him.

The drive to Anthony's home took half an hour. The house was on a quiet street in an upscale suburban development. Nothing pretentious but upscale nonetheless. The BMW in the driveway was the only clue that the house might be occupied. Marco and Al approached the front door with caution. On the drive over, they had speculated on Jules's reason for being a no-show. One of the reasons was incapacity. Marco's policeman instinct leaned toward a violent causation. He'd seen plenty of instances where a key witness or conspirator had been dispatched before police could question him. The circumstances today gave him that uneasy feeling. He followed behind Al with his hand on his gun handle.

The doorbell went unanswered. The door was not locked, so they entered slowly and called out Jules's name several times. The house was still, and so was the body lying prone on the living room floor. Blood had seeped out from under the body and was clotted. The body was cold. This killing had taken place hours ago. Marco went to see if any other victims were in the house. Al could identify the body from photos in the living room as Jules Anthony. He chose not to touch the corpse until a crime scene unit had done its work, but it seemed likely that a gunshot wound or wounds to the chest had done him in. Marco returned after a quick search revealed no additional signs of violence. He called the situation in to the local police and sat down on a chair.

Al just continued to stare at the body.

Marco had his phone in hand and was beginning to place a call. "I'm going to call Brogard's office to establish that he's alive and have him seek safe shelter with the police. I know I'm jumping the gun, but I dislike coincidence as much as you do. He may be the next victim if he hasn't been taken out already. He may also have inadvertently alerted our friend in Tucson that we were looking into Jules Anthony by calling Jules to give him a heads-up."

Marco was shaking his head. "How did all this happen so fast? You just saw Brogard yesterday."

" There's no answer from Brogard's cellphone. Do you have the same uneasy feeling that I do? Covington has little tolerance for potential witnesses. With our breach of his network, we may have set in motion his security system. I wouldn't be surprised if he had a long-term contingency plan to eliminate Brogard and Anthony if he needed to silence them. He's one fastidious clean-up man."

"Here are the local police. I'll fill them in, and then I assume you want to head over to Brogard's house. I share your suspicion that we're going find another corpse somewhere on Brogard's turf."

The suspicion was borne out at Brogard's house. It was the same MO as at Anthony's with the only difference being the addition of a dead wife.

Hours later, Al and Marco were sharing thoughts over a beer at a local brew house. Marco was as pessimistic as Al. "I doubt if the crime scene will offer any clues leading to the perp or perps. These were paid-for executions, pure and simple. They don't as a rule get solved and, considering your clever soul in Tucson, I have even less confidence we'll come up with anything."

"I luckily stumbled on the NSA angle and ended up triggering three homicides. Talk about unintended consequences. I think it's time to let Leslie sell the story she has with the added spice I got from Brogard.

That gives the story credence, even if it doesn't give us Covington. Maybe something will surface without my digging. Serendipity may trump a good investigation. In any event, I want to get Leslie and myself back to a normal life."

CHAPTER TWENTY-FOUR

The phone rang in Jennifer's study and the name on call waiting was a surprise. Eve Burton had been off Jennifer's radar screen since the disc retrieval in Tucson. She had been thanked generously for doing the stunt so effectively.

"Hello, Eve. This is an unexpected pleasure. What'sup?"

"Just wanted to chat and tell you a few details about what went down in Tucson. We never talked, though I know you got my package and I received your hand-delivered bonus. Do you have a few minutes?"

"Sure, Eve, I'm more than a little curious but I was prepared to let it lie, so to speak."

"Well, the seduction went off without a hitch. The guy is a guy and couldn't help thinking that he was responsible for the scene as it played out until I tied him down. He surrendered the disc once he was in a very compromised position and saw no way out. I put him to sleep with a needle and left in an old woman disguise. Oh, one little thing I did on my own initiative. I took a few compromising pictures of him to ensure my safety from any reprisal. If you're interested, I can e-mail them to you."

Jennifer was intrigued. The shoe was suddenly on the other foot. First, she would have to see the pictures to determine if they were as promising as Eve implied. "Eve, can you send them to me right now, so I can see if they have any special value to me? If I do ever use them, you can rest assured your identity will never be revealed."

"Okay. I just sent them. Tell me what you think." Jennifer opened her e-mail and retrieved the pictures.

She was stunned by what she saw. In one, Ed was nude, on his back and his genitals exposed. In the other shot, he was on his stomach with a female's finger in his anus. The female gender was surmised by the finger's arm with a dress sleeve, bracelet, and fingernail polish. It was lewd, and it was powerful stuff.

"Eve, you've done more than protect yourself. I think you've provided the instrument to stifle this very vicious guy. Let's call it a night and put some time between this and our next contact. I'll be in touch."

Jennifer's next move would be a meeting with Al and Leslie.

The pictures were a potential game changer.

CHAPTER TWENTY-FIVE

More than ever, Al was convinced that direct action aimed at Covington was the only recourse. They had taken this case as far as they could within legal bounds and now something extra-legal was necessary. Leslie knew Al was planning some new course of action, but she was not included in his plan. He only indicated that he would be gone for several days and that he would tell all when he returned.

The flight to Tucson went through Dallas and got Al to the Marriott in downtown Tucson in mid-afternoon. After checking in and unpacking, he went to see Ed's office building and penthouse home. As expected, there was a 24- hour doorman. Covington Industries was the only tenant aside from Ed Covington himself who lived in the ninth-floor penthouse. Convenience and luxury coupled with a moderate degree of security. On the ground floor, a 20-foot space ran around the building, making it difficult to approach the only entrance unseen. A full array of video cameras monitored the "moat" and were likely under constant eyeball surveillance. Al had expected nothing less. He would have to meet Ed outside this fortress.

Purchasing a gun was no problem. Newspaper ads for private sales were plentiful and no background check would be necessary.

The business telephone number for Ed Covington was listed on the web page for Covington Industries. Al knew he would have to get Ed's attention and then lure him to a meeting in some less secure setting.

Al called from his cellphone.

A secretary answered on the second ring and cheerfully identified the office of Mr. Edward Covington, President and C.E.O. of Covington Industries.

"Hello, this is George Ryder, an acquaintance of Howard Westlake. I'd like to speak to Mr. Covington."

"May I tell him what the matter is you wish to discuss? Mr. Covington is rather busy today."

"Certainly. I understand. You can tell him I have information regarding Sidney Curtis and Steve Berk that I'd like to share with him."

"Please wait while I put you on hold."

Al thought this introduction might suffice to get him to a meeting.

"Mr. Ryder, Mr. Covington asked me to tell you he understands those two gentlemen are deceased and are of no interest to him at this time."

"He's absolutely correct. They are deceased. That's also true for Jeff Oldham, Peggy Carter and Darryl Edmunds. He probably is aware of those deaths as well. I'd like an opportunity to find out if he knows anything that could connect these deaths together. I have good reason to believe he does."

"I'll put you on hold again."

Al was prepared for the next response. He expected further stonewalling.

"Mr. Covington again indicates no interest on his part. He suggests you leave a business card with me and he'll contact you if anything relevant occurs to him. He further suggests you leave, since he has said his last word to you on your bizarre inquiry."

"That's fine. I'm leaving now."

Al left the building and started back to his hotel on foot. He had no doubt that Covington was more than curious about this intrusive stranger. Interestingly, he hadn't even feigned innocence, only declaring that he was not interested in what was being offered for discussion. Al was sure he would be followed to identify where he was staying but that was of no concern to him. He wanted a private meeting with Ed and this was a step in that direction. He also wanted the meeting to be at a place of his choosing and not Ed's.

His tail was not very professional and arrived at the hotel only moments after Al. In that brief interim, Al was able to tell the desk clerk to give the man arriving shortly any information he asked for regarding him, Mr. George Ryder. He then took the elevator up to his room on the third floor. He next filled an ice bucket from the floor ice machine. He then settled into a comfortable easy chair in his room with some scotch on the rocks and waited for contact to be established.

He hadn't long to wait. Covington himself knocked and Al invited him in. Neither had met the other before, so they each produced photo IDs to confirm whom they were talking to.

"Al Seibolt. A doctor. I have no idea what you're up to, so maybe you'll spell it out for me."

"Why don't you have a seat and a drink before we begin, Ed? There's ice in the bucket and the minibar is unlocked. I've already started on a scotch on the rocks."

"I didn't expect such friendly hospitality after your implied suspicion a few hours ago." Ed moved to the minibar and poured himself some vodka on the rocks. When he seated himself opposite Al, he saw that his host now held a gun in his hand.

"I can see that the hospitality phase has ended. Now what is it you want?"

"I'm here to deliver a warning and offer proof that it should be taken dead seriously. I want to impress upon you that there will be retribution of a very serious nature if you persist in making violent moves toward Leslie Nugent."

"Well, I don't doubt your intention, Doctor. I'm just confused why you think I had anything to do with those deceased souls you enumerated to my secretary. And now your reference to a Leslie Nugent further confuses me."

"Look, Covington, I'm not a fool, and so I don't expect you to own up to your role in the tragic cover-up. I also don't expect you to admit any connection to the two plots against Miss Nugent. We're not going to debate those matters. I'm here to end your attacks against her. I indicated there would be proof of the seriousness of my intent. Since there have been two attacks against Miss Nugent, there will be payback for these, which will also serve as the proof I mentioned. That payback will come at a time and place of my choosing. You're free to go now."

"I don't submit to threats, Dr. Seibolt."

"That's your choice, Covington. Now, please leave."

The threat had been delivered. Now Covington would have no reason to question the motive behind any violence that might befall him. Al would have to think through the time and place of that action. He would check out of the hotel and find other lodging so as not to afford Covington an opportunity for a pre-emptive strike.

His cellphone indicated that a new message had been received. Surprisingly, the sender was Jennifer Henderson. The brief message asked him to call her at home and included her phone number.

"Hello, Dr. Seibolt. I'm glad you responded so quickly to my message. I think you'll find what I have to say very germane to our common interest in Ed Covington."

"You have my undivided attention, Mrs. Henderson. Fire away."

"I very recently acquired some candid photos of Ed. I believe they could be of immense value in getting him to stop his effort to silence anyone seeking to define his role in the White House cover-up. I think when you see them you'll appreciate their potential."

"As I said, you have my undivided attention. And now I suspect you're about to e-mail some photos to me."

"Right. They're on the way. Don't ask any questions about their origin. Maybe we can deal with that after we decide how to proceed."

"I have the photos. They're very interesting. I can see how they fit into a strategy to get him to back away from his homicidal plan to protect the cover-up. I'm not in Washington but will return tomorrow. We can meet with Leslie and plan the next step. We finally have something to work with that could bring closure to this bloody mess."

CHAPTER TWENTY-SIX

A l, Leslie, Jennifer, and Howard were sitting in Jennifer's cozy living room. Al related all that had transpired in Tucson and then let Jennifer introduce the serendipitous photos. Jennifer didn't disclose any details regarding the episode during which they had been obtained. Eve Burton's name never came up.

Al led the discussion, "We're here to discuss how to proceed in the light of this new material. I've given it considerable thought and would like to air some issues.

First, the pictures are very threatening to Ed's concept of his macho image. That's the obvious leverage we could exercise. The threat to let the pics go viral is a nightmare for him. Second, his reaction to the threat is not easy to gauge. What could he do to prevent that from happening or how could he mitigate the damage if they were released? Well, he could argue that it's not him in the photos. We can counter that. The person in the pics does look like Ed. Then, of course, the photographer would have to reveal his or her identity and accept the blame or credit for the photos. That's information you, Jennifer, do not want to see made public.

"Alternatively, he could seek a court order enjoining the holder of the photos from releasing them in a public venue. Since he doesn't know who has the photos, the court wouldn't know whom to enjoin. He could threaten to do violence to all involved in the event of a release. But again, the enemy may remain unknown to him even if he has some suspicion who it is. Ideally, he would just shut down his operation and hope he could ride out the threat posed by the unreleased pictures. The last might be the best we could hope for: a standoff. Any thoughts?"

Jennifer responded, "It's not fair to jeopardize the photographer by releasing her identity. I don't think that's an option. I'm also unclear on the issue of an injunction in such a matter. These pictures are not the Pentagon Papers. Ed may be angry as a hornet's nest, but he may realize that the pictures don't implicate him in the cover-up. Seems it's up to you to sell him on the stand-off. You get him to leave Leslie alone and that was your goal all along."

Leslie gave her slant on the photo strategy, "I agree with Jennifer, Al. A stand-off is a victory. We're no worse off and we can go ahead and try to market the story we have, even without naming the mastermind."

"Let's all sleep on it tonight and see if any additional ideas surface. If no new approach emerges, I'll make an appointment to reveal the photos to Ed and see if he is willing to stand down."

Through all the discussion, Howard Westlake listened closely without offering an opinion.

CHAPTER TWENTY-SEVEN

After a restless night, Al and Leslie discussed how to implement the plan they had devised with Jennifer. There was uncertainty regarding Ed's response once they revealed the pictures to him. Would he cave and agree to give up on his attacks on Leslie? That seemed an uncharacteristic response. He was not one to capitulate and slink away. On the other extreme, he might dare them to release the pictures and choose to challenge their authenticity. If he could weather the exposure, he would be free to continue his attacks on Leslie. The pictures were a stand-alone item with no context. He could challenge them on that ground as well. Just a scam scheme to blackmail a rich businessman.

The more they tried to devise a strategy to use the pictures to rein him in, the more they had to concede the weakness of their position. Maybe he would just give in to avoid embarrassment. That was their best hope, but the dark cloud hovered and might bring more violence rather than a cessation of violence.

"Leslie, I went out to Tucson to threaten Covington and possibly even to inflict a non-fatal but damaging gunshot wound on him after giving him the warning to lay off you. I hesitated out there after getting the call from Jennifer. I thought there might be another way to end his attacks on you. Now, I'm coming around to my original plan. Direct, unambiguous violence seems to be the most certain way to end this. Then you bring the story to the *Post* and see if they'll go for it even without a smoking gun. I think it's compelling as it stands." Al paused, waiting for a reaction.

"I didn't want anyone else in on the actual act of censure. That's why I didn't tell you about my trip to Tucson. Now I'm going to cut you out again. It's all mine, Leslie."

"Al, I think the pictures are worth a try. You talk to Ed and let him know what the score is. See if he bites. He might surprise you and be willing to back off. The problem is knowing if he'll keep his word. There has to be a fail-safe position that places the onus on him; he breaks the agreement, he effectively releases the pictures onto the internet."

"Leslie, I'll go along with that approach. But I must admit, I'm prepared to act decisively to bring this nightmare to an end. I'll make the call to Ed."

Covington took the call in his Tucson office. Al was blunt. He let him know that he had pictures of an embarrassing nature which he would trade for an end to his attacks on Leslie. The alternative was a release on the Internet.

Ed knew he could not destroy the pictures, since they didn't exist in the old-fashioned negative format. The risk of future exploitation could not be totally eliminated. For Al, Ed's agreement to desist could not be guaranteed indefinitely. Each was being asked to accept an imperfect solution.

Covington's first response was, "Show me the pictures." He was more than a little curious. "Here's my e-mail address. Send them now. I'm sitting at my computer."

"Okay. They're on the way. I'm sending you two pictures so that shouldn't take long."

There was silence on Ed's end. Al assumed the pictures arrived and were being studied very closely.

"Are they there? Let me know if the transmission was successful."

"Yes, I have the two pictures." His voice was controlled. There was no evidence of anxiety or any indication that he was in combat mode. He was a cool customer.

Covington said he would have to think about the offer and asked for 24 hours. He also issued a flat denial of any role in whatever acts of violence Al was alluding to.

Al felt he had gone as far as he could at this time. "I'll expect a call from you on my cellphone within 24 hours. Here's the number."

CHAPTER TWENTY-EIGHT

Al related the content and tone of the phone conversation to Leslie. Neither would speculate on the response they anticipated. Their mood was somber.

They decided to use dinner as a distraction and headed for their favorite Italian restaurant.

Twenty-four hours passed and there was no response from Covington. That was unexpected and left them wondering what was going on. A call to his penthouse in Tucson went unanswered. The call to his office found his secretary at a loss to account for his whereabouts. She agreed to call Al as soon as either Ed turned up or called in. An eery silence descended on them.

A call at 2 a.m. woke them from their sleep. Tom Adler of the Tucson police was calling a person named Leslie. "Please identify yourself, Miss."

"I'm Leslie Nugent and Alan Seibolt is right next to me."

"Ed Covington was found dead in his car, Ms. Nugent, the apparent victim of a shooting. A handwritten note on the front passenger seat said to call this number. All it said was, 'Call this number,' and it gave your number, then said, 'Leslie, it's over.' There is no signature. Can you shed some light on what this is all about?"

"Officer Adler, there's a very long and complex story to tell, but that will have to wait for a later date. It may or may not shed light on the event you're dealing with tonight. More to the point, this shooting comes as a complete surprise to me. I have nothing to offer you about the shooting. I'm sorry. I have no idea who wrote that note. Was it Covington? When you hear the story that will come out in the news it may offer some clue to possible suspects."

"Thank you for offering that mysterious insight, Miss Nugent. I hope to hear more about that 'complex story' you alluded to. I'll need to hear it soon since this is a murder investigation and solving it is my first order of business."

"Officer, let me get some sleep now and I promise to call you in the morning. Give me a number where you can be reached." Leslie took his number and then hung up.

"Al, I'm going to the *Post* tomorrow and get my story published. The shooting is puzzling, but my list of suspects is rather short. How do you see it going down?"

"Leslie, I can't process that information now. We both need sleep and will need to be fresh in the morning. I'm going to take a sleeping pill and will be happy to get you one."

CHAPTER TWENTY-NINE

The big jet taxied to the terminal at Reagan International Airport. The nonstop, red-eye flight from Phoenix had taken little over four hours. With no luggage to claim, Howard Westlake was into a cab and at his office by 10 a.m. in time for a conference with the station's advertising execs.

He hadn't shared his plan with Jennifer, so she was truly innocent. He'd arranged a meeting with Ed at a nightspot between Phoenix and Tucson they'd occasionally met at when the two of them planned a weekend of sun and fun at a desert resort. They met in the parking lot before going in and Ed took a bullet to the head while sitting in his car. Howard had little likelihood of being seen on any surveillance cameras. He drove back to Phoenix and flew home.

He felt renewed. Ed had used him and nearly destroyed his relationship with Jennifer. Upon reflection, his years with Ed had been very one-sided. Ed had no conscience and used Howard as the affable partner to help attract female companions. When he brought Howard to Washington and drew Jennifer into their relationship at her most vulnerable time, Ed was manipulating the two of them into a romance that could only have a bitter ending when the true basis for it came to light.

Ed would not be missed by anyone. Howard and Jennifer could now live without fear that Ed could undermine their life together if or when he chose to.

ABOUT THE AUTHOR

A.S. Most is a retired cardiologist with a passion for mystery/thrillers. Harlan Corbin and Michael Connelly are among his favorite authors. Most's first book, No Loose Ends, is a thriller set in Washington, D.C. It follows a newspaper reporter and physician as they attempt to unravel the cover up of a V.I.P.'s medical illness. Most resides in Rhode Island with his artist/educator wife. He has two sons, one an attorney and the other a journalist. He is actively working on his second book.